Dear Susan,

I hope you can enjoy this book despite its lack of sympathetic characters - the central one inspired by a nasty politician from Toronto!

Thanks so much for your caring and support - I feel better already!

Keith
9/5/16

PEACHLAND, B.C 2016

Justice Delayed

A Novel

Keith Fielding

Order this book online at www.trafford.com
or email orders@trafford.com

Most Trafford titles are also available at major online book retailers.

Printed in Victoria, BC, Canada.

ISBN: 978-1-4269-2873-4 (sc)
ISBN: 978-1-4269-3050-8 (e-b)

*Our mission is to efficiently provide the world's finest, most comprehensive
book publishing service, enabling every author to experience success.
To find out how to publish your book, your way, and have it available
worldwide, visit us online at www.trafford.com*

Trafford rev. 03/19/2010

 www.trafford.com

North America & international
toll-free: 1 888 232 4444 (USA & Canada)
phone: 250 383 6864 ♦ fax: 812 355 4082

Chapter One

Had money been no object, John Garter would have traded his aging Volkswagen for a newer, sportier model, long ago. And, but for lack of opportunity and fear of the financial consequences, he might well have done the same with his wife. He was, however, a cautious man: always careful to conceal the impoverished state of both his marriage, and his bank account, in the firm belief that exposure of the truth would interfere with his capacity to someday achieve political office. Why that should be the case he was not certain, but he knew instinctively that for now he must suppress the urge to indulge impulse or fantasy. Those responsible for his misfortunes — his wife and almost everyone else he knew — could pay later.

As he drove toward the main gates of the Aerial Golf Club, he felt combative. Surely he deserved better in life? Had he not always worked hard? Was he not a Chartered Accountant? Had he not been a constant provider? Was he not an exemplary citizen? Had he not earned the right to more respect and recognition for his contributions?

At forty years of age, he had achieved a modicum of success by some standards. For the past six years he had worked as Vice President of Finance at a pharmaceutical company, tolerating a modest salary to savor the prestigious job title, and the prospect of greater things to come. He was active in the local branch of the Chamber of Commerce, and had served as an advisory member on a sub-committee of the local School Board. At work he took pride in his ability to command loyalty, and respect, earned he felt sure, by his policy of always being 'firm but fair'. In reality he was disliked by almost of all of his staff. However, he did not claim to be popular, and believed that those of his colleagues who were, enjoyed that status only because of their unwillingness to demand high standards of performance. On the rare occasions he thought about such matters, it would strengthen his resolve to ensure that popularity did not come at the expense of weakness.

With his indignation mounting, he drew to a halt in the floodlit car park of the Golf Club. It was a cool evening and the air was damp from an earlier drizzle. He slammed the door of his car and crunched his way along a gravel path toward the main doors of the club. This could be a difficult meeting: that pompous ass, Jefferson, might again raise the question of an independent audit of the club accounts. He would have to be careful. The monthly committee meetings seemed to come round faster and faster. As treasurer of the club it was his responsibility to provide statements of account for each meeting and tonight was no exception. Keeping track of the club's financial affairs was not too difficult a task and for the most part was handled by a junior member of his accounting staff who feared to refuse the favor. The capital account he handled himself. Over the past few years the fund had grown larger and, in anticipation of further land acquisition, now stood in excess of five hundred thousand dollars. That the account was twenty thousand below the level it should be, was a fact known only to him.

With his briefcase clutched tightly under his arm, he pushed open the heavy oak door of the clubhouse. A tight knot in his stomach spoke to the possibility of another joust with that interfering nitwit on the committee who seemed determined to raise difficult questions.

*   *   *

Mary Garter's tone was sad, but insistent. "I have to go now Daniel." She uncoiled herself from a tanned, athletic-looking man, some years her junior, kissed him gently and maneuvered her long legs over the side of an ancient, creaky bed. She sat for a moment then turned back towards him, extended her arms on either side of his chest, and looked at him intently. She spoke tenderly. "Daniel, we have to talk… not now, because I have to go, but soon." Daniel raised himself onto one elbow and looked up into large blue eyes, wide-set and gentle. Her face, framed now in a tunnel of light brown, shoulder length hair, carried an earnest expression.

"Maria! You want to stop seeing me?" Mary shook her head.

"I want us to talk. We have to discuss where we are going in our lives. You know that we can't go on like this."

"I know you think so. You have said so before." He looked hurt.

"Daniel, let's meet for lunch, on Tuesday. We'll talk then. Can you do that?"

"I suppose so, if we must."

He grunted, rolled onto one side, and resigned himself to the sad fact that their relationship was about to end. It was not the first time he had been cast adrift by a woman, and he knew the signs only too well: the need to 'talk' always heralded bad news.

Mary walked to the bathroom and turned on the shower, relieved that she had initiated the conversation, apparently without doing too much damage to Daniel's delicate ego. She climbed into the stream of warm water, and allowed the soothing flow to caress her face and shapely body. She nuzzled into the jet spray and reflected on her situation. Yes, the affair would have to end. As much as she had enjoyed her relationship with Daniel, she knew that it had developed for the wrong reasons. Daniel's attentions had allowed her to regain energy, and self-confidence: resources that had been drained by years of fruitless investment in a loveless, childless, marriage. Life with a critical, ambitious, and embittered husband, had taken its toll. But, she had recovered, and Daniel, her Francophone lover, had been the catalyst. They had first spoken, six months previously, oddly, at a moment when Daniel was leisurely wrapping a white flannel dressing gown around his naked body. He had just spent his third consecutive Wednesday evening in front of Mary's night school sculpting class, holding an arduous pose while she and her fellow students attempted to replicate in clay, the contours of his pleasantly toned body. Mary had laughed in response to his question, assuming it to be a pick-up line: would she be so kind as to consider the possibility of posing for him some time while he practiced figure drawing skills? His embarrassed reaction to her laughter, immediately caused Mary to regret the response. In an attempt to repair damage she had offered to talk with him over coffee. One after-class discussion led to another, and despite their differences in age and outlook Mary found that she enjoyed his company. Before long she had developed a genuine affection for him, and felt that his ability to make her feel important, and desirable, more than compensated for clumsy social skills and his propensity to speak at length about himself and his struggling career as a would-be actor. Later, she had decided that some physical intimacy with Daniel might not only be possible, but also therapeutic. She did not regret that decision, but it was quite clear to her that she must now take her life in a new direction.

After a hurried departure from Daniel's basement apartment, Mary drove toward her suburban Toronto home, twenty-five minutes along the highway. It was eight thirty, and she intended to be home before her husband returned from his Golf Club committee meeting, and their marital charade resumed. Drizzle splattered her windshield, and black puddles stared blankly from the road as she approached the exit ramp. Steering confidently with one hand, she switched off the radio, pulled out her cell phone, and pressed the speed dial buttons that connected to the voice mail at home. She retrieved the first of two messages and listened to a practiced, and bored, female tone:

"This is Dr. Fraser's office calling to remind you that John Garter has an appointment for a dental check-up tomorrow, at four thirty. Cancellations require twenty-four hours notice or will be charged. Thank you."

Mary pressed the Save button and listened to the next. A man with a thick, Central European accent, spoke softly and slowly:

"This is your last chance to get it here. Do I need to remind you of the consequences if you don't? Get on with it."

The effect was chilling. The voice was not one that she recognized, and its menacing tone oozed hatred. Was it meant for her? For her husband? Or, was it possibly a wrong number – a message left by mistake? She pulled into the tree-lined driveway of her home, puzzled, but confident that the answer would soon be revealed.

*   *   *

At the Aerial Golf Club, John Garter was trying hard to disguise his irritation with Harry Jefferson, who had once again interrupted his financial presentation with an irrelevant question. "Harry," he said, in the most patient tone he could muster, "while I agree that an external audit does give members the assurance that their volunteer committee is acting responsibly, and that the accounts balance in the way they have been presented, there is a significant financial cost to the club, to say nothing of the time and energy that I will have to invest to steer them through the books. And for what? No one is suggesting there is any impropriety on the part of the committee, so nothing is gained! All that happens is that we spend the club's money and I waste a lot of time." He paused, and stared defiantly at the object of his wrath: a short, stocky man, of about fifty, who was sitting on the opposite side of the table, about three places down.

"Well, that may be true, but we are dealing with large sums of money now, and I think an independent professional view won't hurt." Harry Jefferson peered around the table assessing the support his argument was getting from other members. An impatient voice from the head of the table interrupted his survey.

"Look, I think we've spent enough time on this for tonight". The chairman, a balding, round-faced man in his sixties, was clearly irritated. "Let's put it to the vote, and move on. Personally I don't care either way, but it's not me who has to make the arrangements and guide the process. So, let's see a show of hands on the matter. Who's in favour of an independent audit?"

"Just one moment Mike." A confident female voice interrupted. "Why don't we just defer the issue? That way we can all reflect on it and maybe talk to some of the members to sound them out. I can see that John and Harry both feel strongly about the matter and I think a postponement will help all of us to decide what is best." A flurry of nods and affirmative grunts greeted Julia Miller's comments, and confirmed that her idea had gained substantial support.

"Very well," said the chairman, "let's bring it back in say, two months, and make a decision then. All in favour?" Hands raised around the table.

John Garter reached for the glass of water in front of him, and as he did so, glanced towards Julia Miller. Her eyes were squarely upon him, laser-like in their intensity, seemingly intent on boring a pathway into his brain. He attempted a smile, unsure afterwards whether his effort had drawn even the glimmer of a response.

* * *

No sooner was he back home, than he learned from his wife that a disturbing telephone message awaited his attention. He resolved to not listen until after he had eaten dinner: a resolve that stemmed not from indifference, but from a deep concern about what he would hear. After, fighting with a plate of spaghetti bolognaise and downing two glasses of red wine, the concern had not abated, but he could resist no longer. With a nonchalant air, he picked up the phone, called the message centre, and listened intently.

"Oh damn it! Why the hell didn't you tell me I had a dental appointment tomorrow?" he demanded. "That's just what I need!"

"Because John, I'm not your secretary and I didn't know you had made it!" Mary congratulated herself for not taking the slightest portion of blame for her husband's negligence, dumped her empty plate in the dishwasher, leaned on the counter, and stared at him coldly, while he resumed picking at the telephone keypad.

With a mask-like face, he listened to the next message. At its completion he calmly replaced the receiver, and looked at his wife. "No, it means nothing to me." He stared blankly. "It's just some prankster, or a wrong number like you thought. I have some work to do now."

He strode purposefully through the hallway and into the wood-panelled room he used for a study, and closed the door behind him.

Chapter Two

Garter slumped into the leather chair that fronted his double-pedestal oak desk and resolved to act decisively: his life was becoming far too complex for comfort. He pulled a bottle of Scotch from the bottom drawer, filled a tumbler, replaced the bottle, and reached for a notepad and pen.

In his customary organized way, he carefully drew a line down the centre of the page. At the top of the first column, he printed the word 'Traditional'. At the top of the second column, he printed the words 'Non Traditional.' He then took a drink from his glass, and began to scribble furiously. Five minutes later, the 'Traditional' column contained a lengthy list of items, each headed with a roman numeral. It was a list of ideas, all of them legal, for raising the funds he needed. After he had finished writing he scrutinized his work carefully.

His pen moved up and down the page, pausing at each point as he re-read the idea and considered its viability. With an angry zeal, he scratched a line through the first two items on the list. He continued to stare at the page, deep in thought, and then crossed out the next three ideas. After a further period of study he slowly deleted the remaining items, one after the other. 'Traditional' options were not going to yield the results he needed. He threw down his pen, stood up, and walked over to the casement windows that looked out towards the road.

For a few minutes he stood there, staring blankly into the distance: the grass, paving stones, and rose bushes that decorated the front yard were barely discernable in the shadows cast by the street lamps outside. He reached for the drapes, and carefully pulled them across the window. With a morose expression, he turned, and edged his way around the perimeter of the room, stopping at intervals to examine photographs, paintings, and various framed certificates attesting to his educational achievements and professional credentials. The tour complete, he returned to his desk, picked up his half empty glass of Scotch, and took a large sip before once again settling down to his task.

He turned his attention to the column headed 'Non-Traditional' and for several minutes stared at the page, his pen poised for action but motionless. He was thinking about his company's purchasing practices, attempting to identify among the company's suppliers, people with whom he might strike up a mutually beneficial financial arrangement; people who might be encouraged to 'purchase' his loyalty to their business. He jotted some notes, but as he did so doubts surfaced immediately: the risks were substantial and the connections would take time to put in place. A faster solution was needed.

His mind shifted to new opportunities. Thirty minutes later he had identified several simple, though fraudulent, schemes to generate additional income by exploiting his greedy employer. Two of the more promising ideas, one involving the payroll, and the other requiring him to create a fictitious supplier to the company, were each identified on the page by a single, heavily encircled word.

By midnight he had finished his deliberations. His tumbler had been drained, refilled, and drained again. He felt tired, but excited about the plan now bubbling in his head. He had long previously abandoned the "kickback" scheme, determining that the risks were too great. He had also decided against the payroll and 'phony supplier' schemes, even though they both held some promise and might, he had decided, be useful in the future. By far the most time, almost one hour, had been spent jotting notes on a page headed 'Insurance' with the satisfying result that he now knew exactly what he would do. Of course, the plan would have to be thought through in much more detail, but in all important respects, it was there. It was a plan that would offer quick returns, give a high pay out, and, most importantly, would not be too risky to implement.

After tidying his desk, he switched off the lights, and carefully closed the door. With notes in hand, he walked along a short passageway that led to a downstairs cloakroom. He tore-up the pages on which he had been writing, and flushed the pieces in the toilet bowl. Satisfied that all of them had disappeared, he made his way to the staircase and up towards the main bedroom. A strip of light under the door informed him that his wife was still awake. As he opened it Mary closed the journal in which she was writing, and silently switched her side of the room into darkness. Without speaking, he prepared for bed. He undressed in the bathroom and then ambled to the large walk-in closet at the end of the room. He scanned the side used by his wife and focused immediately on what he sought — a large wooden jewellery casket that sat on a shelf in one corner. He quietly lifted the lid and peered intently at the glittering array of rings, bracelets, necklaces, brooches and ear rings, neatly organized inside. Most of the items were antiques that Mary had inherited from her grandmother. More importantly, most of the items were set in gold and studded with diamonds. He closed the lid, switched off the light, and shuffled to the king-size bed that he continued to share with his wife. As he climbed-in and settled down for the night, he felt more relaxed than he had for many months. It was, he assured himself, an almost foolproof plan. There would be a robbery. He would claim compensation on his insurance policy. He would supplement the insurance proceeds by selling the jewellery when it was safe to do so. Then, he would be debt free and could relax once more. With these comforting thoughts soothing his mind, he quickly fell into a deep sleep.

Chapter Three

As he entered his office the next day, a plump woman in her early sixties was busily organizing files on his desk. She turned as he approached, cooed a respectful "Good morning, Mr. Garter", and handed him a telephone message slip. "You just missed a call from a Julia Miller. She said it was a personal matter and would like you to call her. Here's the number." He frowned. Julia Miller, from the golf club committee: what did she want?

"All right" he said. "I'll have my coffee now Mrs. Bennett, and when you come, bring me the Financial Times". He sat down, and peered at his calendar for a few moments. He then picked up the telephone and dialed the number on the memo slip.

"Good morning. Royal West Bank. Julia Miller's office. Can I help you?" At that moment he suddenly realized that he knew nothing at all about Julia Miller, and had no idea where she worked or what she did. She had been elected to the committee fairly recently as a director-at-large, and they had met there on only two previous occasions. He had recognized her as someone with a sharp intellect, and had noted her inquisitive interest in all matters on the agenda, but he was surprised now to discover that she was apparently a professional career woman with a personal assistant to screen her calls.

"Yes, I'd like to speak to Ms. Miller please."

"Who can I say is calling?" He gave his name and waited. A few moments later Julia Miller's polished voice purred in his ear.

"John. Thanks for getting back to me. I was calling to invite you to lunch! We haven't had much opportunity to talk, and there are a few issues that have come up on the committee agenda that I'd like to pick your brains about. So, is that a possibility? This week ideally." The memory of Julia Miller's laser beam eyes flashed before him. "Yes, of course, I'd be pleased to. I could meet on Friday if that's any good."

"Friday? Yes, that's good for me too." She continued without pausing.

"You're at Bay and King aren't you? So, what if we meet at Henri's? I'll get us a reservation for noon. How would that be?"

After confirming the proposal, he hung-up the phone and jotted an entry in his calendar. At that moment Mrs. Bennett returned, bearing a tray with coffee and the morning newspaper. She deposited both on his desk and left — the tray tucked under her arm and her ears alert to detect whether he had deigned to grunt some form of acknowledgment or thanks. He had not. She did however arrive back at her desk to a buzzer signaling that he wanted her attention. "Mrs. Bennett, please hold my calls and don't interrupt me for the next hour." Thus organized, he settled to some private business, beginning with a call to a stockbroker whose advice, had he heeded it six months ago, would have saved him from the need to embezzle funds from the Aerial Golf Club, and to borrow from the disreputable loan office now harassing him for repayment in full. He sounded tentative. "Yes, it's been a while. Yes, I realize that. Well, I may be able to get back into the market soon. What do you think about Greenridge B? I hear there's some optimism about their explorations. Yes, that's what I thought. Good. Well I can't do anything just now, but I'll check in with you again later."

He hung-up the phone, feeling excited at the prospect of once again indulging his passion for trading in the Futures market. He would, he mused, have to wait a little while until he could execute the break-in and insurance claim, but then things would get back on a more normal footing. What damned bad luck he had experienced over the past year! He looked at his 'To do' list and then at his watch. His hand hovered over the telephone for a moment or two while he collected his thoughts. Then, with an angry zeal, he punched out the number of the Fast Credit & Loan Approval Institute Incorporated. His call connected quickly and was answered with a polite greeting.

"Good Morning. Fast Credit."

"Yes, my name is John Garter. I want to speak to Gustav Illiach. Is he there please?" "

"Just a moment, I'll check." He heard muffled sounds as a hand cupped over the speaker end of the telephone. There was a click.

"Mr. Garter. How nice to hear from you. I take it you have something for me?" The voice was slow, and oleaginous.

"Listen to me carefully. I will not stand for any more of your harassment. If you make any more threatening phone calls to me at work, or at home, I will take legal action against you, and you will regret it. Is that clear?"

"Mr. Garter, Mr. Garter, how very droll!" The response was carefully measured. "I hardly think you are in a position to complain about a legitimate attempt to recover an overdue account on a legally executed loan agreement. In fact, Mr. Garter, it is now so overdue that it is we who will be taking the action, legal or otherwise. Do I make myself clear?" The pained expression on Garter's face made it apparent that he had.

"Look. You'll get your money, very soon. I need about two weeks and I'll be able to pay it off in full, so there is no need for threatening on anyone's part. I just ask that you leave me alone in the meantime." "Mr. Garter. I thought I had made myself clear. Your loan is past due, *now*." His emphasis was practically hissed. "You do not have two weeks. In fact if I am not mistaken there is a recovery order in effect already."

"What do you mean, a recovery order, what's that?" "It's a euphemism, Mr. Garter. It means that we have mobilized someone on our payroll: a debt collector who is very effective at recovering overdue accounts. I believe it has something to do with his physical attributes." There was a long silence during which time John Garter stopped breathing. His reply was finally stammered out.

"You'll get your money. I, er, I'll have it to you tomorrow. How's that?"

"That would be just fine Mr. Garter. If you settle your account with cash, here in the office by noon tomorrow, then I'm sure that the recovery order can be held in abeyance. Do I have your agreement to that?

"Yes, I told you so, didn't I?"

"Very well then, I'll see you tomorrow. Good day to you." The phone clicked in his ear leaving him staring at the receiver. He was still in a state of shock, but clear about what he would have to do. He opened the bottom drawer of his desk and removed a cheque book from an envelope labelled "Aerial Golf Club." He already owed twenty thousand dollars to the club account, but as he now reassured himself, no-one else knew that. Another twenty thousand would settle his debt to the Fast Credit & Loan Approval Institute Incorporated, and the whole forty thousand deficit would be replaced as soon as the insurance plan had been implemented.

As he wrote a cheque payable to cash, he congratulated himself for his foresight in having had two of them pre-signed by the committee chairman who, obligingly, had responded to the suggestion that with two signatures being required, it would be helpful in the event of emergencies. All that remained was to call the bank, forewarn them of the transaction, and pick up the money. Ten minutes later, he had confirmed that the cash would be available at one p.m. that same day. With that business taken care of, he scratched a line on his 'To Do' list and began to jot some notes on a pad. Just as he got started, Mrs. Bennett opened his door and informed him, apologetically, that his wife was on the phone.

"Look... I thought I told you not to interrupt me," he complained, "I'm not going to speak to anyone."

"Yes, but your wife! I thought you would want to talk to her."

"Well I don't. Tell her I'm in a meeting. I'll call her later." Mrs. Bennett persisted.

"I'm sorry, but she knows you are here, I just told her that."

"Oh damn it!" he exploded. "Why am I always surrounded by such idiocy! All right, put her through." He picked up the phone at its first ring. "I thought I told you not to call me at work," he growled. "This had better be important; I've got a lot on my plate." Mary Garter fought back.

"Oh, stop whining, of course it's important! I've just had a car accident and according to the police officer here, it was due to the fact that the tires on my car are worn out and should have been replaced long ago…." Her voice trailed off at her husband's interruption.

"Is it badly damaged?"

"I'm fine. Thank you for asking". Her sarcasm drew no response, so she continued. "And you'll be pleased to know the car is too. However, there's a newspaper box by a convenience store here that has a large dent in its side which the police officer is currently trying to push back into shape. He tells me that he is giving me a repair order ticket and that I have twenty four hours to get a new set of tires or take the car off the road."

"Oh great, that's going to be expensive. I suppose you were speeding again."

"No, I was not speeding. And, expensive or not, please note that I am now going to spend whatever I must to get these tires replaced."

The thought of an additional dent in an already creaking bank account made him cringe. His own set of new tires and a recent brake overhaul had been painfully expensive. But, as he now recalled, what had galled him the most was learning afterwards that had he talked to the manager of a gas station he sometimes used, he could have saved himself half of that outlay, provided that not too many questions were asked about the man's sources of supply. He had consoled himself with the thought that he could take advantage of the connection on some other occasion. And that, surely, was now!

"Look" he said, "I've got an idea. I think I know where I can get a good deal. Let me check into it. Bring your car round here, pick up mine, and I'll get the tires sorted out at lunch time."

"My, my, you are being accommodating" said Mary, her suspicions immediately aroused. "Don't you trust me to do it myself?"

"No, I don't. They take advantage of women like you."

"Like me! And what is that supposed to mean?" she demanded.

"Oh, stop being so prickly. You know what I mean. They take advantage of women because they think they don't know anything about cars."

"Fine. You take care of it, and impress them with your extensive knowledge of auto-mechanics, while I use your car. My only requirement is that I get a new set by this evening. Agreed?"

"That's what I proposed isn't it? Leave your car in my parking spot. I've got a key." He hung up the phone and reached for the telephone directory. He called two suppliers and got a similar quote from each -- both in the astronomical price range he expected. And of course, wheel balancing, old tire disposal, and taxes, would all be extra. The optimistic mood with which he had started the day had long since abated, but the thought of saving half the amount of the quotations he had just obtained, cheered him significantly. He searched through his wallet and pulled out a business card. He peered at it, and found the telephone number of one Tony Angle, Service Manager, Ambrosia Service Station. He dialed the number and was quickly connected to his target.

"Yes, Mr. Garter, of course I remember. What are you looking for?" After explaining his requirements and getting confirmation that the order could be filled at almost exactly half the cost he had just been quoted, he arranged to deliver his wife's car at lunch time. He hung up the phone, glowing with a sense of accomplishment. It was much more than just saving some money. What he was doing was being resourceful, creative, and decisive. He was proud of these qualities, and relished the opportunity to demonstrate them -- particularly when it meant he could thumb his nose at an enemy such as those price-gouging tire suppliers he had spoken to earlier. He glanced at his watch. It was nearly ten thirty a.m. and he was due at a budget planning meeting. There was, he told himself, time for one more piece of personal business. He opened the Aerial Golf Club file and sifted through the contents until he located a list of the names and addresses of the committee members.

He ran a finger down the list alighting on the name of Harry Jefferson. With eyes narrowing, he copied the telephone number and address onto his scratch pad, scowling with indignation as he recalled Jefferson's insulting suggestion that independent auditing should be considered. He tore off the sheet, folded it carefully and placed it inside his wallet.

*   *   *

Tony Angle, owner of the Ambrosia Service Station, was a similar height to John Garter, but slimmer and possibly a little younger. Lank, black hair, topped-off a sharp featured face. Smile creases, etched around his eyes and mouth, suggested good humour, and a happy disposition. But now, his expression was serious. "You'll have to tell the police that you had a spare set of tires, but hadn't got around to installing them. It's the only way, I can't give you a receipt -- not at this price." He paused thoughtfully.

"I'll give you a receipt to show we installed them if you like."

This unexpected snag in his transaction with Tony Angle was disturbing. His under-the-counter deal was to be strictly cash, with no paper record, but somehow, he had to be able to demonstrate to the police that new tires had been purchased.

"Mmm….well, I suppose the installation receipt would work, wouldn't it?" He looked for, and received, a reassuring response.

"Of course, piece of cake! They just want to see some sort of proof. In any case, they can always walk out to the parking lot and take a look at them, can't they?"

"Yes, you're right. Okay then. I'm just a bit nervous about it."

"Don't worry about it. They aren't going to treat you like you were a criminal or something. It's just a traffic offence!" John Garter found himself warming to the idea that the problem had been solved.

"Well, I'm pleased with what you have been able to do here, and I'll know where to come next time I need a bargain."

"Exactly! But just one thing Mr. Garter, I'd prefer if we could keep this transaction to ourselves." His voice ended in a questioning tone. "I let people know about the business when I figure I can trust them, like I did with you, so it would be better if you could avoid talking about this to other people. OK?"

"Oh, yes, I understand. You can count on me". He felt a tinge of excitement at being a confidante in the man's entrepreneurial ventures. As he pocketed the receipt for tire installation that Tony Angle now proffered, a thought struck him. "Tell me" he said, trying to sound as casual as possible, "In your dealings with insurance companies, how quickly do they pay out when someone makes a theft claim?"

"Lost something have you?" Tony Angle grinned, but quickly adopted an air of serious contemplation when he saw the alarmed reaction his comment had drawn. He scratched at his head. "Well, that varies Mr. Garter. Sometimes it's just a matter of days. I know someone who had their radio stolen last week, and they got a cheque the same day. That's fast though. If it's the whole car that's stolen then the police investigate and there's usually a period of time while they wait to see if it turns up somewhere, which it often does, so it can drag on a bit. They're pretty good though -- usually they'll let you rent a car while the claim is being investigated." He paused, noticing the rapt attention being paid to his words. "Oh, I could tell you a few stories about insurance companies though." He gave a knowing wink. "Some of the biggest scams going."

It was now getting a little uncomfortable and John Garter began to regret having spoken about the matter. But, at the same time he was fascinated by the man's seeming familiarity with an area rapidly becoming his own obsession.

"Look" he said, "I'm a bit pressed for time now, but I would like to hear more about that stuff, and maybe get your advice on a couple of related things."

"Sure Mr. Garter, any time. It was a pleasure to do business with you." He extended a hand and crunched heavily on the cautiously proffered palm. "You can catch me most nights at the Fox, on Cross Street."

"Will you be there tomorrow night?" John Garter made up his mind to exploit the moment. "Maybe I could buy you a drink and get your advice on some things." Tony Angle looked at him quizzically.

"Sure. I'll be there at about seven o'clock."

"All right, that's good. I'll see you tomorrow then." He climbed back into his wife's car. It was almost one thirty p.m. and his next task was to cash the Aerial Golf Club cheque. He headed towards the branch where the account was registered, feeling increasingly uncomfortable about the fraudulent transaction he was about to make. His concern did not emanate from any twinge of conscience, but rather from a mounting anxiety that something might go wrong with the plan, and prevent him from walking out with twenty thousand dollars in his briefcase.

As he wove through the lunch time traffic, he reminded himself that he had experienced no difficulties when he made the pre-arrangements on the telephone that morning, and reassured himself that the cash should be ready and waiting. He pulled into the crowded car park behind the bank, and squeezed into the last remaining space, adjacent to a concrete wall.

He walked briskly across the parking lot, and onto the busy sidewalk. It was crowded with lunch time office workers, and the chill wind that gusted down the street, added an air of urgency to everyone's pace. Head bowed, he turned the corner and entered the main door of the bank. Fifteen minutes later, he had completed his transaction. All had gone according to plan, and his briefcase now contained four neat packages, each holding fifty, one-hundred dollar bills. He stepped into the revolving front door, and was disgorged effortlessly onto the street.

Keeping a tight grasp on the handle of his booty, he turned the corner and strode towards the car park. As the cool air ushered his passage, a sense of relief flooded over him. There was light at the end of the tunnel... and it was about time. He backed his wife's car out of the narrow space into which it was wedged, and peered into the rear view mirror to assess his proximity to a metal guard rail. Just as he decided it was safe to turn, his passage was blocked by a black SUV that had swung abruptly through the entrance to the car park, and was now maneuvering into an adjacent area marked "Staff Only". He glared in the direction of the car, and immediately recoiled in shock. His hands locked onto the steering wheel, and his eyes, which now stared directly ahead, gradually crept upwards to the rear view mirror. There, they confirmed, without the slightest doubt, what he feared: it was Julia Miller.

He cursed himself for having been so negligent as to overlook the possibility that Julia Miller may have some connection with the bank where he had just withdrawn twenty thousand dollars of the club's money. He began conversing with himself, furiously posing, and then answering, question after question. That she had some connection with this particular branch was evident, but, did her parking privileges mean that she worked at the branch or that she was visiting on bank business? Either could be true! Was there some risk that the day's transactions would come to her attention? Yes, possibly so! Was there any reason to believe that she would get to see a document showing that the Aerial Golf Club had withdrawn a chunk of money from one of its accounts? Yes, possibly so! If the transaction did come to her attention, what would she make of it? She would investigate! Where were they meeting for lunch on Friday? Elm Street. Had she not chosen that spot because it was close to where they both worked? Yes, she had! Could it be, then, that she was just visiting the branch, perhaps for a meeting? Yes, it could! If she didn't actually work at this branch didn't that reduce the risk of her becoming aware of the transactions? Yes, surely so!

By the time he had finished the self-interrogation, he had convinced himself that Julia Miller did not work at this branch, that she had arrived for a meeting of some kind, and that it was unlikely that, as a matter of course, she would review branch transactions. Thus comforted, he confirmed that she was nowhere in sight, and cautiously resumed his exit from the parking lot, satisfied that the risk of discovery was slight. All the same, he told himself, he would need to concoct some rationale for the withdrawal, in case it did come to her attention. Their lunch meeting was not far off and, he told himself, he could assess the danger more accurately then. For now, he must be patient.

It was two o'clock, and his next appointment, at work, was thirty minutes away. There was, he decided, time to repay his debt now -- he did not wish to risk any misunderstanding with the Fast Credit & Loan Approval Institute Incorporated. He sped off in the direction of their offices to repay his loan a full day earlier than promised. The office occupied by Gustav Illiach, was on the third floor of a drab, Victorian building, whose almost-vertical inclination seemed to owe as much to the iron fire escape ladders in which it was wrapped, as it did to the strength of its foundations. It was his third visit to the Institute and, as before, the building greeted him with a not unpleasant smell of lemon, mixed with dust. He clanked shut the gate of a now do-it-yourself elevator, and ascended slowly, relieved that he was about to rid himself of yet another irritant in his life. He opened the office door and was greeted by a young woman wearing a short black leather skirt, spike-heel shoes, and dyed red hair.

"Oh, hello Mr. Garter, how are you?" She pushed shut the top drawer of a filing cabinet. Mr. Illiach isn't here just now, I think he was expecting you at lunch time tomorrow."

"Yes, I'm earlier than I said. I have the loan repayment for him. When is he going to be back?"

"Do you know, I'm not sure, Mr. Garter. He had lunch with an old friend, and I think he may be out for the afternoon." She looked at him and winked. "Best to get him in the mornings really."

He peered around the sparsely furnished office that Gustav Illiach shared with his assistant, Rose. "Do you have a safe here?"

"Yes, of course we do Mr. Garter, you can't run a business like ours without one, especially with the kind of tenants that come and go in this place!"

"Well, what do you suggest? I've got the money, and I want to make sure he gets it before he unleashes his secret weapon on me." He laughed nervously.

"Oh, you mean Rudolph! That's what I call him anyway -- on account of his nose! Yes, you don't want to be on his recovery list Mr. Garter, although if you ask me his heart's in the right place." She smiled to herself, clearly protective of her misunderstood business associate. "Let me get your file. You can leave the cash with me. I'll put it in the safe, and give you a receipt." She walked back to the filing cabinet and withdrew a brown folder. "It's twenty thousand dollars exactly, Mr. Garter. Is that what you have?"

"Yes it is. I've got it right here." He patted his briefcase.

"All right -- let me have it then. We'd better count it together. Put it over here." She pointed to Gustav Illiach's empty desk top. He opened his case and set four packages on top.

"One hundred fifties in each." he said, confidently.

Rose picked up the first bundle and skimmed deftly through the notes, picking at each with a rubber finger cap, while counting softly "... ninety nine, one hundred!" She repeated the exercise with the other bundles with the same final result. "Twenty thousand exactly--good! Now, let me put this away. She walked to the safe, wedged out of view in the far corner of the room, and spun the dials. "I'll make sure he knows it's here Mr. Garter, and I'll give you a receipt in just one moment." Rose returned to her desk, opened a drawer, and retrieved a receipt book. In neat, practiced, handwriting she filled out the document and handed him the top copy.

"There you are Mr. Garter, all signed and sealed." She smiled reassuringly. "If Mr. Illiach was here, he would say 'Thank you and congratulations!' I don't know why, but he always says that."

Nourished by accomplishment, rather than by food, he returned to his office where he was met by Mrs. Bennett. "Oh, you're back." she observed, "They've started the budget meeting without you. Do you want me to tell them you're here now?"

"No! What would be the point of that? I'm heading there now, so as soon as I walk through the door they will know that I'm back, won't they?" Mrs. Bennett accurately interpreted the reason for what she always referred to as his 'liverish' mood.

"Would you like a sandwich before you go Mr. Garter? There are some left over from the meeting in Room B."

"Er…yes, all right then, perhaps I will." For a moment, Mrs. Bennett thought she detected a look of gratitude on his face.

As she left to find him food, he reflected on his achievements of the past two hours. He had obtained new tires for his wife's car, and saved himself a substantial financial outlay. He had found in Tony Angle a window into the world of insurance fraud, and had made arrangements to meet him the next day to pursue discussions further. He had cashed a cheque for twenty thousand dollars, satisfied himself that his near-miss encounter with Julia Miller was unlikely to be a threat, and just in case it was, he had invented a story to tell her. He had received an assurance from Gustav Illiach that repayment of his debt would result in withdrawal of the "enforcement order", and he had now paid the money in full. Things were going well! The rest of the day could be devoted to company business.

*   *   *

That evening, at the Garter household, dinner was served. It was a cold plate meal that Mary had prepared earlier in the day, and a perfect match for the mood at the table. She stared incredulously at her husband.

"So what am I supposed to show to the police officer when he wants to see a receipt for the tires?"

"I told you, you don't need to give him a receipt. Just go there, tell them the work was completed, and show them the receipt for installation. Lots of people keep a spare set of tires. That's all you have to tell him. Park nearby so that they can have a look if they want to."

"You are such a cheapskate! I can't believe you would take part in some sleazy deal like that and put me in this embarrassing situation all for the sake of saving a measly dollar or two."

"It's not a dollar or two, it's a lot of money, and if you haven't understood that we can ill afford to thumb our noses at saving opportunities like that, then I'm not surprised you were stupid enough to get pulled over for speeding in the first place."

"I was *not* speeding. I skidded into a newspaper vending machine!" She stood up, brimming with indignation. "Look I'm going to the police station now, so if I don't come back you'll know that I have been arrested. Or, perhaps," she mumbled inaudibly to herself, "finally come to my senses and left you!" She snatched from her husband's outstretched hand a piece of paper signed by Tony Angle, Service Manager, Ambrosia Service Station, picked up her purse, and marched towards the front door. "Don't wait up for me, I'm going to visit Ellen afterwards, so I'll be late."

The door slammed and John Garter was left alone with his thoughts and some kitchen chores. After clearing the dishes from the table, he stacked them in the dishwasher, and tidied-up meticulously, all the while thinking about the irksome matter of how to replace the Golf Club money he had 'borrowed'. The burglary and insurance scheme still seemed the best solution to his problems, although the plan was not without risk, and there were still many questions to answer. He wondered how long he would have to wait before being able to sell the jewellery. What was the required cooling off period? And where could he sell the jewellery to ensure he got the best possible price? As he pondered these questions, his conscience, resting conveniently in a state of deep hibernation, failed to register the slightest twitch of concern. He reminded himself that he could not afford to wait much longer: he had lived with the problem long enough, but each day that passed increased the risk of discovery. The best time for the burglary would be when Mary was at her night school class.

He wrung out the cloth he had used to wipe down the counter top, dropped it into a bowl, and then carefully dried his hands. He walked into the hallway and examined the front door. It looked very solid and seemed an unlikely entry point for a burglar. He wandered back into the kitchen, and peered at the back door. It too, was solidly built, but the top half of the door was mostly glass, framed symmetrically with six separate panes of glass. It would, he told himself, be an easy matter to put duct tape over one of panes, and silently bang it out. The gap would then be wide enough for him to reach inside and turn the lock. Yes, that would probably be the way that a thief would make an entry. He made a mental note to have an out-of-reach bolt installed on the door immediately after the burglary.

It was seven o'clock, and he had one more piece of business. He walked to the desk in his study, opened his wallet, and removed the piece of paper containing the name and address of Harry Jefferson, his nemesis on the Golf Club Committee. He stared at it and scowled. What a fool that man was. He opened a drawer, pulled out a writing pad and, in large capital letters, began to print:

MRS. JEFFERSON:

YOUR HUSBAND IS A
LIAR AND A   CHEAT.
HIS PREDILECTION FOR

VISITING PROSTITUTES
PLACES YOU AT GREAT RISK.
PLEASE TAKE CARE.

A WELL-WISHER.

He carefully sealed the note in an envelope, addressed it to Mrs. Jefferson, and placed a stamp in the corner. Five minutes later, the envelope was in the mail, and he was walking back home with a jaunty step. "Let the miserable bugger explain that one!" he smirked.

CHAPTER FOUR

Mary Garter poured herself another cup of breakfast coffee and spoke to her husband for the first time that morning. "I forgot to ask, did you remember your dental appointment yesterday?"

"Oh damn! No, I didn't... damn it!! That means they're going to charge us. Look, call them for me and explain I had an emergency at work... see if they can arrange something else."

"No John, I will not! You can do that yourself. I'm not Mrs. Bennett and I'm not going to mop-up after you like she is paid to do."

"All right, no need to make such an issue out of it." He bit angrily into a slice of toast. "By the way, you didn't tell me what the police had to say about the new tires." He looked up curiously.

"It was fine -- I didn't get arrested and I didn't even have to show the receipt. I just had to sign a piece of paper." Mary smiled to herself as she recalled an amusing, twenty five minute encounter with an outrageously flirtatious desk sergeant: so outrageous that Mary had wondered whether to point out to him that while she had found his banter to be acceptably good natured, others may have seen it as sexual harassment. In the event, she decided against it: after all, the man was still employed, so, presumably, he had some reliable method for reading where personal boundaries lay. How had he figured out hers so quickly? Mary had pondered the question on her return journey, but had not arrived at a conclusion before reaching Ellen's house.

"I told you so!" Clearly relieved, her husband returned his attention to his coffee and toast.

"Don't forget that I'm out tonight at my art class will you?" Mary mentally mapped out her day. It was going to be busy. In addition to her favourite night school class, her schedule included lunch with Daniel, an occasion that would, she reminded herself, be the last time that she would see him. And, there was one other meeting that she had arranged for later in the afternoon: it was with a divorce lawyer.

"I'm out too." he replied. "More committee business. I'll be home first though, so I'll need dinner at six." Mary clenched her teeth and resisted the temptation to bang her husband over the head with her cereal bowl.

"You'll have to get something yourself," she replied," I have a lot on, and there's plenty in the refrigerator

*   *   *

Mary finished the last drains of her after lunch coffee, and replaced the cup in its saucer. She leaned forward across the table. "No Daniel, I can't do that. In fact, I think it is better if we don't see each other again. Look, it's been a wonderful relationship and I care for you very much, but I can't continue like this." She stared at him intently. "We both knew that we would get to this point didn't we? We've talked about it before. We have no future together, and I have to get my life back in order again." She paused while Daniel adopted a pained expression, and straightened himself in his chair.

"Very well Maria if that is how you feel then I must let you go." His thick French accent sounded stronger than ever. "But, I must say, my heart is aching to hear those words." He leant forward, squinting slightly to compensate for his unwillingness to wear glasses. "Never has this happened to me before. You are a beautiful woman. I am a not unattractive man. Surely we can be together somehow?"

"No, Daniel, we can't. I know you feel hurt by what I am saying ... and hurting you is the last thing I want to do, but I have to do this. Besides... an attractive young man like you and a middle aged woman like me.... you'll have forgotten me in no time!" Daniel ignored the opportunity to return her compliment and thought carefully about what he had just heard.

"Perhaps you are right Maria. There will be others.... but I feel the hurt in my heart." He pressed a palm across the top of his stomach, and struck an anguished pose. "I have been loyal to you. You are a passionate woman. I am a good lover am I not? I don't want you to leave me!"

"Yes Daniel, you are, and I know you don't want me to leave." Daniel nodded his agreement.

"Then why must you walk out on me like this?" He was being more difficult than she had bargained for.

"Because I can't carry on like this Daniel. I have to get on with my life. What we have shared has been wonderful and I will treasure it always, but we have no future together. Daniel, I have to stop seeing you now so that I can deal with issues I have been avoiding. You see that don't you?"

"Yes, of course I do Maria, I'm not stupid." Despite a puzzled look he continued confidently. "I am a single man. You are a married woman." He paused. "Of course I understand." Relieved at having reached some new ground in the discussion, she decided to seize the moment.

"Daniel, I am going to leave now." She opened her purse, extracted some cash, and tucked it under the bill that languished nakedly in a black tray at the edge of the table. "That should cover it I think." She reached for one of Daniel's hands and squeezed it between both of hers. "Look, there's no easy way to do this. Let's not make it more difficult than it needs to be. She stood up. "Goodbye Daniel. You are a very sexy man, and I will miss you." She gathered her purse, turned on her heels and walked purposefully to the coat rack by the door, leaving a puzzled Daniel to salvage his pride in her genuinely felt parting observation.

*   *   *

Garter winced as a three inch needle probed into his lower right jaw. "That will just take a few minutes. I'll be back shortly." The dentist shuffled off to an adjacent cubicle, leaving him wishing that he hadn't leapt at the opportunity to avoid financial penalty by accepting a last minute lunch-time cancellation.

While he waited in the chair, he ran over in his mind the elements of his insurance plan. There were two pieces that he worried about the most. How quickly would the insurance company pay up for the losses, and, how and when would he sell the jewellery? He resolved to engineer his discussions that evening with Tony Angle around these points. The important thing was that the money would come through in time for him to replenish the Golf Club account before anyone discovered the shortfall.

A masked-man, wearing a white gown and rubber gloves, bore down on him with an enthusiastic gait. "Okay Mr. Garter, we should be ready to drill that out now."

*   *   *

It was 4.30 p.m. by the time Mary Garter left the offices of Douglas, Douglas, Juby and Cross. Her appointment with Ms. Juby had been extremely informative, and had left her greatly encouraged that her future as a divorced woman need not be spent in abject poverty. In fact, as she had just been reminded, the Garter joint asset pool was much more than the house minus mortgage, plus cars, and meager savings; it also included future earnings, pension plan investments, company share-holdings, and in all probability, profit sharing expectations too.

As comforted as she was by the thought that divorce need not result in financial ruin, Mary Garter now realized that whatever the financial outcomes there would be no turning back. Their marriage was beyond any kind of repair and the love she had once felt for her husband had vanished long ago. The longer she delayed the inevitable, the more painful it would be. Money would be important and he was certainly not going to part with any of that without a fight. However, she felt certain she would manage. At one time she had made a modest income as an illustrator for a publisher of children's stories. For the past two years, she had worked at home, writing and illustrating her own books. She had viewed this work as a creative outlet, a kind of hobby, but she knew that if she put her mind to it, the opportunity was there to turn her work into a professional career.

As she made her way home, Mary recalled her conversation with Ms. Juby. What was that last part?

Oh, yes! Ms Juby had summarized with a four-step action plan proposal. "Remember," she had said, "Four steps: Decide, Organize, Implement, and Treat yourself!"

Mary grinned. The acronym she had just formed in an effort to retain Ms. Juby's message seemed particularly apt. There would be no turning back!

* * *

Julia Miller poured herself another glass of red wine and picked vigorously at the remains of the pasta dish she had prepared for her dinner. Living alone, in the seventh floor of an elegant downtown condominium building was, for her, an ideal lifestyle. She could walk to work in 15 minutes, enjoy her proximity to an endless variety of shops, stores, and restaurants, feel safe at any time of day or night, savour the vibrancy of city life, and, increasingly important of late, reach her fitness club in five minutes.

At 35-years of age she was single, and ascending the career ladder at such a rapid rate that some of her male colleagues had been forced to save face by consoling themselves with the thought that they were victims of reverse discrimination. The truth, however, was that she was extremely bright, and had enough organizational savvy to ingratiate herself with powerful allies, and capitalize on every opportunity that came her way--particularly if that meant the opportunity to expose weakness in the strong, incompetence in the able, and double standards in the smugly pious.

As she ate, she turned the pages of a financial report, stopping every now and again to absorb details, peer cynically at the graphs and tables it contained, and occasionally to make a dismissive noise that was a cross between a tsk-tsk and a cluck. Her study was interrupted by the telephone. She stretched out an arm from her perch at the kitchen counter, and lifted the receiver from the wall mount. "Hello, Julia Miller".

"Oh, yes, this is Harry Jefferson here. I'm sorry to call you at this late hour but I wanted to ask you about your proposal the other night on the committee -- the deferral of my audit proposal I mean..." His voice trailed off.

"Yes, Harry, and what did you want to ask?"

"Why did you do that! Don't you take this seriously? I mean...look...I'll be honest with you...I don't trust that we are getting the best return on the investments we hold, and Garter keeps blocking discussion about alternatives. I think he's getting a commission, or some kind of a rake off. That's not right and I want it all flushed out. The more we delay it the worse it gets."

"I see." Her voice was expressionless. "Harry, the committee made a decision to bring it up again later. I support that--I proposed it in fact-- and I can't see any reason to re-open the matter now". She waited for his reply, enjoying the moment as she imagined Jefferson's discomfort with her stonewall response. When it came she was a little surprised, and if the truth were told, disappointed that he appeared to have accepted it without question.

"All right then. But I don't want the issue to be lost". He paused. "By the way, just a personal thing. When you saw me the other night on Queen Street that was my niece I was with. Her birthday you know...I'd....er...taken her out for dinner".

Julia Miller smiled to herself. She had not seen Harry Jefferson since the last committee meeting, and had most certainly not spotted him escorting a "niece" on Queen Street. "Oh I see. I wondered who she was. And how is Mrs. Jefferson?" There followed for Julia Miller a delightful moment's silence while, in her mind's eye, Harry Jefferson wriggled on a skewer.

"She's fine thank you. Good night".

As she replaced the receiver, her smile gave way to a thoughtful expression. Very interesting! So, despite Jefferson's hunch about John Garter, he in fact knew nothing. Good. She could play this at her own pace.

Chapter Five

John Garter began to feel a little woozy. He had drunk two pints of beer and a third sat on the table in front of him. He advised himself to slow down. The room was crowded and noisy and he had to strain to hear the words of Tony Angle from across the table.

"Anyhow, this time the Fire department realized what was going on, and reported it to the police who traced the whole thing back to him!" The latest Angle story had been delivered to demonstrate that insurance fraud was not always without risk.

"But you're saying that getting caught is the exception rather than the rule?"

"Yes absolutely! How do you think those people with the restaurant on Tulip Street--you know, that place behind the garage. How do you think they built that place? They didn't have two pennies to rub together!" Tony Angle paused, placed his glass in front of him, and stared at John Garter thoughtfully. "Look Mr. Garter, I'm gonna go out on a limb here. You've obviously got something on your mind, and I can probably help you if you'd care to let me in on it! I'm the soul of discretion you know!"

Garter winced. Tony Angle's audacious comment was quite unexpected and for the briefest moment startled him to silence. But, almost immediately, he found himself experiencing a strong urge to open up to this man. Rogue he may be, but he was surely a trustworthy rogue! Almost before he knew it, Garter made the decision to bring this man into his confidence.

"Well...er, well yes, you're right! Okay I'm going share this with you". He leaned forward. "Look, this is just between the two of us, okay?"

"Of course it is Mr. Garter, I can guarantee you that. Tell me what's on your mind".

With a solemnity befitting a man making a death-bed confession, Garter proceeded to share with his new friend and confidante the fact that he was temporarily unable to repay a consolidation loan that he had negotiated with a club he belonged to. He explained that he had been the victim of some extraordinary injustices, and some plain bad luck, but that in all honesty the real truth was he had been badly let down by his stockbrokers. It was, he confided, almost a scandal that a supposedly reputable company could have behaved the way they did. As a professional financial manager, and prudent financial steward himself, he knew the responsibilities that went with positions of trust. He had been betrayed in his trust, but even though he bore no culpability for the financial difficulties he now faced, there was a loan to repay, and he was determined to make good on it at the first opportunity. "So", he concluded, "that's the picture and I'm determined to get back on track".

"Well, you have had a bad run of luck haven't you!" Tony Angle was being as sincere as his sense of humour would allow. "But, if I may say so, aren't you leaving out a piece of the puzzle?" Having delivered his story, he felt surprisingly relieved and almost light hearted.

"Well," he said "those were the highlights. What do you want-- all the gory details?"

"No, no, I get the idea! But what I mean is" Tony Angle leaned forward. "you haven't told me what you are planning to do to get back on track, have you?"

"Oh...no, I suppose I haven't. But I'm coming to that."

"And let me guess, Mr. Garter. Just a wild stab in the dark you understand, but could it possibly have anything to do with... an insurance company!" Tony Angle flashed his roguish grin, took another swallow of his beer, and sat back in his chair with an expectant look.

For a moment, he was silent. Should he, or shouldn't he, bring this man fully into his confidence and possibly even cut him in on his plan? He was satisfied that Angle was trustworthy, intelligent, discreet, knowledgeable, and most importantly had connections that would make the sale of his wife's jewellery a lot easier. He could probably be a useful business partner.

"Sorry if I'm out of line Mr. Garter." Tony Angle began to wonder if his timing had been a little premature. "But I can see what you're struggling with. To tell you the truth, I think I could be useful to you-- and besides, my advice is free!" Garter decided to take the plunge.

"You're right. I could do with some advice." He proceeded then to explain that he held several different kinds of insurance policy: life insurance, car insurance, fire insurance, homeowners insurance, and that over the years he had paid a small fortune in premiums helping insurance companies to get richer and richer. In all that time he had made only a couple of minor claims on the car insurance, while as Angle well knew, the rest of the world were exploiting the system, and forcing the premiums higher and higher. He paused for breath. "So, I think it's my turn to recover some of my investment."

"Of course it is Mr. Garter! That's what I thought you were going to say. And what exactly did you have in mind?"

"Well, I thought a burglary might be possible." He paused, scrutinizing Tony Angle's face for any sign that retreat would be advisable. Finding none, he continued, more confidently this time. "We have some valuables that would be an obvious target, jewellery and so on." He paused again.

"Yes... go on! " Tony Angle paid rapt attention.

"Well that's it."

"What do you mean that's it!"

"I mean, that's the plan! There's a robbery, some jewellery is stolen, I claim on the insurance, get the money, sell the stuff later, and that's it! The details aren't all figured out, I'll grant you, but it should work shouldn't it?" He looked intently at Tony Angle hoping for instant affirmation that he was not wildly off track with his idea.

"What's the insured value of the jewellery?" Tony Angle had a serious expression and peered quizzically at John Garter.

"Well it's not itemized but the policy specifies we're covered for up to sixty thousand dollars."

"Is it worth that much?"

"Yes, possibly a bit more I think."

"Where are you going to sell it?"

"I don't know yet." He looked optimistically at his companion, "Maybe you can help me there?" Tony Angle was not going to be side tracked.

"Who's going to do the break-in and where will you be when it happens?"

"Well…I thought I would do it."

"You...! Are you serious?"

"Well, yes. That's what I'd thought."

"So let me get this straight. You'll wait till your wife is out one evening, break-in the house somehow, collect up the goods that are going to be stolen, and put them, say... in a bag." Tony Angle continued slowly, despite a dubious expression. "You'll leave the house with the bag of stuff, drive off, stash the bag somewhere safe so you can pick it up again easily later on, come back home, and find that there's been a robbery." He paused. "You'll call the police, and tell them that you just got home and found the place had been raided. When they come, you'll still be shocked and amazed, you'll show them how the burglar got in, tell them what's been stolen, and comfort your wife when she arrives back home and finds her jewellery all gone. Oh, and you'll have a story about where you were while the robbery was happening, just in case you need it, and you'll find a way to make sure that no-one saw you coming or going when you were actually doing the break-in. Then, later, you'll make a full report to the insurance company, fill out their forms, answer their questions, and sit back until pay day! Is that about it?"

Garter's face had turned several shades paler. Hearing the steps spelled out so vividly made him realize that he had not yet spent enough time internalizing the venture or imagining how he would feel as the process unfolded. He was a coward at heart, and despite his brusque, aggressive manner, full of insecurities and fears.

"Er, well yes, that's what I had thought, but I'm open to suggestions." He picked up his glass and swallowed the contents in a large gulp. Tony Angle smiled at him before speaking.

"Be honest now Mr. Garter, do you really think you've got the guts to do all that?" John Garter looked nervous.

"I'm not sure...I think so...I have to! Can you help?"

∗   ∗   ∗

At that moment, in a bleak, basement apartment, on the other side of town, Daniel headed toward a kitchen cupboard, pulled out a bottle of schnapps and poured himself a large glass. He had returned home to discover a message from his advertising agent--a man on whom he depended to secure occasional contracts for appearing in television commercials. He had not, after all, been selected as the person to boost the sales of Dude Ranch shaving cream. That news, coming on top of his painful lunch with Mary, was almost too much to bear. Two rejections in one day! Could things get any worse? He took a large swill from his glass.

∗   ∗   ∗

After receiving his invitation to assist in the execution of the Garter burglary and insurance fraud, Tony Angle moved into high gear. "Look Mr. Garter," he said, "as I see it, the problem with your plan is that too much depends on you."

"How do you mean?" He listened intently.

"Well, what I'm saying is that you're doing the whole thing yourself, the break-in, the storage, the police interviews, the wife comforting, the insurance interview, the recovery, the fencing...it's too much Mr. Garter, it's not familiar territory for you!"

Garter thought it appropriate to nod his understanding of the point being made, even though he was not entirely convinced of its merit.

"You think I can't handle it then?"

"No, it's not that you can't handle it Mr. Garter." Tony Angle leaned forward, "What I mean is there's a good chance you're going to slip up somewhere along the line if you don't share the work."

"Well, I have to admit, I do worry about it" he lowered his voice, "particularly about selling the jewellery-- you know, where, when, who to, that kind of thing."

"And so you should, Mr. Garter, that's the most dangerous part. But I'll tell you what else you should be worried about...and that's actually doing the break-in." He paused. "Look, think about it. It will be much easier to brazen it out with the police if you can come home, find a rear window broken, and your valuables stolen, than it will if you've got to do the job yourself first!" His point was well taken.

"Yes, I can see that." He hesitated. "Are you offering to help me there?"

"Yes I am. Not only that, I can help you to get a good return on the jewellery, and I can help you keep on top of any problems that might come up with the insurance claim."

Encouraged by Garter's nod of understanding, he continued. "Look, I wouldn't expect a fifty-fifty cut in the whole thing -- just on what we get for selling the jewellery. As far as I'm concerned the insurance thing is between you and the insurance company. There's a fair bit of work for me on the jewellery side though, and some risk, so I'd have to get cut-in there. Like I said, fifty-fifty would be fair." He paused expectantly, while Garter did mental arithmetic. If he got the proceeds from the insurance company, and half of the sale price, whatever that turned out to be, he would probably still have enough to clear all his debts, with some left over. There was no doubt that Tony Angle could be very useful when it came to selling the jewellery, and, if he was prepared to do the break-in as well, he could be a great help.

"All right" he said. "I'll agree to that.

"You're on! Put it here, Mr. Garter." Tony Angle's hand appeared in front of him, as if ready for an arm wrestling contest. "Here's to a successful joint venture." Their fists locked awkwardly and waggled briefly.

"Yes indeed, a successful joint venture." He quickly disengaged his hand, and reached for his beer.

"Do you know what I'm thinking Mr. Garter?" Tony Angle looked mischievous. "Did I understand you to say that your wife was out tonight?"

"Yes, it's Wednesday, she's at an art class. She doesn't usually get back until late."

"How late?"

"About eleven thirty usually. A group of them go for coffee after the class."

"There's no time like the present Mr. Garter. Let's do it now!"

"Do what?" He was genuinely puzzled.

"Do the break-in of course! The house is empty, right? We've got plenty of time before your wife is back. We can get the whole thing rolling right away!"

"But we haven't organized anything yet, or got the story straight. I've got to explain things to the police."

"It's really not that difficult Mr. Garter. You've been robbed -- you're supposed to be confused! Look it's nine o'clock now. The robbery is my part of the action. What you need to think about is what you will do at..." He looked at his watch "... at ten thirty when you get home and find the place all messed up -- I'll go easy there, just enough to make it look real. That means you've got a whole hour and a half to figure out what to do and say!"

He leaned forward grinning, "And Mr. Garter, if that's not long enough then none of this is going to work is it?"

"Yes, you're right -- I suppose there is enough time to do it now." He became a little more comfortable with the idea. "But we do have some things to sort out, don't we? I mean, you don't know where I live, or where any of the jewellery is, or what the best way to get in..." His voice trailed off at Tony Angle's impatient interruption.

"Mr. Garter, please! You live at 28, Brookmead Crescent, the house with the green double garage doors out front and the back yard with all those cedar trees. Your wife's jewellery will be in the main bedroom -- in a jewellery box that will either be on a dressing table in full view, or in a drawer or in a closet. You've probably got some money lying around within 10 feet of the jewellery, and there will be one or two saleable trinkets, here and there, in the bedroom, the living room, and a couple of other bedrooms. You haven't got a dog, or a burglar alarm, and your back patio lights don't come on automatically when someone walks by." He paused to see the effect. "Am I right or not!" Garter suddenly felt as if he had been found wandering in the street with no clothes. Tony Angle grinned knowingly. "But you're right, Mr. Garter, there are one or two things we need to agree on." He paused. "First of all, if there's anything you want to disappear that really is hidden away, you'd better tell me now -- I won't have long in there." He looked questioningly at John Garter.

"No, what you said was exactly right. The jewellery is in a box in the main bedroom closet. Everything else was right too."

"Good. Then all we need to do is get our stories straight about tonight…just in case. Let's agree that we met here at seven, we had a couple of beers together, we chatted about the future of that car of yours, and then left, at about nine. Agreed?"

"Agreed." Tony Angle had a sudden thought.

"By the way, have you got your car with you? I walked here, so I'm going to need you to drop me off around the corner from your place."

"Yes it's out back."

"Good!" He read Garter's expression. "Don't worry, no-one's going to see me get in the car, we'll meet across the road, behind the supermarket. Okay?" He continued with the instructions. "We left at nine, and went our separate ways. I went home, and you…well, I don't need to know what you did, but you'll have to figure something out though."

"I still haven't eaten dinner so I think I'll go to Aztec and get something there."

"You haven't eaten! God, you must be starving. You could have got something here you know."

"Yes, I know, too busy talking I suppose -- I would have eaten first but I was running late and my wife was going out so I didn't get around to it." Tony Angle looked at him thoughtfully.

"Does your wife work?"

"No, why?"

"Nothing. Just wondered." He was silent for a moment. "Never been married myself." Garter noticed the somewhat wistful tone, but could not help himself.

"Lucky you," he snorted.   Tony Angle looked thoughtful and said nothing for a few moments.

"Okay, then... I say we get out of here and get started. Are you ready?"

"Yes, I think I am."

"Good! You did say the drinks would be on you didn't you?"

They left through separate exits a few moments apart.

*   *   *

"I miss you Maria! I must kiss you, again and again!" Daniel sat on the living room floor of his apartment, propped against a sofa by two large cushions. In one hand he clutched a passport sized photograph of Mary Garter that he repeatedly drew to his lovingly puckered lips. In the other hand, he held a half empty bottle of schnapps. By now, he was certain that she missed him with an anguish as great as his own. He climbed unsteadily to his feet, and addressed her picture once more. "Don't worry my love, I will come for you!"

*   *   *

Garter walked through the back door of the pub, and out into the car park. The air was cold and his breath made small clouds as he puffed his way to where he had left his car. He was soon on his way. He crossed the intersection and circled the block. There was no one about and he glided silently to a halt at the end of a dark laneway where, Tony Angle waiting in the shadows, jumped into the passenger seat with a cheery grin.

"Okay, let's get going. Jeez, it's cold out there!"

"Good job you brought gloves. We don't need you leaving fingerprints anywhere do we!" He chuckled nervously.

"No fear of that, Mr. Garter. Look, you'd better go right at the next lights. You can go round the back of Safeway's and up by the park, then we'll be at the back of your place won't we."

"Yes... Okay, that works." He slowed the car for the turn. "Hey, wait a minute! I just thought of something..." He sounded anxious. "What will you do afterwards? You're going to do a robbery, come away with stolen property and have no car to get away in!"

"I wondered if you'd think of that Mr. Garter. Look, don't worry, I've got that all figured out--and believe me, the less you know about it the better. You'll come home, find there's been a burglary, and you can take it from there. My part will be done, and I'll be home again, safe in bed. You don't have to worry about it." Garter remained puzzled, but let go of the concern.

"We should agree on when to meet again though shouldn't we? We'll need to debrief."

"Yes, we should. Why don't you telephone me tomorrow at the garage?"

"All right. But what about the jewellery? What do we do with it until the investigation is completed?"

"Well you can have it back, or I can hold onto it-- makes no difference to me. Either way we'll have to keep it under wraps until it's safe to sell it."

"Well, I think it's probably best if you hold onto it. I can't very well take it back home, and risk having it turn up again."

"Well, that's true! All right then, it'll be safe with me." He grinned, "And if you get anxious, Mr. Garter, you can come and have a look at the stuff any time you choose."

The corner of the road that ran behind Garter's house was now in view. He pulled around it, and stopped half way along the unlighted street next to a high wooden fence.

"Okay, let me out here. Good luck with the police Mr. Garter! And don't worry; they're so busy these days they aren't going to be spending much time poking about. So you'll call me tomorrow then?"

He stepped from the car and quickly disappeared into the shadows. Garter turned the car around and made his way to the end of the road, confident they had not been seen. At the junction, he turned left, drove through a number of back streets, pulled out onto a main road, and parked outside the Aztec restaurant. He was excited and hungry. He looked at his watch. It was nine thirty exactly.

As Garter drove off to eat, Tony Angle squeezed himself through a space between the back fence, and a hydro pole. He stood next to a row of cedar trees, and surveyed the scene. The houses on either side appeared to be occupied, but both had drapes covering their lighted windows. He moved silently along the concrete path, which meandered through the tree-lined back yard, and up to a large wooden deck. One side of the deck was joined to a family room, and a kitchen, and the other side, to the dining room. He walked softly to the dining room windows and peered inside. He could see that an interior light had been left on, and that it illuminated the front hall and staircase.

He moved to examine the kitchen door, and a window to one side of it. The window was an obvious choice. It was secured by a flimsy casement latch that, he realized immediately, could be flipped with the blade of his pocket knife. He pulled it out, and began probing at the join between the upper and lower sections of the window. In less than two minutes, he had pried the latch, lifted the lower casement, climbed into the kitchen, and pulled down the window behind him. He unlocked the back door, in case he needed to make a hasty retreat, smiled to himself, and muttered under his breath, "Really, Mr. Garter, it shouldn't be that easy!"

The light coming from the hall chandelier was sufficient to guide Tony Angle through the whole of the lower floor. He walked through each room, observing, but without touching, and then made his way up the staircase to the upper level. The first bedroom he came to was sparsely furnished, and he could see that it had a single bed along one wall. He pulled back the bedclothes, and removed the covers from two pillows. He placed one pillow cover inside the other, tossed his makeshift loot bag over one shoulder, and, like Santa Claus heading to inspect his toy factory, strode confidently along the passageway. The main bedroom was directly ahead, but it was too dark in there for him to see properly. He pulled the drapes that covered the front windows, walked into the en-suite bathroom, closed the wooden shutter blinds above the vanity, draped two bath towels across the top of the window rail, and turned on the bathroom light. That was better.

He walked to the closet and immediately spotted the jewellery box. He lifted the lid, eyed the contents approvingly, and tipped them into his pillowcase sack. He tossed away the case, scattered everything that was on the closet shelves, opened every drawer he could find in the bedroom, and pulled out the contents into a jumbled mess on the floor. Once or twice he stopped to add items to his sack--a man's gold watch, the cash that he had accurately predicted would be available for picking, and a silver tray with matching trinket box. In less than five minutes he had scoured the whole room.

He went back to the landing and entered the next bedroom. Like the first, it was sparsely furnished. He decided it needed a ransacked appearance, and he went to work quickly but added nothing further to his sack. He did, however, transfer his loot into a large zippered sports bag that he spotted in a closet.

The last room appeared to be a studio of some sort. It had two easels, an architectural drawing board with a stool, a row of book shelves, and a desk with a computer. In one corner there was a large painting of a child on a swing. He looked around, recognized the room for what it was, and decided to leave it untouched. There was, he told himself, no point in rubbing salt in the wound.

*   *   *

In the front seat of the taxi, the driver fumbled through a small wad of notes, apparently having difficulty finding change for Daniel's twenty-dollar bill. Although still seated in the back, Daniel had his legs on the sidewalk and was organizing himself ready for a standing position. At last he overcame the invisible restraining forces, and clambered unsteadily to his feet.

"I don't need any change, thank you. Not at all-- not a bit, itst all yoursh to keep..." He slammed the cab door, and waved good-bye as the driver made off. He surveyed his surroundings, made a three hundred and sixty degree revolution, and tottered-off, confidently, in an uphill direction towards the top end of Brookmead Crescent. Every now again he would stop, take a sip from his bottle of schnapps, and in a soft, baritone voice, sing out, 'Mar-eeeie!' He came to a wobbly halt, outside number twenty-eight, and called softly again. "Mar-eeeie... Maria my love... are you reaaaady?" He cupped a hand over his ear, and listened carefully. Nothing!

He seated himself despondently on the low wall that fronted the house. His eyes closed for a full two minutes, until his head nodded forward, and he was jarred awake. He tried again. "Hello my love, ist me!" He peered ahead towards the dimly lighted house, but saw no movement. A primitive instinct suggested to him that he would find her in the back yard. He rolled determinedly towards the garage, and along a narrow passageway at its side, staying erect thanks largely to the wall on one side, and a hedgerow on the other.

After he emerged onto the back lawn Daniel saw a garden seat. He sat down, and immediately fell asleep. He was awakened a few minutes later when his body slumped sideways and he tumbled forward onto one knee. He immediately remembered the purpose of his quest. "Maria ish that you?" He looked around but saw no-one. He scratched at his head, stood up, and walked backwards while looking upwards toward the bedroom windows. He cooed softly, "Mareeeie...I'm here now!" He tripped over a large earthenware planter, and tried to steady his fall by grasping the stalk of the tree that the planter valiantly nurtured. He lay on the ground, confused, and with the planter on top of him. As he lay there, wondering whether to stay for a while, a primitive instinct suggested to him he would find her at the front of the house.

*   *   *

Tony Angle walked down the staircase and into the living room. He opened a glass-fronted bookcase and pulled the contents onto the floor. There were two more stops to make before leaving. In the dining room he helped himself to some silver spoons, two silver trays, an antique-looking vase, and a delicate cut glass figurine. He headed to his final destination, John Garter's study. He toppled a small table in one corner by the window, and added to his bag a pair of binoculars and a movie camera that sat on the shelves of a wall cabinet. That would do. There was, no doubt, much more that he could find, but this was sufficient for the intended purpose. He looked at his watch. It was ten minutes before ten -- less than thirty minutes since he had squeezed through the back fence. It was time to make his exit.

He opened the front door, stepped onto the porch, and eased the door into an almost closed position behind him. He made for a shaded area, in front of the garage, where he had a good view of the road outside. While he surveyed the scene, he removed an oversized bunch of keys from his coat pocket. Several cars were parked on the opposite side of the street. Tony Angle cast his professional eye over them. The ageing Buick, parked several houses further up the hill, was the best bet.

Carrying the bag over one arm, and with keys at the ready, he moved through the shadows to the driver's door. He selected a pointed, worn-looking key, and tried the lock. It opened at the first attempt. He slipped inside, started the engine, and before there was time to say "Manager, Ambrosia Service Station" he quietly accelerated away. As he picked up speed and reached to turn on the lights, a figure tottered into view in front of him. He swerved sharply, to avoid the collision, but it was too late. He felt the thud of someone's head on the right fender, and saw the figure rebound, spinning away to his right. "Oh shiiiit!"

To his great credit, Tony Angle resisted the urge to flee and instead jumped out of the car to inspect the damage he had inflicted. As he leant over the figure, he heard it moan. Without hesitation he dragged the man into the back seat of his get-away car, slammed the door, and sped off. A few minutes later, he drew to a halt in a quiet lane. He switched off the car lights, and pulled the man into a darkened area next to a locked car park gate. Through the chain link fence he could see an illuminated sign, confirming what he already knew -- he was less than one hundred metres from the hospital emergency ward. The man no longer made groaning noises, but, as Tony Angle noted with relief, he was at least still breathing. He spoke reassuringly to the slumped figure.

"Don't worry pal, I'm going to get you some help." He quickly returned to the driver's seat, sped down the lane, turned a corner, and drove into the parking lot of the suburban train station located one block down the road. He parked the Buick in a darkened area, grabbed his zipper bag, and walked quickly to the bank of telephones at the entrance to the station.

"Ach, oim just goin' ta say this once, sa please tak noot." In the best Scottish accent he could muster, Tony Angle, took 45 seconds to explain where an injured man could be found, and why it was important that he be found quickly. He hung up, and with his conscience clear, made for the taxi rank at the side of the station.

*   *   *

"It was about ten thirty." John Garter sat at the kitchen table talking to the young police officer seated opposite him. "I checked my watch just before I arrived back." The officer nodded and wrote in his note book.

"And you said you'd been out since about seven, sir, is that right?"

"Yes that's right. As he continued with his note-taking a female police officer holding a flashlight, came into the room from the rear deck.

"Looks like they came through the back yard all right." she said. "There's an ornamental flower pot turned over, and an empty bottle of schnapps on the lawn." She smiled. "I don't suppose you tossed that there Mr. Garter."

"No, I certainly did not." Garter's irritation with Tony Angle became stronger by the minute. Why on earth had he seen fit to create such a mess and to help himself to so much more than the jewellery and a few bits and pieces? His father had given those binoculars to him. If anything happened to them, Angle would regret it!

"Well, that's about all we can do for now, sir." The first officer closed his note book. "Come down to the station tomorrow when you've figured out everything that's missing, and give us a complete listing. I don't want to mislead you though...the chances of us getting it back aren't all that good."

At that moment, Mary Garter appeared in the room. "What's going on? I saw the police car outside! What's happened?"

"We've had a burglar I'm afraid dear." He had not called his wife 'dear' for several years, and it now sounded strange, even to him.

"What! What's been stolen?"

"My binoculars...the digital recorder, the movie camera... your jewellery by the looks of it." Mary Garter looked anguished.

"Oh no! Not all of Grandmother Martin's stuff...?" She put her hands over her face and turned towards the hall stairs. The woman police officer walked over, and curled an arm around her shoulder.

"Let me come up there with you, Mrs. Garter, it's a real mess I'm afraid." They wandered away leaving John Garter alone with the note-taking police officer.

"Where did you say your wife was tonight sir?"

"Art classes."

"Oh yes." He paused. "I guess this is going to be hard for her."

"Yes, hard for both of us in fact."

"We've had a lot of break-ins like this lately, Mr. Garter." He looked thoughtful. "But you know what sir, some houses are easier to get into than others. This one doesn't offer much resistance to a determined burglar." He looked around the kitchen. "No alarm system, no floodlights, poor locking system." He paused. "Look we're doing some security seminars down at the station on Tuesday nights Mr. Garter, why don't you come along for one--might save you from all this happening again." He grinned, "Doesn't alter the fact though, if someone is determined to break in, then they will... doesn't matter too much what you've got in the way of security. But, at least you might as well put a few obstacles in the way and encourage them to go next door instead!" Garter thought that an air of humility was called for.

"You're right," he said. "I suppose we have been a bit lax. But, I've learned a lesson from this I can tell you."

"I take it you have some insurance sir?"

"Er, yes, I think I have something that should cover some of this." He looked dubious. "To tell you truth I'm not exactly sure what the full coverage is, but I'll check it out tomorrow."

"They'll want a copy of the police report but you should get onto them right away. They will probably want to take a look themselves."

"Yes, thanks for the advice, I'll get onto them first thing. You will be looking for the culprit though won't you? We'd much prefer to get everything back again."

"Yes I'm sure you would, but the fact is the chances are very slim." He began to recount the gloomy theft recovery statistics, and seemed to John Garter to be unnecessarily pessimistic at a time when crime victims, such as himself, needed to be reassured. Mary Garter and the policewoman appeared in the doorway.

"It's horrible." Mary Garter shuddered. "I feel like I've been violated. All my jewellery, my gold rings, my bracelets, that diamond necklace of my mothers, all gone! It's horrible." The policewoman nodded sympathetically.

"Mr. Garter." she said. "Your wife mentioned that there was an anonymous threatening telephone call the other day. What do you think that was all about?" Garter was startled, but tried hard to disguise the fact.

"Oh yes, that....er, well it didn't make any sense to me…I assumed it was a wrong number." The other police officer pricked up his ears.

"What exactly was it sir?" Mary answered for him.

"It was a really nasty sounding voice, threatening, saying that our time was up and we'd better get it here fast, or else. Something like that. It was left on our voice mail."

"Better get 'it' here fast?" repeated the officer. "What would 'it' refer to I wonder?"

"Well, like I said, it makes no sense to me." Garter felt increasingly uncomfortable with the direction of the discussion.

"Do you think there could be a connection to this?" Mary gestured around the kitchen. "If someone was threatening us then maybe this is the 'or else' piece!"

"Have you deleted the message now?" asked the policewoman.

"I didn't," said Mary. "Did you John?"

"Yes, I believe so," he said, "I remember now... I didn't think it was worth saving." He knew that he had done no such thing, but hoped to bring an end to the matter.

"I'll check." Mary reached for the telephone, and dialed the message centre. "No, it's still here!" She passed the telephone to the policewoman who listened attentively. She passed the telephone back to Mary.

"Can you replay it for my partner please? You should hear this Nick." He pressed the receiver to his ear and listened. He whistled through his teeth.

"That is what I call a menacing telephone call." He reached for his note book once more and began to write. "When did you say that was left?" he asked.

"It was Monday," said Mary, confidently.

"And neither of you can think of anyone who might want something from you, or have cause to be aggrieved over something you did or didn't do?" He looked from one to the other.

"No, I can't," said Garter.

"I can't either." The police officers looked at each other. Officer Nick made a few more notes, closed his book, and sighed.

"Well," he said, "maybe it was a wrong number, but if you think of anything or anyone that might be connected to the call then let us know right away, okay? I wouldn't want to rule out some connection just yet". Garter cursed himself for not having got around to deleting the message.

"We'll be sure to let you know officer." he replied.

"Oh, and don't delete the message just yet, if you don't mind. We may need to listen to it again." He looked at his partner. "In fact, we should probably tell OgoPogo about this." John Garter was puzzled.

"OgoPogo! Who's OgoPogo -- I thought that was a lake serpent?"

"Oh, I'm sorry sir; I shouldn't be talking like that." The police officer appeared embarrassed. "It's a nick name we give to the Detective Inspector at our station. Bad taste really, his name is Ogopoulos and he has a bit of a hump back." His eyes twinkled, but he resisted the temptation to add that he also was not seen very often, and had a reputation for finding it difficult to keep his head above water. "He lives somewhere round here I think. Anyway, I think that's all we can do for tonight. I'm sorry about all this; I know what a shock it can be."

"If I were you I'd get all this cleaned up as soon as possible" said the policewoman, waving her arms around the room. "It will make the bad taste disappear that much faster." Mary Garter sounded despondent.

"Yes, I'm sure you're right. I'll get started right away." They walked to the hallway and watched the police officers disappear down the driveway. Mary Garter spoke her thoughts out loud. "This is so miserable! How can anyone be so mean as to do all this?" John Garter shook his head.

"It beats me," he replied. He walked to his study to begin the clearing-up process. Before going to bed, Mary made several tours of the house, noting with mounting distress everything that had been moved, toppled, broken, or stolen. She seldom wore any of the jewellery that she had lost, but the pieces were heirlooms and she was deeply attached to every item. The anger and sadness she felt was tinged with guilt. All of the items had special meaning. She was guardian of these inherited pieces, and they had been lost while entrusted to her keeping. She decided to take the policewoman's advice and began clearing up immediately.

As she tearfully completed her reconstruction of the bedroom, John Garter worked downstairs, replacing toppled furniture, re-stacking books, and rearranging items on his study bookshelves. His initial indignation about the thoroughness of Tony Angle's sweep through the house began to diminish. It had taken him only a few minutes to straighten the downstairs rooms, and, as he told himself, provided that no harm came to his binoculars, no real damage had been done. And, it had worked! Clearly the police were not the least bit suspicious, and they had even given him some advice about contacting his insurance company. Of course, there was that incident with the telephone message from Gustav Illiach. He cursed his wife for having brought it up, and chastised himself for not having deleted the message. Could any connection be drawn there? The more he turned it over in his mind, the more he became convinced that nothing would come of it... unless, that was, the police had some way of tracing who had made the call. Despite their request, he decided to erase the message once and for all. He dialed into the message centre and quickly made the deletion. If they asked about it again, he would have to say that he had erased it by accident.

Chapter Six

The next day, Garter prepared for work in high spirits. An important component of his recovery plan had been successfully implemented, and everything in the house now appeared back to normal. As he ate his customary cereal and toast breakfast, he observed that his wife still appeared upset. He frowned, and offered her some words of encouragement. "Don't worry," he said, "you'll get over it. I'm off now."

When he arrived at his office the first thing on his agenda was to contact Tony Angle. He picked up the telephone and dialed the Ambrosia Service Station. Tony Angle answered almost immediately.

"Oh, hello Mr. Garter. So, how did you get on? Everything all right?"

"Well, it went okay with the police, but I do have a bone to pick with you. You took my binoculars -- I don't want any harm coming to them, they were a present to me...and, you made a hell of a mess in the bedroom. It took my wife a couple of hours to get it straight again."

"Okay, okay, I'm sorry... but it had to look realistic, didn't it? You can have the binoculars whenever you want. They're quite safe, along with everything else." He paused. "Tell me what happened when the police came."

He gave an account of the police arrival, and their investigation, but left out the piece about the threatening telephone call, and the recorded message. Tony Angle didn't know about problems with the Fast Credit & Loan Approval Institute, and there seemed to be no need to get into those details.

"So, they left around twelve thirty in the morning. They even advised me to contact my insurance company right away. We just have to go to the police station, and give a description of what's been taken, and the values. By the way, how much money did you take?"

"About eighty bucks I think, why?"

"I'll probably bump that up a bit, when I report it -- I don't see why not."

"Yes, of course, why not." Tony Angle paused. "My end of it was okay too". He had decided that John Garter need know nothing about the accident, and so did not mention it.

"Yes, good. So all in all we're doing all right here." At that moment Mrs. Bennett knocked on the door and entered the room carrying a tray of coffee and a newspaper. "Look, I have to go now. I'll call you over the week-end." He hung up the telephone and beamed appreciatively at Mrs. Bennett. "Thank you Mrs. Bennett, just what I need, a good cup of coffee."

"Don't forget you have to go to the R&D meeting shortly, Mr. Garter. I've brought the file. You will have to chair it as the C.E.O. is away--you'll be the only V.P. there." He looked up blankly.

"Why can't Chan do it? He's in charge of Research."

"Because he's away at a conference."

"And Arthur? What's he up to?"

"Mr. Gordon is going to be late. Oh, and by the way, I'll be acting as secretary as Margaret is off sick today." Reluctantly, he accepted that he would have to pay a little more attention than usual to the string of progress reports, and updates, which formed the agenda of the monthly meeting of the Research & Development committee. Not being a scientist, and not being particularly interested in pharmaceutical research, he usually sat through the meetings and attempted to stay awake while a succession of presenters gave excuse after excuse for their lack of results, and failure to justify the excessive budgets they had been given at the beginning of the year.

"Oh, very well Mrs. Bennett. Thank you for the coffee." Mrs. Bennett frowned. She was not accustomed to being thanked for her services, and the remark fueled her already strong conviction, that something could be amiss in the personal life of her boss. She looked at him quizzically and left the room.

He picked up the file that Mrs. Bennet had left for him, and spent the next few minutes sipping coffee, browsing the agenda, and reading previous minutes. Then, armed with the necessary materials, he made his way to the conference room, nudged a path through several people hovering around a large coffee pot that was located off to one side, took his place at the head of a long, polished table, and with a resigned expression, signaled his readiness to begin the meeting.

* * *

Mary Garter completed typing out a list of the items that had been stolen. She was surprised how difficult it had been to reconstruct in her mind the contents of her jewellery box, but eventually decided she had remembered most of the pieces. She added descriptions of the lost crystal and silverware, and the items that her husband had listed for inclusion--binoculars, camcorder digital recorder, and approximately two thousand dollars in cash.

Two thousand dollars! What was all that money doing in his drawer--weren't they supposed to be having a difficult time balancing the household budget? She made a mental note to ask him about it, and entered the amount on her list without thinking to question the truth of his claim.

The robbery had shaken Mary, but now, as she drove to the police station to deliver the list of stolen items, she felt angry. And, pity the culprits, if she ever got hold of them! She imagined what they looked like, and decided they were dressed in black, and wore balaclava helmets. As the crime unfolded before her eyes, she cursed at the shadowy figures in the imaginary scene, and upon seeing one of them rifle through her dressing table drawers, allowed herself the pleasure of conking him on the head, with a china pot. She suddenly realized she was driving much faster than was safe, and checked herself, just in time to make the turn into the now familiar parking lot of the local police station.

There was no one at the counter when she entered the lobby, but several doors opened into the office area behind, and she could see into three of them. In one office, a woman sat writing notes on a yellow pad, while a young boy, and an overweight woman, whom Mary presumed to be his mother, both sat with worried expressions on the other side of the desk. In another office, two uniformed officers stood, fidgeting with open notebooks, while a portly man, wearing what might once have been a respectable business suit, sat hunched forward, his elbows planted on his desk and his hands wrapped around a coffee mug, from which he occasionally slurped. In the third office, a man without a jacket, but otherwise in uniform, thumbed his way through the top drawer of a filing cabinet. The pear-shaped build was unmistakable, and she recognized him right away as the sergeant she had spoken to about her new tires. He had his back to her, and was clearly engrossed in his search.

As she stood patiently wondering whether to twang the bell on the counter, or to wait until someone spotted her, a young woman appeared from the side, and enquired politely how she could be of assistance.

"Yes, my name is Mary Garter. There was a break-in at our house yesterday, and two officers came to investigate." She pulled out the cards they had given her and passed them over to the clerk. "They asked me to drop off a list of items that had been stolen, and to put down a description... I've done that here." She passed over the two sheets of notepaper that now detailed the losses. The woman scanned the list and looked at the business cards.

"These two are both off duty until this afternoon, Mrs. Garter, but I can give this to them when they come in. Would that be okay?"

"Yes, I should think so. They just needed the descriptions for their investigation. Perhaps you could tell them I came in with it?"

"Yes, of course Mrs. Garter. Would you like a copy of this?"

"Oh, yes please! I didn't think to print off one for myself. Thank you." As the clerk disappeared in the direction from which she had come, Mary looked up, and noticed that the portly man in the business suit, was now engaged in conversation with the pear-shaped sergeant, and that both were glancing in her direction. She smiled towards them, apparently causing an end to their conversation, and the sergeant's return to filing cabinet duty. The portly man ambled purposefully towards her.

"Hello," he called cheerfully, waving a podgy hand as he approached the mid-point distance, "and how are you today?" Mary Garter found herself wondering about his accent. What was that? Not French for sure. Was it Greek? Yes, possibly. Before she could answer his greeting, he thrust out an oversized paw, and introduced himself, ending her debate about his accent. "Good morning to you. I'm Inspector Ogopoulos." He blanketed Mary's hand in his own, and shook it vigorously. "Can you spare me a few minutes of your time Mrs. Gater?"

"It's Garter" she corrected.

"Mrs. Garter, of course, my apologies. Thank you for coming. Let's go into my office." Mary nodded warily, and followed the inspector into a room that appeared to have been equipped with rejected Salvation Army furniture donations. She sat down on one of the three unmatched chairs that faced his desk, and looked up, in time to see him walking backwards out the door. "I'll just be one moment," he assured her, and then disappeared from view.

Obviously, the Inspector's invitation to talk had something to do with the burglary, or the threatening telephone call, or perhaps both; Mary was unsure as he had given her no indication. After a few moments, he returned, lumbered around his desk to an ancient swivel chair, and sat down heavily. As he did so, Mary noticed the distinctive shape of his shoulders: wide bulges that seemed to disappear into his head without any trace of a neck. What was it the two police officers had called him? Yes, OgoPogo! How cruel! He clasped his podgy hands in front of him, and looked serious.

"Mrs. Garter. I have a photograph I would like to show you. I'd like you to tell me if it is anyone that you know."

He opened an envelope and passed across the table a glossy 8" x 10" print. Instantly, Mary recognized Daniel's face, staring alluringly from one of his promotional studio portraits. She looked up, with an expression that to a sensitive observer, would have communicated surprise, anxiety, embarrassment, and concern, all in one.

"Is it anyone you have seen before Mrs. Gator?"

"Yes, I do know him! It's Daniel; he's a friend of mine. But why are you showing this to me? Is anything wrong?" Her mind raced. Had anything happened to him? Was he wanted by the police? Had he committed a crime?

"Yes, Mrs. Gator I'm afraid there is something wrong. He's dead." The delivery was matter of fact and struck home with brutal effect. Mary Garter's mouth opened but no sound emerged until the initial shock subsided.

"Dead! When? How? Please...tell me what happened!"

"All in good time Mrs. Gator. Actually, I'd like you to tell me what you know."

"But I don't know anything! There's nothing to tell. Tell me what's happened."

"When did you last see him?"

"Yesterday. We had lunch together. How did he die? What happened?"

"What time was that Mrs. Gator?" Mary Garter began to lose patience and raised her voice in an angry tone.

"It's Garter not Gator. I left him at two p.m. and I insist you tell me what has happened -- he was my friend! I need to know." Inspector Ogopoulos decided that there was a strong probability that Mary Garter was about to get hysterical. And if there was anything worse than having to deal with a tearful woman, it was having to deal with an hysterical one. In his best, bedside manner, he leaned forward reassuringly.

"All right, all right, just calm down please, and I'll tell you what I know." Mary Garter grit her teeth, and decided to ignore his patronizing manner.

"There was a telephone call to the hospital last night, from an anonymous party. The caller said a man had been in an accident and could be found at a certain place. The party then hung up. A security guard and an ambulance attendant went to look, and found him dead." He gestured at the picture of Daniel "They took him to emergency but he was definitely dead."

"Well how did he die? What kind of accident was it?"

"I'm afraid I can't tell you that just yet, Mrs. Gater, er...Garter. It's not public knowledge." He looked pleased with himself. "I'm treating this as a suspicious death which means I will be investigating it to find out all that I can about what happened and why? If there was any hanky panky I want to know." Mary Garter assumed that his use of the words "hanky panky" referred to the general circumstances of Daniel's death, but she was not sure.

"Well at least tell me whether he suffered. Did he?" Inspector Ogopoulos considered the question carefully.

"I would say, 'yes'. But then again, I can't be certain of that. There's no doubt he was alive before he died." He stopped himself, and smiled a toothy grin. "Sorry, that didn't come out quite right, but I think you know what I mean. He didn't die right away, is what I'm saying."

Mary Garter felt sad. In reality Daniel had not been a loved one: he was more of a partner in an arrangement that provided a temporary accommodation of mutual needs. She had found it impossible to communicate with him at anything but the most superficial level, and was frequently exasperated by his posturing and vanity. But, despite his flaws and insecurities, she held a genuine affection for him. He could be a charming companion, and while she had not for one moment believed his impassioned declarations of love, she had enjoyed his attentions, luxuriated in the ego-boost they provided, and savoured the pleasure they had both derived from satisfying a mutual physical lust. She bit her lip, and then addressed OgoPogo.

"Why did you show his picture to me?"

"Aha! I wondered whether you would ask me that. And since you have, I will tell you. It was because you were recognized."

"Recognized? Recognized where?"

"You were recognized as the woman in the picture!" Whether intentionally, or otherwise, OgoPogo had a way of raising her wrath that no others, husband excepted, had ever been able to do so rapidly.

"Stop being obtuse!" she demanded. "Please explain to me what you are talking about, and be direct. I have no patience for games. A friend of mine has died and I want to learn, through an adult discussion, what is going on." She glared at him intently. "What picture are you referring to?" OgoPogo looked surprised and a little hurt. He slid another envelope towards his belly, opened it gingerly, and carefully placed a small passport sized picture of Mary Garter in front of her.

"This picture was found in the victim's coat pocket. The sergeant here…" he nodded towards the office next door, "saw the picture early this morning, recognized it was you, and alerted me to the fact you were here in the station." He leaned back and clasped the podgy hands, which Mary now thought of as two flippers, behind his head. "And that, Mrs. Gator, is why I asked whether you knew the victim. It is you in the picture isn't it?" Mary tried to gather her thoughts and composure. There had seemed no point in denying that Daniel was her friend, but she was now wondering whether the true nature of their relationship was about to be revealed to the world, and if so, whether she really cared. She wasn't sure, but her instinct was to keep as much of it as private as she could, particularly with a divorce pending, and a husband who would then be intent on making her life as miserable as possible. It was distressing that Daniel had met with what sounded like a horrible death, and on top of that, the Inspector seemed to be implying that she knew more about his death than she had disclosed. She decided that honesty was the best policy. If it came out that they had been lovers, then so what? She would have to deal with the consequences. The important thing was to help the police get to the bottom of it.

"Look, Inspector Ogopoulos, I want you to know that Daniel and I had a very close relationship for the past few months. Yesterday we had lunch together, and I told him that I would not be seeing him again. He was a bit hurt, but the news was not entirely unexpected and when I left him I was confident he would get over it very quickly. That was the last time I saw him."

"I see. You were lovers. He carried your picture to keep you close. And yesterday you dumped him. Is that correct?"

"Well... I wouldn't have put it that way, but yes, essentially that is the case."

"I see. Did he have any other enemies that you know of?"

"Inspector, I was not his enemy, I was his friend."

"Yes, yes, of course. I meant did he have any enemies?"

"Not that I know of. He used to act in television commercials and appeared in advertisements. He has a sister, in Montreal I believe, but no other relatives here. His parents are both dead. He was a French Canadian."

"Was he?" To Mary's surprise, Inspector Ogopoulos appeared to have been unaware of that fact, and seemed to have found the information significant.

"Where did he come from?"

"Quebec City I think. He left there when he was thirteen years old." OgoPogo looked thoughtful and made a note on his pad.

"Where were you last night, Mrs. Garter?" She stared at him intently. Was this man suggesting that she had something to do with Daniel's death?

"Inspector, are you aware why I came to the police station today?" He thought for a moment.

"Sergeant Dawson mentioned tires. Something to do with that?"

"Inspector, I am here because I am delivering a list of everything that was stolen from my house in a burglary that occurred last night while my husband and I were both out. Two police officers from this station spent a considerable amount of time interviewing us and have a full account of where we were, what was taken, and have promised us they will do their best to recover our property. Surely I don't have to go through all that again -- can't you just talk to them? I understand they are expected in this afternoon." OgoPogo frowned.

"You're upset."

"Yes, of course I'm upset! You asked me to step into your office for a moment. You tell me that someone I care for has been in an accident and has died. You ask questions that imply you think I am some kind of suspect. You still haven't told me how Daniel died. You seem to be unaware of something I should have thought you would been briefed on before you called me in here... Yes, I'm upset... I'm very upset!"

"Yes, I thought so." Inspector Ogopoulos was pleased by the accuracy of his diagnosis. "Look, I won't need to keep you much longer but I will want to talk to you again later so please let me know before you take off anywhere far away. And please understand, Mrs. Garter, I am not thinking of you as a suspect. Your information has been helpful. I didn't know he was French and I didn't know that when he was left unconscious at the hospital -- with a wallet and all his ID still in his clothes-- that we would find out so quickly about the photograph in his pocket." He paused and leaned forward as if to take her into his confidence. "I think he was hit on the head by someone, Mrs. Garter, and that his assailant, or someone else, took him to the hospital and telephoned for help because they wanted to help him without being identified. He resumed the train of thought "There was much I didn't know... your information is a big help. I will see what we have found out about the burglary at your house, and establish if there is any connection. Oh, and I will need to speak to Mr. Gator." Mary interrupted his musings.

"Connection? To the burglary? What kind of connection?"

"Well, let us suppose for a moment that this man, Daniel, was feeling vindictive... because you dumped him. Maybe he decided to get back at you by breaking into your house and stealing your things." He ignored Mary Garter's dismissive retort. "That's an angle I will have to check out. And by the way Mrs. Garter, does your husband have any knowledge of your infidelity?"

"My infidelity! You mean my relationship with Daniel don't you? No, I'm sure he does not. Look, is it necessary for you to tell him? I don't see much benefit to either of us by advising him what I've told you." OgoPogo considered the matter.

"Mrs. Garter. He probably doesn't need to know. However, I can't rule out the possibility that he already does. Perhaps he decided to get even with the party who cuckolded him, and inflicted the injury that resulted in death. I'll have to talk to him." Mary was astonished by the connections that Inspector Ogopoulos was apparently making, and alarmed that a man of his insensitivity was about to wade-in, and un-pick the delicately woven fabric of her life and relationships. "Where do you live Mrs. Gator?" As he was poised to write down the address he looked up in surprise.

"Brookmead Crescent! Me too! In fact we're only a few doors apart. Well, well, well. What a small world. A pleasant neighbourhood don't you think? Except," he paused for a moment and frowned, "seems like the tone of the place is going down -- some hooligan stole my car last night."

Chapter Seven

John Garter decided to take a taxi to his lunch meeting with Julia Miller. There was nowhere sensible to park near their meeting place and he could claim the taxi fare on his expense account. Whatever they would discuss over lunch he could no doubt find some connection to his company's interests, and that being so, his conscience, or more precisely the risk-analysis matrix that passed for his conscience, had no difficulty endorsing the idea.

By the time he arrived at Henri's, he could see that Julia Miller was already seated at a table, with a view of the entrance in one direction, and a quietly flaming log fire in the other. As he proffered his coat for installation on the rail in the lobby, he waved his acknowledgement of her hand signal and was promptly escorted to her table.

As he approached, she stood to greet him. The Julia Miller now standing in front him with her hand extended, looked quite different from the woman who sometimes sat across from him at the committee room table of the Aerial golf club. This Julia Miller wore an expensively tailored navy blue jacket, and a matching knee length skirt, a white cotton blouse with an open necked collar, non-sensible high heeled shoes, a gold swan-shaped lapel pin, and a delicate gold necklace. She was tall, slim, elegant, perfectly groomed, and carried herself with a poise and confidence that he found attractive, but also disconcerting. This was not a woman to be under-estimated. He continued to absorb the vision: high cheekbones, an oval face, perfect features, shining hair that gently framed a graceful neck, clear, penetrating eyes—green, and wide-set: eyes that without doubt had mind-reading capability. On this occasion however, her gaze was softer, and as John Garter noted with some relief, tinged with what seemed to be amusement, or was it perhaps, pleasant anticipation? Was she going to confront him about his fund 'borrowing'? He extended his hand and felt Julia Miller's soft palms and long fingers encircle his own in a carefully measured grasp.

"Good to see you John, I'm glad you could make it."

Yes, me too. I'm sorry if I kept you waiting, the traffic was worse than I expected."

As they settled into their seats a waiter deposited a basket of hot bread on the white tablecloth, poured iced water, gave a detailed description of the day's special dishes, and asked whether they wished to order anything to drink. Julia Miller was quick to reply. "Yes, I should think so... John, what if we share a half litre of their house red? It's usually quite drinkable." The idea met with John Garter's approval, and the waiter left them alone to review the menu and consider conversational openings. Having quickly settled upon his luncheon choice, Garter folded his menu and glanced around the room.

" I like this place. I'm glad you suggested it."

"Oh, me too." Julia Miller folded her menu, and decided to order the third of the day's special dishes. "It's one of my favourites – especially for a business lunch."

"So, that's two things we have in common, a liking for Henri's, and a liking for golf. We've not played together though, have we? Do you get out much?"

"Two or three times a week in the summer, usually with clients, and I sometimes play with a friend at the weekends. How about you?"

"Now and again, but not as often as I would like." At that moment the waiter returned with their carafe of wine, poured two glasses, took their food order, and disappeared once again.

"Well, we'll have to play sometime John." She moved her glass to a spot where the stem could rest comfortably between her thumb and index finger.

"I'd like that. Hard to imagine it though with the weather like this isn't it?"

"Yes, that's true, but I like to plan ahead. It will be something to look forward to." Her observation gave him cause for optimism. At least her vision of the future had him free to play golf, and did not appear to include supervision by a prison officer. He relaxed, more certain than ever that his fund-dipping activity was known only to himself.

"Speaking of looking forward to things, I'll be quite glad when this week is over. It's been crazy at work, and to crown everything our house was burgled on Wednesday." He waited for the reaction.

"Really? How upsetting. What happened?"

"Well, the police say there has been quite a lot of this going on. Someone broke through the back windows when we were both out, rifled through all our stuff and stole quite a lot of our valuables – jewellery, cash, my binoculars, some crystal and cut glass, things like that." Julia Miller appeared sympathetic.

"Oh, that's too bad. I hope you had it well insured?" She stared one of her brain piercing gazes. "Not the same as getting it back, but it will help to ease the pain. Your wife must be upset."

"Yes, she was." Julia Miller noted with interest his use of the past tense. "She seldom used most of it, but there were lots of heirlooms."   He continued with the story and responded to Julia Miller's questions until their food arrived. "So," he concluded, "all in all, it's not been the greatest week."

"No, indeed. I'm sorry you've had all that trouble." As they began their meal, she gently probed into his personal life, and found him more than willing to discuss his job, the company he worked for, children--or lack thereof, his role in the Chamber of Commerce, and his thought of someday running for political office. Julia Miller had shown considerable interest in his political ambitions and learned that his goal was to better serve the community where he lived. He had not yet decided whether this would require his entry at the Provincial, or the Federal level, but the important consideration was to apply his talents wherever he could make the greatest contribution. Julia Miller picked up her glass of wine.

"So, to change the subject John, I'd like to move on to what I wanted to talk to you about today." She paused, and stared at him directly, "I'm curious about the club's financial position. I'd like to know how you see things."

He decided to interpret the question as an invitation to launch into a financial overview, and proceeded to give his customary analysis.   For a member-owned venture, the club was in excellent shape. There was no debt, revenues were high, expenditures were below average for the industry, and there was adequate funding for expansion should the members want to develop the asset further. Not only that, there was a lengthy waiting list of potential members anxious to join. Of course, a golf club was not necessarily the highest and best use for the land, but that was why it existed so the issue of selling it for some other purpose was moot. All things considered, it was a well-run, well managed, facility. He stopped short of congratulating himself for these excellent results, but his smug expression made it clear where he felt the credit belonged.

"And what about the capital account John?" The self-satisfied look on his face gradually faded while he stared intently at Julia Miller, trying to read the full import of her question. There seemed to be glint in her eye, but he wasn't sure.

"What about it?" He asked.

"Do you think the capital account is safely invested?" She sat back in her chair, and smiled sweetly at him. Ah, so that was her angle! She wanted to propose some alternative investment strategy. One where there would be some commission benefit for her, perhaps?

"Well, as you know, some of it is in cash, some in bonds, some in blue chips..." he paused, "I think it is safely and sensibly invested, but I'm open to suggestions." Julia Miller stared hard into his eyes.

"Why do you think Harry Jefferson wants the accounts audited?" John Garter made a dismissive hiss.

"Because he's a narrow minded, mean spirited, hypocrite who likes to criticize."

"Well, I wouldn't disagree with that summation John, but he does have a reason you know. He believes that a different investment strategy is needed. As far as I can make out he feels that he hasn't been heard on the issue, and that an audit will point out the wisdom of his position." Garter gave a contemptuous grunt.

"Huggh -- what the hell does he know, the man's a grocery store clerk!" He dug into his food and considered Julia Miller's comments. He looked up. "Am I to take it that you agree with him?" She stopped eating, picked up her wine glass, and stared at him before replying.

"No John, I do not agree with him. But, there again, neither do I agree with you." She paused as if carefully considering her choice of words, all the while studying his reaction to her blunt observation. "The capital account may, or may not, be sensibly invested, but it most certainly is not safe. And, we both know why, don't we?" She sat back in her chair and smiled, clearly savouring the moment.

He considered pretending that he had no idea what she was driving at. However, from the expression on her face, and the gleam in her eye, he knew instantly that it was pointless to do so. He had just been nailed between the eyes. She knew what he had done; she had confronted him squarely, and now she had him where she wanted - writhing at the end of her harpoon. There was no escape. So, surely then, he should at this moment be feeling frightened, scared, embarrassed, fearful of imminent exposure, concerned about prosecution, worried about public scorn and ridicule? But he did not! Instead he was experiencing a moment of inner calm and tranquility.

It was then that he recognized an important truth: one that came flooding into his consciousness, uninvited, and unimpeded. Julia Miller had no intention of exposing him. She wanted to play! The rules of her game, and its objectives, were not yet clear, but without doubt they involved two critical elements: her pleasure, and his submission. His participation would be mandatory, that much was clear. Beyond that, he was unsure. Could this be something from which he could emerge unscathed? Was he about to participate in something that might even prove to be enjoyable?

As the lunch date neared its conclusion, Garter attempted to understand the rules of the game into which he had just been conscripted. Some of them had become crystal clear. He had two weeks in which to place forty thousand dollars into the golf club account. He would be proffering his resignation as treasurer at the next committee meeting, citing workload as the reason. He would point out that he had taken the liberty of sounding out potential replacements, and would say that he had reason to believe Julia Miller would be willing to take over if invited to do so. He would lobby as necessary to implement that change.

These instructions had been communicated with a courteous, matter-of-fact delivery, much as if he had been receiving an itinerary briefing from a travel agent. However, there had been no concealing the almost erotic pleasure that oozed from Julia Miller as she had elaborated her requirements: it had enveloped him in a sensual, intoxicating, wave.

Now, as they sat across from each other over silver coffee pots, other requirements were unfolding. " I want a written confession. A note that explains what you did, and why you did it. I want it hand-written, signed and dated. Is that understood?" He nodded. "And another thing," she looked at him with an expression he found positively seductive, "you will meet with me whenever I tell you, so that I can review the progress you have made with our contract. Is that clear?"

"Yes, yes, of course, whatever you say." After delivering her specification of terms for his redemption, and having received a satisfactory, indeed, an eager and emphatic assurance of his willingness to comply, she proceeded to the finale.

"Very well, now repeat to me slowly, and carefully, everything you have agreed to." As he complied with her instructions, her eyes absorbed every detail of his changing facial expressions, while her tongue gently moistened her lower lip. She stared at him intently, while he finished the summary. "That is very good Jonathon. Very good indeed." She sat back in her chair, and waited for him to speak.

"Can I take it that this contract will be known only to the two of us?"

"You may."

"And that your purpose is..." his voice trailed off as he recognized the possibility of multiple agendas, "to ensure that there is full restitution without the need for... unpleasantness?" Julia Miller considered his question and smiled gently.

"Jonathon, you have been a naughty boy, and a careless one too. I found you out, but I am going to give you a chance. I have decided to take you under my wing. You need to be helped Jonathon, especially if we are going to make you into a political star." She leaned forward. "I can forgive naughtiness Jonathon, in fact I find it an endearing quality, but I cannot abide hypocrisy." She stared at him. "You and I have a lot in common. The difference is that I can admit to being rapacious, egocentric and ambitious, while you cannot. But you will. In fact you will soon be sharing your innermost thoughts and fears with me. We are going to travel together for a while Jonathon, and while we do, you are going to enjoy it. Is that clear?"

85

CHAPTER EIGHT

The clutch of envelopes in the Jefferson mail box held, for the most part, no mystery: a bank statement, a telephone bill, a charity begging letter, and an invitation to subscribe to a book club. But there was one that was different. This envelope, with its blue ink and bold printing, appealed to the eye, and offered the possibility of a personal greeting. The postmark showed it to have a local origin. Mrs. Jefferson carried the haul into the kitchen, sat down at the table, and once again studied the blue writing before then proceeding to satisfy her curiosity. Could it be an invitation? How nice! It had been a long time since she had been anywhere pleasant.

*   *   *

Tony Angle finished loading his pick-up truck with the essentials to sustain him for an extended trip to the west coast. Inside the cab, concealed under the seat, was a small bag filled with the contents of Mary Garter's jewel box. A pair of binoculars and a note to John Garter sat on the passenger seat in a plastic bag.

The need for his unscheduled vacation had become apparent the moment he had discovered that the man he had deposited at the gates of the emergency department had died shortly thereafter. The news was disconcerting, and he was upset to learn that his efforts to save the stranger who had wandered into his path, had been fruitless. The collision was not his fault, and there was nothing he could have done to prevent it. But, the man's death was upsetting, and raised the stakes dramatically. If he was implicated in any way in the Garter burglary, then he risked being found guilty, not just of fraud, but also perhaps, of manslaughter or murder. All in all, it felt sensible to close-up shop for a while, and put some distance between himself and the scene of his misadventures. Thus resolved, he dropped-off John Garter's package, and began a westward trek. He would, he decided, call John Garter from British Columbia and explain the situation then.

*   *   *

After what seemed like the longest day he could remember, Garter walked slowly towards his car. When he opened the door he immediately saw on the passenger seat a plastic bag with an envelope attached to it. He climbed in, shut the door behind him, and peered into the bag. His binoculars! He quickly tucked them into his briefcase, and opened the envelope. Tony Angle's note was brief. "Here they are, safe and sound. I'll call you next week." He crumpled the note and envelope, and, as he drove past the exit gate, ditched both in the trash can that stood there on sentry duty. What a week! He joined the queue waiting to merge with four lanes of almost motionless expressway traffic, and for the tenth time that afternoon, replayed in his mind the details of his lunch meeting that day with Julia Miller.

They had shared a cab on their return from lunch, during which time she had asked him how he felt about their discussion. She had volunteered that for her part she was pleased they had reached a mutual understanding, and was optimistic their contract could now be managed without any further awkwardness or discomfort. She had said she hoped he would be able to look upon their emerging relationship as being one of equals. There was of course a power imbalance, but that was a fact of life and he would have to accept it. For his part, John Garter had confessed to feeling humbled by the experience of being brought to task for his misdemeanors, and was determined that he would make amends no matter what it took. He was grateful to her for giving him the opportunity to prove himself, and redeem his self respect. At that point the cab had drawn to a halt to deposit him outside of his building, whereupon Julia Miller had taken his hand, kissed him softly on the cheek, and whispered in his ear. "Jonathon, you are *so* full of shit -- but I intend to enjoy you anyway!"

He edged his way into the centre lane, and continued his slow crawl home. Some aspects of his encounter with Julia Miller puzzled him, but he felt sure that he would be able to escape from her web relatively unscathed. And besides, it seemed possible that her agenda might even be enjoyable. What was that nonsense about a journey together? Well, whatever she had in mind, he was willing to participate if it meant he was to be permitted the opportunity for some intimate engagement with this intriguingly sensuous woman. There was no getting away from it; she was an exquisite creature! He allowed himself the unaccustomed luxury of a smile, and reluctantly forced himself to other areas of reflection.

She had given him two weeks in which to replace the stolen money--or as he now thought of it, the 'account deficit.' Would the insurance company pay out in that time? He wasn't sure, but if it didn't, then he might have to do some fast talking--she had been quite adamant about the two week deadline. And why did she want to take over as treasurer? He had decided against any enquiry in that direction at the time of their meeting, but resolved to find out when they next met. It certainly wasn't an enviable role--unless of course it was to assist with personal budget planning. Could that be her angle? He left the questions unanswered as he turned from the expressway, and headed into the exit that would take him to Brookmead crescent.

When he entered the house, Mary was on the telephone to her friend Ellen. She deftly changed the subject from the death of Daniel, to the break-in and robbery, and watched as her husband deposited his coat and briefcase by the front door. He nodded to her vacantly, and wandered into the kitchen in pursuit of an alluring aroma that he was disappointed to discover emanated from a meat-stew mixture, intended for the cat. He poured himself a large measure of Scotch, and picked up the local newspaper. The front page showed the picture of an ugly, not too recently shaved, man with dark hair, and an unpleasant scowl. Alongside the picture was a caption that read: 'Local Actor Dies in Suspicious Circumstances'. The text quoted an Inspector Ogopoulos who apparently wished to hear from anyone in the vicinity of Queensway hospital at about 10.00 p.m. the previous night. He wondered whether that invitation might not apply to several thousand citizens, and turned his attention to a story outlining the possible need for a mill rate increase to balance next year's municipal budget. What a bunch of losers! His talents were sorely needed in the political domain.

Mary interrupted his musings. "There's an Inspector at the police station who wants to talk to you. He seems to think you might know something about..." She pointed at the newspaper, "the death of that man. He'd like you to give him a call."

"What on earth are you talking about?" He stared at her blankly.

"When I was at the police station delivering the list of stolen property, the inspector they call OgoPogo, was there. He wants to talk to you. Don't ask me why--you'll have to check that with him. All I can tell you is that in addition to suspecting you of murder, he probably thinks you stole his car, and that if it wasn't you, then it was the Queen of England." She looked at him with a blank stare. "Don't ask. The man is crazy, but I suggest you call him anyway." She held out a card. "Here's his number."

* * *

At the Jefferson courthouse, a jury of one, had reviewed the evidence, deliberated, and found Harry Jefferson guilty of being a contemptible worm. His punishment had been determined, and partially implemented, the moment he returned from work, when, as he had approached his wife to deliver the customary peck to her cheek, he had received an excruciatingly painful knee to the groin. His recovery had been slow, and remained incomplete at the point when Mrs. Jefferson delivered the balance of his sentence. He was to be banished immediately. His protestations fell on deaf ears.

"I don't care! Go and stay with your mother, she's the one responsible for your birth." Mrs. Jefferson slammed the front door, leaving her distraught husband inside with twenty minutes to pack his bags.

* * *

On Saturday morning, John Garter arrived at the police station for his meeting with Inspector Ogopoulos. He had been assured on the telephone that only ten or fifteen minutes of his time would be required so he was confident of being back in time to meet with the insurance investigator who had promised to call that morning.

"Can I offer you some coffee Mr. Garter? There's probably some left in the pot." Garter declined. "I take it you don't mind if I do?"

"Not in the least." Inspector Ogopoulos picked up a cracked mug and rolled toward the end of his credenza where he inspected a stained pot sitting on a small electric hot plate.

"Mr. Garter, I'll come straight to the point. I want to eliminate you." John Garter's alarmed reaction quickly turned to amusement.

"Not literally I hope!" He smiled expectantly, but received no acknowledgement of his joke.

"Do you know this man Mr. Garter?" OgoPogo passed Daniel's studio portrait across the table.

"No, I don't. I saw this picture in the paper today, and that was the first time I had set eyes on him."

"So you were not with him last Wednesday night?"

"With him? Of course not. Am I accused of something?"

"No, no, Mr. Garter, I merely wish to demonstrate, to my complete satisfaction, that you had no involvement in this unfortunate affair. There are lots of people I have to talk to."

"But why would you even think that there is the remotest possibility that I did meet him on Wednesday? Or are you planning to interview and ask the same question of the whole of Toronto?" Inspector Ogopoulos laughed.

"No, that won't be necessary. I don't think he was that much of a Lothario." He continued earnestly. "It's a sensitive matter Mr. Garter. He was considered to be a good-looking man and something of a celebrity. People did fall for him you know, so we shouldn't rush to judgment. Anyway, it would be understandable if there were...let's say, jealous emotions involved." John Garter tried hard to comprehend but without success.

"He was good looking?" Inspector Ogopoulos appeared not to have heard the questioning edge to John Garter's reply."

"Yes, wasn't he. Did you know him well?"

"Look, I didn't know him at all! I have never met him in my life. What on earth are you driving at? You seem to be implying that I was jealous of him. Are you suggesting that I had something to do with his death because I had some kind of relationship with him? " Inspector Ogopoulos looked interested.

"Well, did you? I have to cover all possibilities Mr. Garter."

"No I did not! What on earth makes you think I even know him? And besides I'm not in the habit of having sexual relations with men. Now, I have a lot to do this morning, and I would like to get way from here as soon as possible. So, please understand that I have not the faintest idea who this man is or why you should think I might. In fact..." he stood up and glared at the Inspector, "I think I deserve an apology, and a full explanation!" Inspector Ogopoulos was alarmed.

"Mr. Garter, please. I was not trying to imply anything. Your sexual orientation is of no interest to me, and if you tell me that you have never seen this man before, then that is good enough." He paused to assess the damage. "I do have just one question though if I may? And, please, do sit down Mr. Garter, this won't take a moment." With a bemused and weary nod, Garter complied, while Inspector Ogopoulos continued. "Where were you on Wednesday night, between nine and eleven in the evening?" He had expected such a question, and, anxious to return to the comparative sanity of his home, quickly rattled off his rehearsed reply.

"I was with a friend at The Fox & Hounds pub on Cross Street--until about nine, and then, as I have no doubt the staff will confirm, I had a late dinner at Aztec, on Main Street. I then went home, and, as I am sure you are aware, found that my house had been burgled."

"Yes, yes, I know about that."

"Good - I'm pleased to hear that. Anyway, that's it… end of story. All of the details have been taken down by the officers who came to investigate." He looked hard at the Inspector. "So, if that is all, I would like to get back home now."

"Yes, yes that's very helpful Mr. Garter. I'm sorry to have taken up your time. And I hope you can be forgiving--he was a good looking man, and these things do happen." He grasped John Garter's hand, and shook vigorously. "I'll let you know if I need anything more. And I do hope we can get your valuables recovered soon, people are working on it. Who did you say you were with in the pub?"

"I didn't"

"So tell me please--in case it should become important." Inspector Ogopoulos picked up a stubby pencil and listened to the response. "Spell that for me please." As Garter obliged, he looked up curiously. "Oh, French is he?"

"No...at least, I don't think so. He doesn't sound it." Inspector Ogopoulos frowned.

"Hmmm, I'll check it out. You can't be too sure. Thank you Mr. Garter

* * *

When he returned home from his bizarre encounter with the Inspector, Mary and a tall, slim man, who had to bend his head to walk through the doorway, were emerging from his study. Mary introduced the insurance investigator to her husband.

"This is Mr. Davies. He's come to check out the losses." Mr. Davies walked forward to take John Garter's hand, and as he did so rattled the hall chandelier with his head. He stood in the midst of it for a moment, giving the appearance of someone wearing a glass hat made in the shape of a wedding cake. Mary Garter smiled to herself and gently maneuvered the party to safer ground. Mr. Davies was the first to speak.

"So, I see we can cross the binoculars off the list Mr. Garter!"

"Oh, those! Yes, they hadn't been taken after all - I found them behind my desk."

Mary Garter looked at her husband but said nothing.

"But I take it everything else is still missing?"

"Oh, yes. Isn't it dear?" He looked at Mary whose nodding head and sad expression confirmed the point.

"Mr. Garter, why did you have two thousand dollars lying around the house?"

"Oh that. Well I'm treasurer of a Golf Club and I sometimes receive dues and fees for deposit. Sometimes I'll exchange the cash for a personal cheque of my own to simplify the banking. Makes it easier to deposit."

"Yes, I see. So was it your money, or the club's money, Mr. Garter."

"Mine. Is it important?"

"Well yes. If it's not your money the owners will have to claim for the loss under any policy they may have. But if it is yours, then it can be counted as part of your contents." He paused. "So it was yours, and you had deposited a personal cheque for that amount in the golf club account. Is that correct Mr. Garter?" He cursed silently to himself. There was no such deposit, and a bold-faced lie was too risky as the story could easily be disproved if he was unable to back it up with the documentary evidence. Damn! He had just blown two thousand dollars. He struck a thoughtful pose.

"Well, you know, I'm just thinking about that. In fact, I received the money on Monday, at a committee meeting, but I hadn't yet got around to making the cheque deposit, so I suppose that technically it was still the club's money.

"Ah! So that's something else we can cross off from the list, Mr. Garter. I'm afraid the club will have to look for some other avenue to get that back." He looked triumphant, while John Garter resisted a strong urge to grab him by the throat.

The meeting continued with a tour of the house, during which time Mr. Davies wrote in a notebook, inspected the exact location of every missing piece, and thanks to extraordinary good luck, twice narrowly escaped decapitation by ceiling fan. By the time he was ready to leave, he had delivered a stern warning about home security, specified a number of enhancements the Garter's would have to implement to maintain insurance coverage, and filled an envelope with several ancient photographs brought to his attention by Mary Garter because they featured ancestors wearing various items of jewellery on the stolen goods list. He assured them he would be in touch when he had received the police report and could establish if progress was being made in the recovery operation. He thanked them for their patience, cleverly folded himself into the compact car in which he had arrived, and disappeared from view.

As she closed the front door, Mary sighed, and turned her attention to a matter that had been troubling her. "How did you make out with OgoPogo?"

He glared at her, still fuming at the escape of two thousand dollars. Reluctantly, his mind shifted to the police station. "Oh him! I haven't the faintest idea how I made out. He thinks the dead man and I were having a sexual relationship." He looked at her blankly, and wandered into the kitchen, calling out behind him. "I denied it." With an astonished look on her face, she followed him in.

"He did what!"

"He kept alluding to his good looks, and how understandable it would have been if I had been jealous of him, and where was I when he died. I told him I had never seen him before, and that he wasn't my type." He paused reflectively, "The man's an idiot. He didn't accuse me of stealing his car though."

Mary was relieved that she did not have to launch into a defence of her relationship with Daniel. From what she could gather, it sounded as though Inspector Ogopoulos had created as much confusion for her husband as he had for her. That, she presumed, had diminished the chance of any connections being established.

Garter picked up a piece of paper lying on the kitchen table. It was a computerized summary of his insurance policies, and had obviously been left there by the investigator. He folded it quickly, and placed it into his pocket, but not before Mary noticed him do so.

"Yes, I meant to ask you about that. It says there is a two hundred thousand dollar life insurance policy for me. I didn't know we had that?" Garter stared blankly.

"Didn't you? Yes, it was a special offer they called about recently. I thought I had mentioned it. It's just an extension to the policy on my life." He turned and headed towards the door, leaving his wife to digest the news that he considered her life to have value. She called after him.

"And how much do I get if you die?" He turned and smiled benignly.

"The same as before of course, five hundred thousand." Unable to resist the temptation, he added a qualifying observation. "But don't get your hopes up, I'm not intending to kick the bucket just yet."

* * *

"I'm not sure exactly, maybe a couple of weeks. She'll probably forgive me before too long." Harry Jefferson's 82 year-old mother seemed dubious as her son attempted to negotiate temporary board and lodging.

"Two weeks! Well, you'll have to do your own laundry dear." He looked pained.

"Yes, all right then mother. I'll sleep in the back room if that's okay." It was more a statement of intent than a question. The location was important. He anticipated some late night comings and goings while his detective work unfolded, and this spot was close to the back door. He was going to get to the bottom of the anonymous note, and whoever it was that had tipped off his wife, was going to regret having done so.

"And you'll have to get your own breakfast." He resigned himself to the news, knowing that his negotiating position was weak and entirely dependent on maternal good will. He decided to take his leave before new conditions were imposed.

"I have to go out now mother. I can let myself in so don't wait up will you?" He promised not to wake her on his return, and left, anxious to get on with his investigations.

Although neither man knew the other, Harry Jefferson and Inspector Ogopoulos shared the same approach to detective work. It was founded on the idea that a theory, once postulated, should hold true until it can be disproved. And, that being so, it was the job of a detective to formulate a proposition and attempt to pick holes in it until it collapsed under the weight of facts or logic. The possibility that a proposition might survive thanks to some deficiency in the investigative talents of the detective, rather than because of the strength of the proposition, was not a matter to trouble either of them unduly.

Harry Jefferson's working hypothesis was simple: Julia Miller did it. So far, he had uncovered no evidence to the contrary, and his conviction was growing stronger by the minute. But the search for the truth was not yet complete. He needed to find out about this woman and intended to track her every move until he was satisfied.

For his part, Inspector Ogopoulos had not yet formed a proposition. He felt sure that one was not too far away, but for the time being he was content to ponder connections. If past experience was a reliable guide then a powerful unifying theory would spring to mind before too long. It was Saturday afternoon and supposedly a time for rest and relaxation.

Chapter Nine

Had she not been so focused on making preparations for leaving him, Mary Garter may have noticed some changes in her husband's behaviour during the past ten days: he was even less communicative than normal; he was spending more time than usual in his study; his liquor consumption had increased; and in the past week he had twice taken the afternoon off from work. But, as it was, her thoughts were almost entirely fixed on the third step of her lawyer's Decide, Organize, Implement, Treat-yourself injunction and she was now more than ever determined to DO-IT. She had paid a rental deposit on a studio apartment, set up a separate bank account, arranged for the divorce papers to be filed, contacted a removals firm to transport various items of furniture, packed her clothes, secured a part-time temporary position at the publishing house where she had once worked as an illustrator, and was now ready to reveal to him her intentions. He would be leaving for work in a few minutes, and the moment she had been anticipating, had now arrived. She poured herself a coffee, and steeled for the scene that was about to unfold.

"John, would you sit down please, I want to talk to you." There was a grunt from her husband, but no other acknowledgement or sign of compliance. He continued with his silent shuffle around the kitchen, and she tried once more. "John, did you hear me? I have something to say to you, and I want you to sit down and listen to me."

There was a determination in her voice that efficiently penetrated his sullen pre-occupations.

"What? What do you want?"

"I have something to tell you."

"Go on then, I'm listening." He continued to shuffle.

"I'm leaving you." He stopped in mid-shuffle.

"You're what!"

"I'm leaving you John. I want a divorce." His reply came without a moment's pause.

"Don't be so stupid, we can't afford to divorce!"

"I don't care about that. I can't stay in this ridiculous relationship a moment longer. I'm leaving you, and that's that. I've seen a lawyer, and my requirements for a divorce settlement have all been spelled out. You'll be hearing from her in the morning."

"What are you thinking about!"

"I'm thinking about regaining my sanity and my pride. Something I should have done years ago."

"Don't be ridiculous. If you think I'm going to finance this..." he fumbled for words, "this stupid, self indulgence, then you are wrong! How are you going to live? Who's going to pay your rent? I'm not!" He stared at her in astonishment. "I can't believe this! Do you want to ruin us?" As the financial implications began to focus more and more clearly, he could barely contain his anger. "Have you gone completely mad?"

"I'm leaving today John. I'm sorry, but this is it."

"You're sorry? You will be sorry; I can assure you of that!"

"Don't threaten me! I'm sick of your bullying ways and I'm not going to put up with it anymore. Our marriage is a failure. It's over, and I'm going."

"Our marriage is a failure you say. Well, let me tell you something..." he paused, searching for verbal weaponry, "you are the failure!" He continued with the assault. "It's a good job you couldn't have children because you would have been a lousy mother just like you are a lousy, useless wife, who is too stupid to see what side her bread is buttered. Well, let me tell you... my lawyer will make sure you get nothing out of this! Without me you would have nothing anyway."

There was a time when such an attack would have caused her unimaginable distress. She had anguished over the idea that she could not have children, and each reminder, whether accidental, or heartlessly deliberate, would cause her great pain. Now, however, coming from a man that she had learned to despise, it had barely caused her to flinch.

"Tell that to your lawyer John. I'm clearing out this morning." That said, she stood up and left the room, leaving her astonished husband staring after her in disbelief.

* * *

The possibility that the Garter burglary was staged, rather than genuine, was a thought present in Mr. Davies' mind even before he began his tour of the Garters' house. The idea was not based on any particular evidence or suspicion. Rather, it was a consideration that he brought routinely to any insurance investigation of this kind, and his house tour with Mary had done nothing to eradicate the idea. Some items that he would have expected to be stolen, remained: a laptop computer in John Garter's study, some easily portable pieces of art work, and all the contents of the well stocked liquor cabinet. The omissions could, of course, all be explained so they did not give any particular cause for concern. Nevertheless, fuelled somewhat by John Garter's attempt to recover two thousand dollars in cash, the idea that it could have been an inside job remained with him when he went to speak with Inspector Ogopoulos about the status of the police investigation.

Seated across from Inspector Ogopoulos at the police station, Kenneth Davies opened the conversation he had requested. "So, do you have any leads yet Inspector…any suspects perhaps?"

"A few. We're working on it." The Inspector was not in a conversational mood. Kenneth Davies waited, hoping for some elaboration.

"Really?" he said, hoping to communicate his interest. Evidently he was unsuccessful.

"You sound surprised." The Inspector's voice had a testy edge.

"No! Not at all. I was hoping we might compare notes."

"Notes? You have a theory then?" OgoPogo looked interested. "What is it?" Kenneth Davies was startled. His only theory so far was that the stolen goods were unlikely to be recovered and that his insurance company was going to be the loser. He hesitated before replying.

"Well, I'm not totally convinced that it was a professional job." Inspector Ogopoulos stared at him.

"You think that burglary is a profession?"

"Well, yes--not an honourable one of course, but for some people it's an art form!" This was not going well. "What I meant was that I wonder whether the burglar was…let's say, inexperienced. Whoever did the burglary missed quite a few obvious pieces."

The Inspector grunted, asked for examples, and jotted down some notes when Kenneth Davies repeated his list. He did not appear too impressed.

"Anything else?"

"Not really, but…" he hesitated. "I thought it a little odd that Mr. Garter had two thousand dollars lying around the house."

"I saw that on his list. Don't you believe him?"

"I don't know. Anyway, as it turns out it wasn't his; it belonged to the Aerial Golf Club. He told me he is the club treasurer and that he hadn't got round to banking it." Inspector Ogopoulos grunted.

"Golf…pahh!" He was evidently not a devotee. "I may talk to someone about it though…couldn't hurt."

Kenneth Davies decided to push a little. "Look, Inspector, I'm sure you are doing whatever you can, but what I need to know is whether you are optimistic about catching anyone and getting any of the valuables back again. There's quite a lot of money at stake for my company, and if there's anything I can do to help, then I will." Inspector Ogopoulos did not encourage the thought.

"I can't think of anything at the moment, but I'll let you know if I do." He was mistrustful of amateur dabblers. "And, by the way Mr. Davy, not everyone drinks liquor these days. There are lots of dead heads out there who just want drugs." He paused. "Not that I am implying you don't know that of course." Kenneth Davies wondered if the comment had been intended as an insult. He decided it had not.

"We've been thinking about a reward for information."

"Have you indeed." The Inspector paused. "Well it would have to be your money. We haven't got any."

"Yes, we'd post the money. I had in mind twenty thousand dollars, but we would have to get everything back of course." Inspector Ogopoulos grunted.

"Twenty thousand eh? And here I am, trying my best to get everything back for you, free of charge! Something wrong there don't you think?" Kenneth Davies was unsure how to respond to what sounded like a rhetorical question.

"Well, we hope the money will surface some leads that wouldn't otherwise be found."

"I don't want you making deals behind my back, Mr. Davy. If there are any nibbles because of your reward I expect you to tell me about them. I want an arrest. That's the business I'm in."

"I understand what your interest is, Inspector, and I think you understand mine. Hopefully we can satisfy both." Inspector Ogopoulos stared at him.

"I'm not sure that you appreciate the difficulties we police investigators face Mr. Davy. Do you know how many cases I have on my desk right now?" He didn't wait for a reply. "No, I thought not. Well I'll tell you. There are forty seven different files that I currently regard as *priority active*." He added a clarification. "And by that, I mean files that have not yet been moved to an *unsolved pending* file, or to the *completed* archives. Forty-seven of them! They range from burglary, to car theft, and from forgery, to dead Frenchmen. They also include arson, missing persons, and next year's budget proposal." He stared at Kenneth Davies. "Is it any wonder that we can't always catch the villains responsible? I do my best, but it's never good enough. Headquarters want reports and statistics all the time, and all I've got is one of me, a quarter of a secretary, and whatever the police officers here can contribute when they're not in court, or taking notes at a traffic scene, or doing one of hundreds of things they have to do all day." His indignation seemed to be gaining momentum. "It's too much!"

Kenneth Davies thought it appropriate to offer a sympathetic ear.

"I had no idea you were so short staffed. It must be very difficult for you." Inspector Ogopoulos seemed pleased with the response.

"Yes, it certainly is!" He smiled and looked a little sheepish. "Forgive me for going on like that, but it gets to you now and again."

"Of course, I quite understand." OgoPogo continued.

"Can you believe that headquarters actually wanted to set up an 'Inspector of the Month' competition? Inspector of the Month! Can you imagine it: all of us competing to outdo each other instead of co-operating?" He paused, an expression of incredulity lingering on his face, but he stopped ranting.

"You'll forgive me for not being enthused about rewards, won't you Mr. Davy. I think they are…" he searched for the right word, "insulting!" He clasped his enormous hands behind his head and stared at the ceiling, as if inspecting it for cracks or cobwebs. Finally he leaned forward onto his elbows, and smiled before speaking.

"I have to get on now, Mr. Davy, I've a car thief to catch."

Kenneth Davies decided that for the time being the Inspector had been as helpful as he could, and prepared to take his leave. He had learned nothing about the investigation and was forced to conclude it was because there was no progress to report. A reward would probably do nothing to change that, but it was worth a try. Maybe there was a disaffected party involved who was ready to provide some information. It wouldn't hurt. He stood up and extended his hand. It was immediately crunched in a hammer-lock and shaken vigorously. To his great relief, the clamp was eventually released, allowing him to speak.

"Thank you Inspector. I'll be sure to let you know if anything surfaces. If it doesn't, then I'll settle the claim with my clients." He added as an afterthought. "John Garter seems quite anxious for a settlement. He's on my case quite often." Inspector Ogopoulos stared at Kenneth Davies, but said nothing.

*   *   *

Seven steps, and a short corridor, separate the parking area under Julia Miller's building, from the interior lobby. A security camera monitors the passageway, and a security attendant monitors a bank of screens from behind the lobby desk. Entry to the garage requires use of a magnetic striped plastic card, while exit from the garage requires only that a vehicle approach the doors and pass through an infra red light beam. The exit doors can be opened by passing a hand through the beam. A pedestrian, following a car out the exit doors, has 35 seconds to walk through before they close, and if such a person wishes to do this unobserved, there are a number of places, concealed from camera view, that allow swift egress. All of this information, including the location of a camera blind spot in the passageway between garage and interior lobby, was uncovered by Harry Jefferson, early on in the surveillance operation he had mounted to record the pattern of Julia Miller's arrivals and departures.

Now, intent on finishing his garage research, Harry Jefferson was once again prowling the parking lot of her building. With notebook in hand, he sidled between the concrete pillars, pacing out distances, recording notes, and drawing diagrams, all the while puffing frosty breath clouds, as he went silently about his business in the cold evening air. Time was of the essence. He would have to act soon: before Julia Miller's hate campaign ruined his reputation, and his marriage.

Chapter Ten

The piercing bleat of a cell 'phone roused OgoPogo from what he customarily referred to as his state of *creative reflection:* a condition that because of its outward resemblance to an after meal nap, would often confuse the less perceptive of his colleagues, and induce amusement in the uncharitable. With some difficulty he managed to press a button and position the device alongside his ear. "Hello, Inspector Ogopoulos here".

"Ogie, it's me. I've found our car! It was parked at the railway station."

"What! Are you sure?"

"Yes, of course I'm sure. I just got off the train and spotted it right away."

And, so it was, at nine thirty on Monday evening, that Inspector Ogopoulos learned from his wife that she had been able to accomplish what neither he, nor the combined resources of the Division, had been able to do during the time that had passed since Tony Angle borrowed it to make his escape after the Garter break-in. Although its discovery meant that he would now have to part with the comfortable rental car that his insurance company had allowed him to acquire, OgoPogo was delighted to know he would soon become reunited with his old Buick, confident that his examination of the car would yield important clues to the identity of the hooligan who had stolen it.

Having established that his wife had not attempted to enter the vehicle, and that she would now wait for his arrival, OgoPogo sped off to join her at the railway station where, after a brief greeting, they exchanged cars and Inspector Ogopoulos was left to begin his search for evidence.

The first thing he noticed was a dent on the passenger side fender. It was one of several, but without question, one that had not been there previously. He examined the damage carefully, all the while muttering to himself. He continued his tour of the exterior and was relieved to discover no other visible signs of damage. He turned his attention to the interior and gingerly opened the driver's door. It smelled familiar and looked at first glance to be in its usual state of reluctant readiness for travel. He leaned over the front bench seat and carefully examined the floor for clues. After several minutes of scrutiny he decided that there weren't any and turned his attention to the back. Aha! What was that? He picked-up a small piece of crumpled paper and unfolded it. It was blank. Damn, that wasn't of any use! He continued scouring the floor, and after a few minutes reluctantly rendered a verdict of 'clueless'.

He decided to make another tour of the outside of his vehicle. His second inspection at first yielded no new information, but it did raise a question in his mind about the cause of the dent. Obviously there had been a collision of some kind, but with what? The dent was rounded and looked as if someone had driven a football at it. And what was that discoloration? Unless he was very much mistaken...yes! That was dried blood! It gradually dawned on Inspector Ogopoulos that the hooligan who had stolen his car had also hit some living creature. Whether it was animal or human, and what had happened to the unfortunate entity after the contact, he did not know, but he would certainly find out.

The next day, Inspector Ogopoulos drove his car to the police forensic centre where he was able to pose a number of questions to the science officer in charge. Was it blood that he had found and if so, was it human? What could be told about the previous owner of the blood? What type of accident had occurred?

Despite his best efforts to curry favour, seek sympathy, and finally to pull rank, he was disappointed to learn that workloads at the centre meant that it would be at least two weeks before he could get an official response to any of his questions. And, even more disturbing, he would have to leave his car there to avoid contaminating the evidence. There was however another option -- one that he eagerly accepted; an unofficial, off the record, off the cuff opinion could be offered there and then.

By the time he left the centre, OgoPogo had much to chew on. The information had been delivered in matter of fact style by a young man who, in the best tradition of Sherlock Holmes, had uncovered it with the help of a large magnifying glass. It was human blood, Type O, and came from the head of a man with black hair. He had been struck while the car was accelerating and travelling at approximately twenty five kilometers per hour. Whoever drove the car did not leave fingerprints on the wheel or door. The car had not been cleaned thoroughly in several years, and was in need of a service. It had not been hot-wired meaning that the driver had a key and could be a member of the family, a locksmith or have some connection to the auto industry. Since the vehicle had little value it had not been stolen for resale. The thief therefore probably wanted it as a getaway vehicle. DNA samples of the hair could be taken and there would be a two-month delay before that information could be made available. Even then, the information would be useless unless it could be matched to a known person. Finally, the crumpled piece of paper that the Inspector had thought to be blank was actually the faded copy of a visa slip. The credit card had been used to purchase something at a store called 'Western Books Galore' and belonged to someone whose last name ended in 'opoulos'.

OgoPogo returned to his office to think. He had always known that everything in the universe was connected to everything else, but he now felt sure that some important connections existed between the theft of his car and some of the matters remaining in his in-basket. The particular matters and the types of connection were not yet in focus but the feeling in his gut told him that he was on to something important. Equipped with a mug of coffee, a note pad, and a pencil, he began to engage the task with remarkable gusto.

He checked the date his car had been stolen, and decided to log everything that had come to his attention on that day, and the next. He then checked the daily activity summary for the whole station, and ended up with a single list of all events that had been reported. If the information was immediately available, he then wrote the names of all persons associated in any way with any of the events. This gave him a lengthy list of names, some of which appeared more than once. He cast his eye over the list to see which names occurred most frequently and numbered them in descending order. The names at the top of the list held the greatest interest and offered the strongest possibility for making breakthrough connections. Number one on the list with eight entries belonged to Mary Garter. She had been burgled. She was married to someone who had been burgled. She had received a threatening telephone call. She was married to someone who had received a threatening telephone call. She had committed a traffic violation. She had complied with the terms her traffic violation. She was the ex-lover of a man found dead in mysterious circumstances. She lived on Brookmead Crescent.

The second name on the list belonged to a man that OgoPogo had arrested the previous week, and charged with fraud, following the discovery that a large number of senior citizens had been persuaded to part with cash for unnecessary roof repairs. Several names--each with five entries--shared third place, including among them John Garter. Having decided to advance John Garter to a clear third place position by virtue of being married to the person in first place, Inspector Ogopoulos then threw down his pencil, and leaned back in his chair triumphantly. His task was now clear: he must establish as many connections as possible between the theft of his car, and anything having to do with the Garter household.

It took Inspector Ogopoulos a further five minutes of contemplation to decide that one such connection concerned the death of Mary Garter's ex-lover. The idea was reluctant to arrive and had hovered fuzzily for a time before accelerating into the brilliant focus it now presented. Forensic proof would be helpful, particularly for court purposes, but for now, the certainty of his conclusion made it irrelevant: that dead Frenchman had been struck and killed by the stolen Ogopoulos car. Whoever had killed the Frenchman, was the hooligan he was seeking!

It took another five minutes to establish a second blinding truth: that same hooligan was the Garter burglar making his escape. What luck, there were now two possible avenues that could lead him to the car thieves.

Chapter Eleven

Tony Angle paced up and down the deck of a British Columbia Ferry. It was a beautiful day, and the sun shone brightly. The wind was light, and there were few waves to impede the ship's journey as it surged effortlessly through the water, transporting its cargo of several hundred passengers and their cars from Vancouver to Vancouver Island.

A charming array of islands dotted the route, and as the ferry passed between, and around them, he could see rocky shorelines, bays, and beaches. Partially concealed by trees and foliage, houses and cottages sprinkled the landscape, many of them homes where people lived all year round enjoying the peace, freedom, and seclusion of their water-locked communities. The contrast to his life in Toronto was startling, and he could not help but wonder whether there would ever be a time when he could extricate himself from the survival pressures of urban life to take up a simpler, more peaceful, existence: a time when he would not have to work long hours every day in order to meet deadlines, balance demands, organize suppliers, satisfy customers, and worry about revenues and expenditures.

His thoughts of Toronto reminded him that he should call John Garter. He had arrived in Vancouver the previous day after a spectacular drive through the Rocky Mountains, and had wasted no time in tapping into his business network, the result of which was a meeting set up for the next day in Victoria. The meeting was with an old business associate: someone he hoped would prove to be a suitable purchaser for Mary's jewellery when the time was right. Feeling a little guilty that he had not spoken with Garter since starting out on his journey, he decided to correct the omission and make contact again.

As he pulled out his cell phone and began to pick at the keypad, John Garter in Toronto was desperately trying to figure out how he could satisfy Julia Miller's demand that the Golf Club money must be replaced by month end. As she had gently reminded him that very day, he had only one week left to do that. Although he had assured her that all would be settled well within the agreed time limits, he had only the vaguest idea about how he could comply. His burglary and insurance plan had all been pieced together on the assumption that he need not worry about returning the cash he had embezzled for some time to come. That meant there would be plenty of time to receive his share of the proceeds from the jewellery sale and to collect the insurance money before replacement became urgent. But, that was then, and this was now. A new reality meant that different solutions would have to be found. He was in the midst of just such an enquiry when Tony Angle's telephone call interrupted him.

"You! Where are you? Where have you been? I've been worried..."

"Been worried that I did a bunk have you? Really Mr. G, you'll have to be a bit more trusting than that! Anyhow, I don't need to tell you that there are some things you can't trust, like for example cell phones, if you know what I mean, so be careful won't you?"

"Yes, yes, of course."

"I'm out west at the moment. Decided I needed a bit of a break. Thought I'd combine some business and pleasure." He had not told John Garter of his getaway accident and despite the remorse he felt over what had happened he still saw no reason to do so.

"Tell me about the business part."

"Okay, I will. I'm meeting tomorrow with someone who may turn out to be a suitable buyer down the road... when we're ready with the product."

"That's wonderful, I'm very pleased. But, look… here's the situation. You know those financial obligations I told you about?"

"Financial obligations...?   Oh! You mean your temporary pecuniary embarrassment?"

"Yes, yes I suppose so. Well here's the thing. They've got worse... my obligations that is... and I have to act a lot faster than I had thought. I want to ask you a favour. I want us to accelerate the selling operation..." He cut off an interruption from Tony Angle. "I know, I know... just hear me out please. In addition to a very fast sale I need you to..." he paused, "to let me have all the proceeds and not just half. You can have your split later, after the second stage is completed. I'll make it worth your while of course, with some added commission, say another thousand. How would that be?" Tony Angle was quick to reply.

"I don't like it at all, Mr. G. There are too many risks. It's just too soon for the product to come to market. Don't get me wrong though, it's not the delayed commission thing, I'm willing to talk about that if it will help you out, but I think we should wait."

"Well, I'm pleased to hear that you're willing to wait for your share, but the point is it won't be of any help to me unless we can get the product to market right away. I need both of those things, a delayed split and proceeds from a fast sale. I haven't got much time." Sensing Tony Angle's discomfort, he pressed on with his argument. "Look, getting the product and putting it on the market always carried some risk didn't it? And that's going to be the case whenever we do it, so I say, let's do it as soon as possible, and have done with it."

"It will make quite a lot of difference to value."

"Well if it does, it does. Just do the best you can and let me have the amount as soon as you possibly can. I have a deadline coming up that I have to meet." Tony Angle considered John Garter's plea.

"Let me think about it Mr. G, and get back to you."

"No!" There's no time for that. I need your agreement now!" The words practically leapt from his mouth. "If it's a money thing I can make the extra commission two thousand if that will help?" Tony Angle suddenly felt some concern over the mental state of his business partner. He was obviously extremely stressed, and now sounded both desperate, and aggressive. The last thing he needed was an irrational John Garter throwing his weight around.

"Look calm down will you. I'm not ruling it out... I'm just urging caution. I don't believe in taking unnecessary risks. So please, just relax a bit will you? " Garter appeared to take the advice.

"Yes, I'm sorry, I didn't mean to shout." Tony Angle continued to voice his concerns.

"Look Mr. G. I'm taking quite a hit here. There's no immediate fifty percent for me, and if we bring the product to market that quickly, the pie is going to be a lot smaller than we thought, isn't it? You'll have to sweeten the pot a bit I think, after all you'll still get the ins... er, the reimbursement amount won't you. Don't you agree that would be fair?" Convinced that he was about to be gouged, Garter immediately went into a defensive mode and countered with a cautious enquiry.

"What did you have in mind?" Tony Angle thought for a moment before replying.

"Let's wait and see what the market will deliver first. When we know that I'll let you know about a commission bonus."

"No! That's not good enough. I need to have a clear ceiling on this. I've proposed two thousand and if that's not sufficient tell me what is." John Garter's anxiety was getting the better of him, and his indignant, aggressive tone, genuinely offended Tony Angle. His proposal to wait until they both knew what they could get for the jewellery, had been intended to avoid an exaggerated demand, but he was now forced to state his terms. Very well then, he thought, he would.

"I should think ten thousand, Mr. Garter."

"What! Are you mad? That's way out of line. I can't agree to that."

"You can't... and why not? I thought you wanted me to do you a favour."

Garter was silent. He could not deny the truth of Tony Angle's observation, and realized that he was entirely dependent on him to deliver the fruits of their scheme. Tony Angle did not wait for a reply before continuing. "Look Mr. G, the heat for this comes in my direction first. You should remember that."

"Yes, and it stays in your direction doesn't it?" He regretted his comment the moment he made it.

"What do you mean by that?"

"Nothing. Nothing at all, I'm sorry. I didn't mean that."

"Yes you did Mr. Garter. I know exactly what you meant. Well let me tell you something. This is a joint venture, and if you have any thought that you can make it appear to be a solo deal on my part if it all blows up, then I have some news for you." The idea that John Garter could, if it became necessary to save himself, deny all knowledge of his own involvement in their scheme had occurred to Tony Angle before they had even finished hatching their plans. He had therefore taken out some insurance of his own: a precaution that had already yielded three small tapes containing recordings of mutually incriminating conversations with his partner. This wasn't the time to reveal his secret weapon, which at that very moment was earning its keep, and he decided to content himself with the caution he had just issued.

Garter quickly attempted reconciliation.

"Tony, I'm sorry. I didn't mean to imply...I wouldn't do a thing like that! In any case, this isn't going to blow up is it? I've put my trust in you, and you can do the same with me. I know I'm a bit uptight right now but the truth of the matter is I have to come up with about forty thousand in a few days. Unless I get the proceeds by then I'm in a very difficult spot."

"Well can't you cash some RRSP's or something? Surely things aren't that tight? You could put that amount on a credit card!" John Garter winced. If only it was that simple. The unfortunate truth was that he had already exhausted all investments and credit lines with his impetuous stock trading binges.

"No, I can't." He said nothing more and left Tony Angle to draw whatever conclusions he chose.

"I see. Well, we don't have too many options then do we?" He paused. "But Mr. G, surely you must realize that even if I withhold on getting my half for the time being, you aren't going to get anything like forty? The best we can expect bringing the product to market so fast is about fifteen-- twenty at the most."

"Fifteen or twenty! They're worth well over sixty or seventy. You know that!"

"Mr. G, it's a very hot product. Any trustworthy purchaser knows that, and will purchase accordingly. That's why if we wait a few months the product can go for a lot more-- like we talked about before, maybe thirty, or even forty if we're lucky."

"I don't have a few months. To be exact I have seven days." Tony Angle frowned.

"All right, if that's the way you want it, leave it with me. I'll get you as much as I can and have a courier deliver it as soon as possible. Tell me where I should send it?" As obvious as it was, the question took John Garter by surprise.

"Oh.... that's a good point! Let's see, if you send it to my office Mrs. Bennett will open it, which won't do, and I don't want to risk my wife getting her hands on it at home, so..." Tony Angle interrupted his musings.

"Look, I'll tell you what. I'll send it to my service station and you can pick it up from there. My brother Alfred is looking after things while I'm away. He'll have it all for you. I'll tell him to expect it, and to let you know as soon as it's arrived. How's that?"

"Excellent, that sounds just the thing, but..." he paused, "I suppose your brother is, er... reliable?"

"Now, now, Mr. G, would I have a brother who wasn't? Of course he is! I promise you he won't even open the packet!" Tony Angle had resumed his customary, teasing style, but as he now reminded himself there was an important and unfinished part of their conversation. "Mr. G, I'm being quite serious when I say that as soon as the second phase is completed I will want my half of whatever I send to you now, plus ten. I hope I have your agreement to that, otherwise it's all off and we wait until the market is better." John Garter experienced a sharp pain between his shoulders as he reluctantly accepted that he had no real choice in the matter.

"Well, I think it's a bit steep, but if that's what you demand, then I can't do much about it can I?" Tony Angle became impatient.

"Mr. Garter, don't mess about with me. You and I both know that it's a fair arrangement so don't give me any of that carping and whining. Just tell me: do you, or don't you, accept the deal?"

"Yes, I accept. Of course I do." With an injured tone, he added a final shot. "Forgive me for looking after my interests won't you." Tony Angle was quick to reply.

"Far be it from me to damage your interests, Mr. G, but speaking of interest, you'll notice that I've made no attempt to recover lost interest on my delayed payment won't you. Maybe I should rethink that part..."

"Very funny. Ha, ha. Now if that's all, I shall get on and wait for word from your brother. Needless to say, the more you can get, the better. Please remember, I'm in a jam here."

With their call completed, John Garter returned to his scratch pad and sums, while in British Columbia, Tony Angle switched off his recording device, leaned on the upper deck rail of his mini cruise ship, and frowned at the horizon. He didn't like John Garter, and their recent discussion did nothing to endear him. He had agreed to his proposals against his better judgment, and despite his conviction that after the insurance company pay out, John Garter would happily renege on his promises if he thought he could get away with it. He would not be able to do so of course, but even so... Yes, the fact was, he was dealing with a greedy and untrustworthy man.

Then and there, Tony Angle decided on a little chicanery of his own. Unlike his business partner, he had made some extremely shrewd investments during the years he had been at the helm of the Ambrosia Service station, and as a result, he could afford to make other investments when suitable opportunities arose; and one such opportunity was arising now. Yes, the more he thought about it, the more it made sense: he would sell the jewellery to himself! In a couple of days Garter would receive…say twenty thousand, that would be very generous…and he would no doubt be delighted that the sale had gone through so quickly. Then, after the insurance payout, Garter would owe him ten thousand for his share of the proceeds, and ten for the bonus they had just agreed to. So, he would then get his twenty thousand back again, he would have the jewellery to sell at a much better price later on, and could keep all the proceeds for himself. He would have kept his end of the agreement with Garter, and Garter would have most of the insurance money. It was an excellent plan, and an ethical one too! Feeling extremely pleased with himself he continued his promenade around the upper deck, all the while breathing deep, cleansing gulps of sea air, and marvelling at the view as the ship continued its passage across the blue-green waters of the Strait of Georgia.

*   *   *

As was her custom, the last few minutes of Julia Miller's work day had been spent updating performance review notes on her staff. As some of them had come to understand, the main strategy for avoiding being the subject of a negative entry in her famous journal, was to perform one's duties happily, efficiently, and without question. Others believed that salvation could be achieved by demonstrating independent thought and a willingness to take risks; she had, after all, been known to declare these qualities the ones she valued most. They, however, had failed to understand that such virtues were not transportable from private life to her workplace and, as a result, frequently found themselves the subject of her journal entries.

She glanced at her watch, smiled to herself, and began packing her briefcase. It had been more than one week since she had confronted John Garter about his misdemeanors and now it was time to follow up with his contract. She took the elevator to the underground shopping mall beneath her building, the nucleus of an interconnected network of shops, stores, restaurants, and hotels, that spread for miles under the street visible city above, and walked briskly along a familiar route that took her past fountains and water features, through marble paneled walkways, along carpeted 'streets' and up an escalator to the hotel lounge where they had agreed to meet. When she arrived, John Garter was already there, off to one corner, lounging in a comfortable wing-backed chair, and sipping at a drink of Scotch. She approached the table and slipped into the chair opposite.

"Jonathon dear, it's lovely to see you again. I haven't kept you waiting I hope?"

"No, not at all. I just got here. What do you want to drink?" He conveyed the information to a passing waitress and beamed a charming smile across the table. "It's nice to see you again. How are you?"

" I'm fine, thank you Jonathon. And how are you?"

"I'm well, thank you, and I'm pleased to report that I have things firmly under control and that I expect to be back on the straight and narrow in no time at all. Does that surprise you?"

"No, Jonathon it does not. In fact, nothing about you surprises me, you are a very predictable man." Garter looked hurt. She continued. "But, don't fret about it -- predictability is not such a bad thing."

"No, I suppose not. Better than being irrational anyway."

"Those two things are not mutually exclusive you know."

"Oh, I see. So does that mean you find me predictable and irrational?" He glared defiantly across the table. Julia Miller smiled, picked up the drink being delivered to her, and remained silent as she returned his stare.

"Tell me Jonathon, have you written your confession for me yet?" He leant back, crossed his legs, and patted at his inside jacket pocket.

"Yes, I have, but..." he paused, in obvious discomfort, "I'm not so sure that it's a good idea for me to... er, to show it to anyone."

"Jonathon, I am *not* 'anyone'". Julia Miller's voice was icy.

"No, no, of course not... it's just that..." Julia Miller cut him off.

"Jonathon, that is the first and last time that you will ever attempt to escape your duty to me. Do you understand?"

"Yes, of course. I wasn't trying to get out of it, I was just..." Julia Miller held out her elegantly groomed hand.

"Give it to me." Without further ado, Garter retrieved an envelope from his inside pocket and passed it to her. She opened it and read in silence while he fidgeted in his chair. After a few moments, she made a contemptuous snort and threw the paper across the table towards him. "Just as I thought it would be… this is quite inadequate… completely unacceptable. You will do it again Jonathon, and next time you will get it right. Is that clear?" John Garter was genuinely shocked.

"What! What do you mean it's inadequate?"

"You really don't know, do you?" Julia Miller's icy tone changed to amusement. She reached for the piece of paper and read aloud scornfully " '…when I noticed the shortfall I immediately resolved to correct it since it was my responsibility as treasurer…'" her voice quivered into an incredulous snigger " 'to get to the bottom of the problem!' You really do think that those words constitute a true confession don't you! But, am I surprised? No Jonathon, I am not. In fact, I am not the least surprised you could not bring yourself to write the truth because I know who you are, and what you are." She sat back, and with obvious pleasure, watched as Garter struggled to come to terms with her message and to marshal his defence. It did not come to him easily.

"Well I do admit I have been a little circumspect …I wasn't trying to…I mean I can tighten it up somewhat.

Are you expecting a longer statement...or something more specific?"

"Jonathon, a moment ago you asked whether I see you as irrational as well as predictable. Well, I suggest that you now give serious consideration to whether it is rational for you to continue to shirk from the task I have set you when the alternative, I can assure you, will be substantially more painful." John Garter was quick to absorb the full intent of her words and looked pained.

"Jonathon do you have a pen with you?"

"Yes, of course."

"Then get it out, and write this." She began to dictate. "I, John Garter, confess that I have stolen from the Aerial Golf Club ... I'll leave you to fill in the exact amount Jonathon, which of course will be not less than forty thousand dollars, thereby betraying the trust and confidence placed in me by the members of the club in the performance of my duties as club Treasurer." She paused to allow him time to catch up with her dictation, all the while looking at him as if he were an errant schoolchild. "I have acquired the stolen money by cashing cheques drawn on the Aerial Golf Club account taking advantage of the naiveté of our Chairman who, without any knowledge of, or involvement in, my fraudulent actions countersigned the cheques while they were still blank. The reason that I chose to steal these funds..." she broke off, "you can fill that in the explanatory piece later, but I want it to be honest, specific, and concise." She continued. "The reason for this confession is that my dishonesty has been discovered and I am frightened that if I do not confess to my crime I will be exposed to the police and to other persons who would use the information against me." Julia Miller smiled while her pupil scribbled furiously. "Keep writing Jonathon… I do not regret my actions, but I do regret having been discovered. I have agreed to replace the stolen funds in full and have committed to do this by…" she looked at her watch, "the twenty seventh of November." Her dictation completed, she added a final instruction. "You will write this out in full, sign it and date it, and deliver it to me at our next meeting."

By the time he had finished writing, John Garter's indignation and anger were bubbling furiously, controlled only by a sense of helpless resignation. He had no choice but to comply with this humiliating performance, and he knew that he must contain the temptation to express his fury. He averted his eyes from those of Julia Miller and read over what he had scribbled. He frowned as he did so, and twice re-read the sentence that stated he did not regret stealing the money -- just that he regretted getting caught. He looked up and spoke.

"I thought this confession was supposed to also express my regret?"

"It is supposed to be an honest confession Jonathon."

"But surely you know that I regret what I did and am embarrassed by it and want to make restitution right away? I mean this looks as if I don't even care." Julia Miller stared at him intently.

"Jonathon. For once, please try to be honest with yourself. It is true that you are embarrassed. You are embarrassed that I have found you out. I have uncovered things that you wanted to keep secret and the revelation of those secrets is painful. You have even embarrassed yourself because you have mismanaged your finances to such an extent that you have had to embark on this scheme. That is embarrassing because it does not fit with your image of who you are. So yes, you are embarrassed at being exposed and frightened too. But, let us not for one minute delude ourselves into thinking that you regret what you have done. You regret only one thing and that is that you have been found out. If you had got away with your plan you would have had no regrets whatsoever." She drew closer and stared into his eyes. "Jonathon, you need never be embarrassed to admit the truth to me, whatever that truth is. Until you can learn to do that ..." she paused, "and believe me I have every intention of helping you to do so... there can be nothing between us except play acting. So, admit to me now that you do *not* regret what you did and that you would do it again if needs demand." She beamed an encouraging smile and waited for his reply.

John Garter was not a man to spend much time in a state of introspection. However, even to someone with his capacity for self delusion the truth of what she had said was inescapable: he was indeed capable of believing his own lies! Undoubtedly the birth of this revelation was assisted as much by her confrontational delivery as it was by any flash of insight, but the effect was powerful. This was unfamiliar territory, and he found the sensation intriguing. "You are right!" he said earnestly, "I do regret being caught out, and the fact of the matter is I could live with myself perfectly well if that had not happened. In fact, I would not have lost a wink of sleep." He paused and continued enthusiastically. "There! I have said it to myself, and I have said it to you. You are an exceptional woman Ms. Miller, you have..." he struggled for words "made me feel... comfortable with myself." Julia Miller smiled.

"Well, well, Jonathon, I am pleased. That is much better. We may be making some progress now."

At a safe distance, shrouded by the fronds of a large potted palm tree, Harry Jefferson peered across the hotel lounge and focused intently on a side view of Julia Miller. He had taken up his position some thirty minutes earlier having followed her there on the journey from her office. Every now and again he would blow his nose and scribble in a note book. This was the most rewarding day of sleuthing so far. Other days had been spent on routine surveillance: discovering the location of her condominium; the layout of the underground parking area; the location of her office; the car she drove; what she did at work. Once, after a whole day of sleuthing, all that he had learned was that Julia Miller sometimes spent long hours at her office before going home; no doubt to then hatch plots to destroy happy marriages such as his own. Today, however, his perseverance had been richly rewarded. There, before his very eyes, were Julia Miller and John Garter engrossed in intimate conversation.

Harry Jefferson was quick to reformulate his working hypothesis regarding the origins of that spiteful note maligning him in the eyes of his wife, and it was now crystal clear: Julia Miller did it, but Garter was in on the act. And, without question, they were both manipulating club funds for personal gain. More significantly they knew he was on to them! It was almost certain that they were, at that very moment, discussing how to silence him. He would have to be careful, they were a dangerous pair.

Julia Miller began to organize for her departure. "We will meet again in two days Jonathon. You will deliver to me your homework text, which of course will read exactly the way we have now established, and we will continue our discussion which will focus, warts and all, upon your plans for replacing the money by the twenty seventh. Is that understood?" Her penetrating gaze instantly eradicated from his mind any thought of disagreement. "Good night Jonathon."

Chapter Twelve

Mary's move to her new quarters had been completed with relative ease. Her new home was on the top floor of an old Victorian mansion that, despite having long ago been converted to a number of self-contained apartments, managed, with its elaborate system of chimneys and fireplaces, its leaded windows, and its liberally scattered, although regrettably now ineffective, servant-summoning bell pushes, to convey an air of elegance, decadence and privilege--characteristics that Mary found both whimsical and ironic. Eaves sliced into the sides of her new living room that, at one end, led to French doors and a railing to prevent entry to a nonexistent balcony, and at the other, to a kitchen and dinette. Her bedroom, which would also serve as her studio, was large and bright, and looked out over a broad expanse of backyard grass, edged by tall trees and dotted with bushes and shrubs.

It had been almost one week since she had moved there and it already looked comfortable and inviting. With the help of her friend Ellen, she had hung paintings, erected bookshelves, made drapes for the windows and acquired various items of furniture to supplement those she had taken from the house. She had not yet completed the set up of her computer but had just settled to that challenge after her morning coffee when the door buzzer signaled a visitor. She was not expecting Ellen but, as she jogged down the three flights of stairs, Mary felt sure it would be her waiting at the door. However, that notion was quickly dispelled when, as she approached the hallway she could see a distinctly un-Ellen like shape looming at her through the frosted glass panes. For an instant she wondered if it was wise to open the door to a stranger, but her instincts told her it would be safe to do so, and she reached for the door latch without hesitation. As she swung it open the figure took a step backwards and in a movement that looked like a cross between a curtsey and a bow, revealed itself to be Inspector Ogopoulos.

"Good evening Mrs. Gator. My apologies for this uninvited arrival, but I heard that you had moved and I would like to talk to you if I may." To Mary Garter the inspector looked awkward and out of place in the real world of her doorstep. It was a cold morning and as he stood there in his baggy woolen suit, wearing a hat, but no coat or scarf, she found his presence quite incongruous and could barely suppress a giggle.

"It's Garter, not Gator, Inspector -- like the things that used to hold up women's stockings." She paused to assess the impact and noted a slight flushing of the cheeks as he proffered an apology. "Don't worry about it Inspector, I'm not offended." She opened the door wider. "Come in won't you. There's no-one here and I'm not doing anything that can't wait a moment or two."

Inspector Ogopoulos trundled into the hallway and followed Mary Garter up the stairs to the top floor, panting as he climbed what seemed like an endless mountain of steps. She ushered him though into her living room, pointed him towards an armchair, and offered him a choice of coffee or tea. He declined both and wedged himself awkwardly into the seat.

"So, I see you have moved out then Mrs. Garter." Inspector Ogopoulos appeared somewhat hurt. "You didn't tell me you were going to do that, I had to learn it from Mr. Garter."

"Yes, I suppose I should have told you... I'm sorry about that, but I have had lots on my mind and calling you about my move wasn't one of them."

"Mr. Garter didn't know where you were... said you hadn't left a forwarding address! I had to track you down through the telephone company. I must say though, he seemed quite angry Mrs. Garter."

"Inspector, I have no doubt he was angry. I have left my husband and intend to divorce him. He's not pleased about that... thinks it will be expensive." She paused, wondering whether to elaborate further, and decided to say nothing more.

"I see. Was it because of the dead Frenchman?"

"No it was not. He had nothing to do with it." She decided to provide a little more information. "Inspector, our marriage has been in a very bad shape for many years. This is the culmination of many things. I've left him and am making a new life for myself." She paused. "But I'm sure you haven't called at my house to discuss the state of my marriage... what did you want to see me about?"

"I'll get to that in just a minute Mrs. Garter, but first I do need one more piece of information about your marriage and your affairs..." She cut him off abruptly.

"That should be 'affair' Inspector, in the singular. There was only one." Inspector Ogopoulos looked puzzled and then let out a loud guffaw.

"Oh, no, no, no! I didn't mean your adulterous affairs! No, no, no they are between you and your lovers." Mary clenched her teeth and said nothing. "I'm talking about your domestic affairs." He smiled to himself and continued. "I just need to know if you will be staying at this address from now on or whether you will be moving again. If so, I must insist that you let me know this time." He looked up expectantly.

"No, Inspector, I do not anticipate moving again in the near future, and yes, I will most certainly let you know if I do." She paused. "But I'm not sure why that is important to you. You make it sound as if I am under some kind of suspicion." Inspector Ogopoulos looked thoughtful.

"Well... not really Mrs. Garter... I have no legal grounds... it's just that with all these loose ends I may need to get hold of you. That's all."

"Are you referring to loose ends about my stolen jewellery, or about the death of Daniel?"

"Yes... about both of those, and of course, my car."

"Your car? What do you mean?"

"Forgive me. I can't be too precise about that just yet." Oblivious to her puzzled expression, he continued. "Do you drive Mrs. Garter?"

"Would you like to see my license Inspector?"

"No, no, just curious! I assume you do?"

"Yes I do. Quite an achievement for someone with my limitations, don't you think?" OgoPogo seemed thoughtful.

"Indeed... indeed." He paused before continuing. "What about golf Mrs. Garter?"

"What about it?"

"Do you play?"

"No, I don't! I can't stand the game." The Inspector nodded approvingly.

"Me neither. Do you know any people at the club where your husband plays; people your husband might hang out with? Someone on the management side perhaps?"

"No, I don't. Why don't you ask my husband? The only person I've heard him talk about…" she corrected herself, "I should say, 'complain' about, is someone called Jefferson. I gather they sit on the same committee." The Inspector made a note in his book.

"Thank you Mrs. Garter. I'll check that out." He paid no attention to the amazed look on Mary's face. "But that wasn't why I came here. My purpose was to let you know we are offering a reward for information about the theft of your property." He paused triumphantly.

"That's wonderful Inspector! Is that usual? How much are you offering?"

"Oh it's quite common when the circumstances are right... the reward is twenty thousand dollars Mrs. Garter. It's an amount suggested and posted by your insurance company. We don't have much of a budget for those things ourselves. Anyway... you never know, it may turn up something." He smiled. "I just wanted you to know that we are working on it... the insurance company tell me that you are anxious for a cash settlement. I understand Mr. Garter has telephoned several times."

"He has? I didn't know that!" She paused. "Actually that's very upsetting information…I don't want a cash settlement I want my jewellery back!" She looked at OgoPogo curiously. "So my husband has been calling you say?"

"No, not to me Mrs. Garter, to your insurance agent... or at least that's what I gathered from him recently when we were talking about the reward. Maybe you should talk to him yourself?"

"Yes, I most certainly will! Thank you for that information. Inspector you do understand how important it is to me that I get this jewellery back don't you?"

"Yes, yes of course. Don't give up hope Mrs. Garter. I too have a vested interest in a satisfactory outcome." He leant forward in a confidential pose. "I haven't told you this Mrs. Garter but I think that whoever stole your jewellery was the same person who stole my car."

"Really, why? "

"I have my reasons Mrs. Garter, and I am sharing this with you because I want you to know that I am dealing with a serious matter. You'd be very surprised to learn the number of cars being stolen in this area." He paused. "To say nothing of the dead man and your jewellery of course."

"But surely you don't think there was any connection between the theft of my jewellery and Daniel's death, do you?"

"I haven't ruled that out Mrs. Garter. It may have been an accident but it may not. People can be very clever at covering up their tracks you know." He paused. "Mrs. Garter, you told me that your husband knew nothing of your affair with Daniel. But, how can you be sure of that? Isn't it possible that he found out somehow and then decided to get even with your lover? After all he would have been very upset, I'm sure, and he is an impulsive man isn't he?" Mary Garter laughed.

"John, impulsive! No, inspector, I think constipated would be a better adjective. Although, I must say, when he finally makes up his mind he does get on with things. Anyway, if he did know about my relationship with

Daniel I can assure you that it would not be Daniel he would want to get even with... it would be me! So, I think we can safely assume that he is quite unaware of any connection Inspector, and with your assistance, I hope to keep it that way."

"I see. Well, there's one other thing. On the evening you were burgled your husband says that he spent part of the time at the Fox and Hounds pub with a man by the name of Tony Angle. Was he a friend of your husband's Mrs. Garter?"

"Tony Angle? I've not heard that name before Inspector. If they were together it must have had something to do with business because my husband doesn't have any friends, only acquaintances. Why don't you ask my husband about him?"

"Yes, all in good time Mrs. Garter. Just wanted your thoughts about it." He stood up and with a hopeful expression looked around the room for his hat. It suddenly appeared in Mary Garter's hand, and he accepted it gratefully. "I'll be off now then. Thank you for your time Mrs. Garter, I'll see myself out. And, like I said, please let me know if you are thinking of moving again." He lumbered to the hallway, disappeared from view down the top flight of stairs, and trundled his way out the front door and back to his car.

* * *

The afternoon following her visit from Inspector Ogopoulos, Mary Garter decided to call the insurance company to get an update on Mr. Davies' progress. She had been alarmed to discover that her husband had been attempting to accelerate a settlement and wished to make it quite clear that her own priority was for the stolen jewellery to be recovered. Besides, if there was to be a settlement the money should come to her since it was her jewellery and not her husband's. When she reached Mr. Davies at his office, she was surprised to hear that his voice had a decidedly testy edge.

"It's really no different from what I told you yesterday Mrs. Garter, we do want to explore the reward money approach first before…" Mary Garter interrupted him.

"Excuse me, Mr. Davies, we did not speak yesterday. In fact we have not spoken since the time you came to the house after the burglary."

"No, no, that's quite true." He sounded taken aback. "I was referring to your husband's calls – I'm assuming he has told you what we discussed?"

"Well, you assume wrongly, Mr. Davies. My husband has neglected to tell me that he has been in contact with you, and although I could now ask him what was said I would rather hear it for myself if you don't mind."

"Yes, of course, Mrs. Garter. I thought he was calling for both of you. My mistake." He paused, "So, am I to take it that in future I should deal with you both separately?"

"Yes you may. My husband and I are now living apart pending a divorce."

"Oh, I am sorry to hear that!" Mr. Davies appeared genuinely upset at the news. "My, my, so that does explain things. Are you still living at the house?"

"No my husband is, for now at least. I've moved out. Here, I'll give you the address and telephone number, in case you need to reach me." She heard a keyboard clicking as Mr. Davies entered the information directly into his computer.

"I'm not being nosey Mrs. Garter but just for the records here, can you tell me when this separation happened: you were still living together when the burglary occurred weren't you?"

"Yes we were. This is much more recent, I left about a week ago. Does it make any difference to anything?"

"Yes, it might if you get divorced Mrs. Garter, you'll probably want to separate out some of your policies. The policy covering your burglary losses is in your joint names and your life insurance is a spousal plan so that would have to change. However, there's no rush we can sort all that out later… at least, I assume we can, you're not getting divorced immediately are you?"

"No, it will take a while yet." Mary Garter felt a flood of bitterness as she considered the time and effort she was going to have to invest, and the acrimony she would experience, while managing herself through the next few months. She attempted to suppress the feeling. "So, please, tell me what is happening."

"Yes, of course, Mrs. Garter. You will have gathered from what I said before that we have posted funds for the police to offer as a reward for information leading to the recovery of the stolen property? We are doing that because it sometimes does help to give us a lead on what's been going on."

"Do you have any leads so far?"

"No, not really Mrs. Garter. Like I say, the reward approach may help to turn up something. The police don't seem to have much success in these cases but the prospect of a reward often pulls something out of the woodwork. There's certainly no harm in trying and if it does prove helpful we save money in the long run and you get your valuables returned."

As she listened to his assessment, Mary Garter became increasingly indignant. What right had that toad of a husband to press for an insurance settlement on her stolen jewellery, apparently assuming that the cash would come to him, and that when it did, everything would be satisfactorily resolved! She blurted out a demand. "Mr. Davies I want to get something very clear. It is my jewellery that has been stolen. I do not want a cash settlement and I most certainly do not want my husband to get a cash settlement. What I want is for my jewellery to be recovered and if my husband should call you any more, pressing for a settlement, please tell him that you have instructions from me to the contrary and that without my consent, and my lawyer's involvement, there can be no question of anyone, especially him, getting a cheque." She paused long enough to draw breath. "Is that understood!"

"Yes that's quite clear Mrs. Garter. In fact, given the circumstances…your separation, and the fact it is a joint policy, your mutual consent will be a required anyway. I'll make sure Mr. Garter understands that, if he calls again. And, in the meantime, we'll press on with the reward approach and continue working with the police. All right?" He sounded hopeful.

"Yes, Mr. Davies. Since we now seem to understand each other, it is quite all right. And I assume you will let me know as soon as there is any news to report?" He assured her that she would be the first to know of any development in the case, apologized once more for his mistaken assumptions, and wished her a pleasant afternoon.

CHAPTER THIRTEEN

After finishing her morning coffee Mary tidied up the kitchen, gathered up her purse and keys, and skipped down the three flights of stairs that led to the front door. Once in the main hallway she stopped, fished in her purse and pulled out the piece of paper she was looking for: the receipt for tire installation given to her by her husband after his cheapskate deal with…she examined the document, *Tony Angle, Ambrosia Service Station*. Well, Mr. Angle, she said to herself, I expect new tires to stay properly inflated! She made for her car and peered at the front passenger wheel where the night before she had noted that the tire was distinctly flatter than it should be. She decided that despite the fault it was still driveable and pulled away cautiously, resolving as she did, to remain calm and polite when she reached the garage. What was that saying about flies and vinegar? Well, whatever it was, she didn't feel in the mood for a fight. Yes, honey… that was what was called for!

Until that morning she had not had occasion to look at the receipt bearing the name and address of *Tony Angle, Ambrosia Service Station*, and it was not until she was approaching the garage that it dawned on her that this was the person that Inspector Ogopoulos had asked her about when he had come to call – the man her husband had met at the Fox and Hounds pub the night they were burgled. Well, how interesting, why would he be meeting with a garage owner? She steered into the forecourt, and parked by a door marked 'Office'

Seated at his desk adjacent to the only window in the room, Tony Angle had a clear view of all visitors to his garage. Although he had never met Mary Garter previously, he had most certainly met her car, and he realized immediately who she must be the moment she approached. His first reaction was one of alarm. He had returned from Vancouver only two days previously, confident that his new arrangement with John Garter had given him sufficient control to make possible his safe arrival back home. The stolen jewellery would not be marketed for a long time to come, and the deal-making risks were no longer of concern. However, he now felt decidedly uncomfortable at the approach of the woman who had been the principal victim of their scheme, and worried that her presence meant he was about to discover something unexpected that could link him to the robbery, or even worse, to the get-away accident.

As she approached, the smile on Mary Garter's face reassured him and caused his concerns to retreat. "Hello" she said, "I'm looking for Tony Angle. That wouldn't be you would it?"

"Right first time." He rose from his chair and extended a hand in greeting. "And, if I'm not mistaken you must be Mrs. Garter-- I recognize the car. What can I do for you?" Mary was taken aback.

"Well, well! I am surprised – you're quite the detective. I didn't know my car was so distinctive."

"I know, but it is to me. I had a good look at it when Mr. Garter bought it in last month. It's been re-sprayed at some time and the colour isn't standard." He paused wondering whether to comment on the tire deal they had completed and decided to avoid the subject. "Still clunking along OK is it?"

"Yes it's going just fine apart from one of the new tires you supplied – it's sprung a leak. Come and see." She led him outside and pointed at the bulging front wheel. "Something wrong there I think you'll agree."

"Yes, Mrs. Garter, there certainly is. I'll get that fixed for you right away. It's probably a faulty valve." He called out to a young man who came ambling towards them through an open garage door, wiping his hands on a rag. "Take a look at this flat Dirk. See what you can do and let me know when it's fixed." The young man nodded and set off to get tools and a jack. "Would you like some coffee while he's doing that Mrs. Garter – it shouldn't be too long."

"Yes, thank you." She pulled up a chair to Tony Angle's desk while he filled two plastic cups and brought them over in a cardboard tray laden with packets of creamer, sugar, and stir-sticks.

"Here you are. Just help yourself if you want sugar and stuff." He pushed the container towards her and watched as she picked out a napkin. He noticed immediately that she wasn't wearing an engagement ring or wedding band and with a sudden flash of guilt, wondered whether they were among the collection he had stolen from her and which, at that very moment, lay not more than five feet from where she sat, hidden from view on a cupboard shelf in a canister marked 'shop rags'. For the first time, he thought about what the loss must have meant to her, and immediately felt embarrassed. She was so obviously a nice woman… pleasant, attractive, dignified….and, adding to his feelings of discomfort and guilt, had something about her that seemed sad, and vulnerable.

"So, I understand that you know my husband quite well." She looked at him curiously.

"Mr. Garter? Yes I know him…not that well really. He comes in for gas now and again."

"Oh I see." She decided not to press the matter further and to come at it from a different angle. "There's quite an interesting co-incidence. Your name came up in a conversation recently. It meant nothing to me at the time, and it wasn't until I looked up your address this morning, that I realized you were the person referred to."

"Mr. Garter been talking about me has he?" Tony Angle sounded a little anxious.

"Oh no. In fact he and I aren't talking at all at the moment…" she hesitated, "but that's another story." Tony Angle looked at her with a puzzled expression curious about both of the discussion topics she had now opened.

"Go on then." He picked up his coffee container and took a large gulp.

"I was referring to the police Inspector who is investigating a burglary at our house." She broke off, mistaking for confusion, the look of panic that darted across Tony Angle's face. "Sorry, I should explain. Our house was burgled last month and we lost a number of things including some irreplaceable jewellery that was very important to me." Tony Angle shook his head and made a sympathetic clicking noise with his tongue. "Anyway, the detective investigating the case came to see me last night to tell me there was a reward being offered. He was the one who mentioned your name." Tony Angle absorbed the information with mounting trepidation.

"Really? What did he say?"

"He just wanted to know if I knew you. He said that my husband had told him that the two of you had a drink together the night it happened." Tony Angle frowned.

"Yes, we did meet at the Fox once." He sounded a little doubtful. "That was when he was thinking about how much longer he should hang on to that car of his. So, that's when you were burgled eh? It was about a month ago now."

"Yes that's right." Tony Angle was unsure of his ground.

"I wonder why he asked about me?"

"Oh, just part of his checking up process I suspect. I have to say, he's a very strange man. Always leaping to wrong conclusions and suspicious about everything. He's also obsessed about finding out who stole his car. He lives just up the street from our house and the same night we were burgled someone took off with his old Buick. He thinks it might have been the burglar, which I suppose it might have been, but he does make odd connections." She paused, and despite the temptation, decided there was too much explaining involved to mention that he had also suggested the possibility that her husband might have killed Daniel while in a jealous rage.

"He really is very odd."

As she spoke, Tony Angle listened intently-- anxious, but with his mind clear and focused. Nothing that she said was, in itself, cause for concern. The pub meeting was not supposed to be a secret and he already knew from an earlier discussion with John Garter that it had been brought up during his meeting with Ogopoulos. Checking up on the story would be quite routine and it probably meant he could expect a visit himself at some point. The fact that he had chosen to make his get-away in a car belonging to Ogopoulos was a surprise, but an amusing one and no more dangerous or incriminating than if it had belonged to anyone else. He had expected a connection to be made between the car theft and the burglary, so that was all right too. No mention had been made of a connection between the car, and the death of the man he had hit, which might mean that none had been made. All in all, there seemed to be nothing new to worry about, although he found it curious that he had learned this new information, from Mrs.Garter and not from her husband. He began to relax.

"I'm sorry to hear about the burglary Mrs. Garter. What did you lose?" Mary gave an abbreviated account of the stolen items, but it was obvious from her expression that she was deeply upset about the lost heirlooms. He pressed on. "Did I understand you to say that there is a reward being offered?"

"Yes, by the insurance company. It's for twenty thousand dollars."

"Oh, that's interesting. I think that usually means they don't expect to catch the person who did it--not without the help of an informer that is."

"Well, I don't hold out any hope of OgoPogo catching anyone."

"OgoPogo?"

"Oh, that's Inspector Ogopoulos. He's the one investigating. They call him OgoPogo at the police station I understand."

"Do they?" Tony Angle smiled to himself. "I didn't know that, although I do know Inspector Ogopoulos. And you're right; he's certainly an oddball. I wouldn't underestimate him though." He paused. "How's Mr. Garter taking all this?"

"Mmm…as I mentioned before, we aren't talking at the moment. But to answer your question I don't think he is taking it at all well. He wants an insurance settlement as soon as possible, whereas I don't. All I want is to have my jewellery back. Besides…and you might as well know this, I've left him and am seeking a divorce, so if it does come to a settlement I'm going to make damn sure he doesn't get any of it." She paused, noting Tony Angle's surprised expression. "Sorry if that sounds bitter… it's just that I am!" He grinned at her cheerfully.

"Yes, I can see that! It's been a while since I last saw him, so I didn't know any of this…not that he would have mentioned it necessarily." He looked at her thoughtfully. "Mrs. Garter, I know this isn't my business, but was he in some kind of trouble?" She paused for a moment before replying, apparently weighing the question.

"Well he was certainly a troubled man. But, I don't suppose that's what you mean. What kind of trouble did you have in mind?"

"I'm not sure exactly…I just got the impression he was feeling really worried about something, debts and things I suppose. He said something about his stockbrokers having let him down badly, but I got the impression he was anxious about something else too… don't know what though." He suddenly felt awkward and wished he hadn't said anything. "Oh well, like I said, it's not any of my business, I was just curious." Mary Garter listened carefully.

"No, that's okay, and I think you might be right too. He was… is, I should say, always obsessed about money, but he has been particularly anxious about things of late". She looked thoughtful and added. "And there was a threatening telephone call that was left on our answering machine, and even though he says it was left by mistake, I still worry that it was meant for him and that the threat was that we would be burgled."

"Really? What did the threatening call say?"

"Oh, I can't remember exactly, but it was quite menacing. Something like 'get it here or else.' It was a few days after that we got burgled, and I lost all my jewellery." Tony Angle winced as he noticed Mary fighting back her tears.

"So you didn't ever find out what 'it' referred to." He asked, gently.

"No, I didn't. Whoever the message was intended for was definitely required to deliver something urgently, but I've no idea what the 'something' was." Tony Angle was silent for a few moments as he recalled snippets of conversations he had had with her husband.

"You know what?" he said. There are a lot of villains out there who make their living by lending money to people who find themselves in a financial bind… and, they get very nasty when they don't get paid back on schedule." He looked at her inquisitively. "Maybe that's why he's been a bit anxious lately?"

"Mr. Angle, I don't know you from Adam, so I don't know why I am telling you all this, but I have been quite silly in the past, not keeping a close eye on our financial situation. John is an accountant and he took care of all the transactions and I didn't bother with that too much myself. If he said something wasn't affordable I accepted it. But then I came to realize that more and more things were becoming unaffordable and that there was a disparity between what I understood to be our situation and what he was saying. Suddenly we were becoming poorer and poorer, and it took me a long time to realize that he was bingeing away our assets on reckless, get-rich-quick, stock market transactions that often went bad. I made him promise to consult with me about any trading investments he was thinking about before he made them, but I'm more and more convinced that he just carried on regardless." She broke off, looking rather sheepish. "Our financial troubles aren't really the reason I am divorcing him though. However, I am now coming to realize that in addition to all the reasons I do have for wanting him out of my life, that he may well have been driving us down some path of financial destruction." She paused. "I've been very foolish and far too trusting, and you may very well be right when you suggest that the threatening telephone call had to do with an overdue loan. I hadn't thought of that, but the more I do, the more it makes sense. Maybe he got into something, over his head, and began some dealings with loan sharks!" She sat back in her chair. "I thank you for that insight Mr. Angle."

"You're welcome!" He grinned at her cheerfully. "Sounds like you need a good lawyer Mrs. Garter."

"Yes… and I do have one. She's really getting on top of things now."

"Oh, well that's good." He paused. "Like I said before, I don't really know your husband that well, but I can see that he could be difficult to get along with at times."

At that point Dirk stuck his head around the office door and pointed to Mary's car. "It's all done now" he said, "I put a new valve in. Shouldn't give you any more trouble."

Tony Angle rose and escorted Mary to where her car waited outside the office door. She extended her hand. "I enjoyed meeting you Mr. Angle. Thanks for fixing the tire… and thanks for the idea about that call."

As she slipped into the driver's seat and pulled away across the forecourt, Tony Angle made a decision: Mary Garter would get back her jewellery just as soon as he could figure out a safe way to conduct a deal with the insurance company.

***

Harry Jefferson paced up and down the corridor that led from his mother's front door to her kitchen. For the past five minutes he had repeatedly made the same journey, striding from entranceway to kitchen, perhaps thirty times or more, without once stopping to adjust the crumpled hallway rug that, with its ever-increasing midriff bulge, now threatened to trip him on each lap. The anxiety that induced his hand wringing and pacing had manifest itself twenty minutes previously, shortly after Inspector Ogopoulos had called to ask whether he might ask a few questions in connection with an investigation he was undertaking. The request was not in itself, particularly worrisome. Since the start of his sleuthing operations Harry Jefferson had been feeling unusually confident: more certain than ever that he had been right to stop taking his prescription medication; a dosage that his wife referred to as his "calming tablets". I am no longer in need of artificial controls, he had told himself. And now, he was energized and focused -- fully capable of tracking down and revealing his quarry for what they were: malicious, spiteful, frauds who had to be exposed and taught a lesson. Empowered by this sense of rightness, he had not hesitated to agree when Inspector Ogopoulos called and asked to talk.

The conversation opened pleasantly enough with an observation by the inspector to the effect that the weather was a little chillier than he preferred. Harry Jefferson had responded with a suggestion that the inspector wear some additional clothing, possibly a sweater or an overcoat. For some reason, known only to himself, the unsolicited advice had triggered a thought, leading the inspector to enquire whether Harry Jefferson was French. As it happened, Jefferson did have a Francophone heritage and informed the inspector accordingly. At that news the inspector had edged back a step or two, adopted a wary expression, and asked whether he also played the piano. Harry did not seem to find the question unusual and explained that despite having had some lessons as a child he had no mastery of the keyboard. He enquired whether the inspector was a pianist himself, and after what seemed to be a moment of anguish for the inspector, learned that he did not play, but that a piano lid had once dropped on his hand. Harry Jefferson had apologized and then led the inspector to a seat in the living room.

With the opening pleasantries completed, the Ogopoulos-Jefferson conversation had turned to business matters. No, Jefferson did not know the unshaven man in the picture. Yes, he did know John Garter. No, he did not consider him a friend. Yes, they did serve together on the Aerial golf club management committee. No, he had never owned a 1989 Buick. No, he did not have mechanical expertise. Yes, he was married. No, he lived with his mother because of a disagreement with his wife. No, his wife was not French. Yes, women could be perplexing. No, he had not met Mrs. Garter. Yes, John Garter was an unpleasant character. No, he was not aware that Mrs. Garter knew the unshaven man in the picture. No, he was not aware that John Garter had been burgled, but it was probably nothing more than he deserved.

It was not until the Inspector asked where Jefferson had been the previous Wednesday night that Harry surmised the true reason for his visit. It came to him in an instant: Julia Miller had told Ogopoulos about seeing him on Queen Street with that young woman from the escort service! Yes, that was it. No doubt she had sent an anonymous note to the police as well as to his wife. That was why the inspector had called and that was what he was fishing to find out. Angered by the deception, Jefferson had jumped to his feet and articulated a stream of incomprehensible bluster. In between Jefferson's finger-wagging, OgoPogo had caught only a few words that he could understand: "my business", "mighty mouse Miller", "dear wife", "Queen Street", "bitch", and "NOW!"

With his arm fully extended Jefferson had pointed at the front door and repeated the "now" word several times. Having deduced correctly that Jefferson wished to be left alone, the Inspector had stood up and excused himself, citing urgent business elsewhere. He had then begun to rummage around the room in search of his hat causing a noticeable escalation in Jefferson's level of agitation, so much so that by the time the inspector had retrieved it from its hiding place on a peg behind the living room door, Jefferson was hopping from foot to foot and his face had turned a bright red. Seemingly oblivious to Jefferson's discomfort, the Inspector had waved a cheery good-bye, paused briefly to admire a paint-by-numbers seascape hanging in the hallway, and returned to his car, feeling sure that Jefferson was not implicated in the theft of his Buick.

After completing several more of his pacing laps, Jefferson stopped abruptly, donned an overcoat and gloves, and strode purposefully out the front door allowing it to slam shut behind him.

Chapter Fourteen

Ever since he had learned of his wife's ridiculous plan to file for divorce, John Garter had been beset by a sense of impending doom. He had arranged an urgent consultation with a male equivalent of Ms. Juby--a lawyer with whom he had once been partnered at a golf club tournament who had impressed him with his no nonsense manner. The man clearly knew his stuff, but the advice he had given did nothing to quell John Garter's fears of financial ruin, and, had there been any to hide, would have sent him rushing to conceal as many assets as possible. He had left the meeting feeling like a wingless fly: a condition about which, thanks to childhood experimentation, he was not unfamiliar.

But now as he sat at home in his office, his mood was optimistic. Thanks to Tony Angle's swift delivery of twenty thousand dollars, and the almost eager enthusiasm of Gustav Illiach to supply the shortfall, he had at last been able to fulfill his contract: the golf club money had been replaced in full. It was a moment of great satisfaction and relief, and one that he had eagerly awaited ever since Julia Miller's brutal lunchtime confrontation.

It had been almost one week since his latest meeting with her. On that occasion she had summoned him to an after-work meeting in a coffee bar so that he could deliver to her the final version of his confession. She had stayed just long enough to review and approve the carefully written document, supervise the addition of his signature and the date, pronounce him an "improving student" and remind him that under the terms of his redemption contract the deadline for restoring stolen golf club assets was fast approaching. He had impressed upon her that there was no possibility of him failing to deliver the money by the due date, and had received in return, a charming smile, an assurance that she had not the slightest doubt he would meet his commitments, and, as she had taken her leave, a softly whispered promise, gently delivered to his ear behind her cupped hand, of a reward for good behaviour when compliance was demonstrated. His imagination danced with unaccustomed vigour, as he picked up the telephone to call her private number.

"Jonathan! You just beat me to it. I was about to call you".

"Really? Well, I was calling you to say," he paused for effect, "that the contract is now completed!"

"Yes Jonathon, I know that it is, I've checked already. And that's why I wanted to reach you. You have done very well and we can now move on." She continued speaking before he had a chance to reply. "Now listen. I want you to come to a dinner engagement with me." Her tone was instructional rather than invitational, and as he immediately realized, the arrangement was not open to negotiation. "It's this Saturday at the house of a business acquaintance. You will be available won't you?" Although this did not sound like the invitation he had been anticipating, he confirmed that he would be pleased to attend.

"And what is the occasion may I ask?"

"It's a business matter Jonathan. I'll tell you more on the way. You can pick me up at seven at my place and we'll take a taxi from there... you do know where it is don't you?"

"Yes, at Church and Queen isn't it?"

"That's right, I'll be waiting in the lobby."

As he slowly set down the telephone, his anxieties were pushed aside by a wave of optimism that better times lay ahead. Julia Miller was unlike any other woman he had met, and he was rapidly becoming obsessed by her alluring power, sensuous movement, and elegant beauty. With her silky voice still alive in his head, he began to indulge his imagination until, a few seconds later, Mrs. Bennett, bearing a tray laden with tea, biscuits, and a file binder marked 'confidential', bounced into his room and coarsely interrupted his daydream.

* * *

"Oh, I should say 'promising' would be the appropriate word." There was a note of hesitancy evident in John Garter's voice as he attempted to answer an unexpectedly direct question from his dinner host, a man in his sixties, who sat on his right, and whose body and face appeared to have been inflated with a bicycle pump. Seated opposite John Garter, at the elaborately decorated and crystal-adorned dining table, was Julia Miller who, in sharp contrast to their host, radiated a beauty, poise, and elegance: a presence that enveloped him with its energy and hypnotic allure. A youthful, East Indian man, with large brown eyes, who had smiled extensively but had barely spoken all evening, sat to his left.

During the taxi ride to the inflatable man's massive, North Toronto home, Julia Miller had explained that their host was a business client, someone she assisted with difficult international financial transactions. She had gone on to say that while the evening was intended to be a social occasion that he should expect to engage in a business discussion: one that she had no doubt he would find of interest. She had declined to elaborate any further, except to stress that he could set aside any misgivings he may have about the trustworthiness of their host, and should expect to converse in an open, honest, and confidential manner, entirely free from any confabulation or hypocrisy. And that, she had reminded him, was, as he well knew, a requisite condition for any meaningful relationship between them. Having thus prepped him for the occasion, she had proceeded to cement his loyalty to her agenda with the captivating suggestion that after dinner they return to her apartment to enjoy a nightcap and, as she had put it, to "debrief".

Conversation at the table had suddenly turned from the general to the specific and, just as he was beginning to feel more comfortable in his strange new surroundings, he was taken-aback by his host's direct invitation to explain the status of a highly confidential pharmaceutical research program about which he should have been completely unaware. The project had been known to John Garter for several years, and, as he had learned only a few day's previously, it was no closer to fruition now than when it was first authorized. He looked cautiously across the table to Julia Miller who spoke softly and directly.

"Jonathan, I warned you to expect honesty and directness. You can trust everyone at this table to protect your interests completely." He decided to add a little more information.

"As I said, 'promising', but only in the sense that the researchers have been promising to deliver something on it for several years, and are, well frankly, nowhere close to doing so."

"Yes quite so." replied the blimp-like figure to his right. "But it's a different story with the Crylex research isn't it?" Noting the puzzled expression on his guest's face, he reached out and grasped a large crystal decanter. "Here have some more wine."

"Crylex?" replied John Garter. "That's not one of ours."

"Oh, but it is, my dear chap. And a most promising project it is too."

"I'm sorry, but you're mistaken" he persisted. "We don't have a project by that name. I can assure you, I would know if we did."

"John, let me tell you something. There are some research projects in your organization that not even your Research Director knows about. I, however, have information that comes to me because of my, shall we say, 'funding support' and special relationships with some key researchers on your payroll." He paused, and took a sip from his wine glass. "You see Jonathan, many of your company's research resources are considerably underutilized. You have wonderful laboratories, dedicated staff, and some very talented scientists, one of whom, I won't tell you his name, is, extremely loyal to me. I am, after all, something of a benefactor to him." He looked pensive, and continued. "Yes, a very talented resource John, one who has made a most interesting breakthrough with an unofficially sponsored project." Julia Miller smiled across the table to her bemused escort.

"That's the Crylex project, Jonathan. It really is most promising." Julia Miller paid no attention to Garter's look of bewilderment, and allowed their host to continue.

"I can see that all of this must be quite confusing to you, but it really is quite simple Jonathan. Julia and I have a business relationship--and I can assure you it is strictly a business relationship, isn't that so Julia?" He beamed at her, as she nodded in confirmation and patted his hand.

"Exactly so, Marco. Exactly so." The East Indian man, coughed gently, and began to assemble empty dinner plates in front of him, promising to attend to dessert.

"And, although you do not know it, one of our business interests happens to be the Crylex project, which, courtesy of your company Jonathan, and of course our dear researcher, promises to make us a most profitable return on investment." He turned to Julia Miller. "I'll let you fill in some more of the details my dear."

"There aren't too many Jonathan. I provided some bank financing to a venture project related to pharmaceutical research at your company, knowing the project concept to be illegal, and knowing that with some minor maneuvering it offered me the potential for considerable personal financial gain with virtually no risk." She continued quite unabashedly in a calm, matter of fact, voice. "It was not until I discovered that you were VP of Finance at the host organization that I decided to check into your credentials a little more closely, whereupon I was delighted to discover that you were everything you appeared to be, and that with a little cultivation on my part, you would make an excellent associate. And what a discovery you have been Jonathan." She leaned back and gazed at him in apparent admiration. John Garter was incredulous.

"You, engaged in an illegal venture! I can hardly believe my ears. You, who demand absolute honesty, and hold me accountable to the highest standards of morality. You, a person I thought to be of exemplary character:

someone who held herself accountable to the same high standards that she demanded from me. Well, well, this is a revelation!" The blimp man said nothing, while Julia Miller calmly responded to John Garter's emotional outburst.

"Jonathan you are sometimes very naive. What I value, practice, and expect, is honesty in interpersonal communication. I don't expect it from everyone, I don't get it from many, and I demand it only from those who are, or who aspire to be, close to me. That type of honesty is quite different from whether any given behaviour that you, or I, or anyone else might engage in, happens, by someone else's definition of morality, to be considered honest or dishonest."

"Well said!" congratulated the host. "Trust, transcends truth, and morality is in the eye of the beholder."

"Well, well." said John Garter, leaning back in his chair, and for the first time that evening, beginning to feel at ease in his unfamiliar surroundings. "So you don't, as I had believed until now, claim any moral superiority over me. How very interesting, I can't tell you how pleased that makes me!"

"Of course I don't Jonathan, and I am distressed that you could possibly think that of me. My contract with you has been for your own good, to prevent you from sinking further into the mire--although I do have to admit, it is also to provide Marco and I with some safeguards as to your, as yet, untested trustworthiness as an associate in our venture. Let's be quite clear Jonathan, I am as vulnerable to temptation as you, I am probably more devious, and I am certainly greedier. There, I hope that makes you feel even better." She beamed him a charming smile and squeezed his hands across the table. "And that" she said, turning to the head of the table "brings us, I think, to the business portion of our discussion, Marco." She released her grasp, and made room for the dessert platter now being positioned at centre table by the young Indian man.

"Yes indeed. Let me continue with a little more about the project at your company, and by the way, I was of course teasing you just now, asking about Crylex-- I knew that you would not have heard of it. Present company excluded, no-one has, other than our loyal, scientist friend, who has made the discovery using the facilities and freedom you have so thoughtfully provided him."

"And what discovery is that?" asked Garter, half expecting his question to be ignored. The blimp man continued.

"It's an exciting discovery John. What our man has invented is a toxin that when absorbed through the skin, induces a quite painless and unexpected death approximately one hour later." He paused, as if lost in thought. "It comes in various forms…only a dab is needed…a touch on a hand with an applicator tip does the job." He leaned forward in a confidential pose. "And, here's the really interesting piece, John, the toxin leaves absolutely no trace in the body after death. Needless to say, I'm sure, the product is highly marketable in many circles. Dividends will be in the millions." John Garter was silent while his eyes, wide with amazement, alternated their gaze between his host, and Julia Miller, as if searching for some indication that he had misheard or misunderstood. Finally he spoke.

"A toxin you say?"

"Yes, Jonathan, you do know what that is don't you?" Julia Miller smiled gently as she watched her dinner date struggle for comprehension.

"Made by one of our scientists, on our payroll, in our laboratories, without anyone knowing?   Not even Chan?"

"Especially not Dr. Chan" replied the blimp man. "He wouldn't have approved."

"No, he wouldn't. You're right there..." John Garter broke off his musing. "Tell me," he said, "how long has this been going on, and how many people are involved -- scientists that is. How many on our payroll and yours at the same time?"

"Three or four, Mr. Garter. That is all we have needed. Until now that is."

"Until now." repeated John Garter.

"Yes, until now."

"Meaning that you now need more help?"

"Yes, exactly so, Mr. Garter, in return for which, we will ensure that you receive a handsome dividend, down the road, when marketing is further advanced. At least six figures, I would say."

"You want me! Why? What do you want from me? It sounds from what you have told me that you have refined your product to the point where you are ready to go into production. Or did I get that wrong?" The blimp man leaned forward in his chair and spoke in an earnest tone.

"I may have given an incorrect impression there. We are very close to being able to go into production mode, but there is a snag. You see, unfortunately our Crylex chemist has recently been..." he paused, "I believe that 'laid-off' is the correct euphemism?" He glared at John

Garter with a decidedly hostile, expression. "Sadly, it seems that on your orders there is to be a thorough cost benefit evaluation of the official project to which he, and a number of other dedicated team members, have devoted a large portion of their lives, selflessly seeking a glorious pharmaceutical solution to a perplexing ailment affecting the male prostate." He paused to assess the impact of his words, and continued, as a glimmer of understanding became evident in John Garter's face. "As a result of this unwelcome intrusion into his second-favourite project, he no longer has access to some critical pieces of equipment needed to stabilize Crylex and make it safe to package in useable container forms. He is not happy Mr. Garter, and neither are we!" He leaned back in his chair and scowled at his guest.

"So you want me to get him back into production. Is that it?

"Precisely."

"But I don't involve myself in laboratory operations, that's all Chan's business."

"Yes, perhaps so, Mr. Garter, but you do involve yourself in funding decisions don't you? And our man's bread and butter project, giving him access to everything he needs to finish our venture, has, at your instigation been unceremoniously, chopped -- causing I might add, immeasurable turmoil and strife in the lives of all those unfortunate employees and their families."

"Bah - they've all been getting government assistance, haven't they? Anyway, look what's been going on! How many of them have been doing private research at our expense? I don't have any sympathy for them – it's no wonder the project got canned." He paused, thoughtfully.

"However, I suppose that's neither here nor there as far your interests go, is it?" Julia Miller spoke.

"Jonathan, we don't really care how you do it, or what rationale you use, but we need that team to be refunded for at least another three months." She gave him one of her laser beam stares. "You can do that, can't you Jonathan?" Despite some uncertainty as to whether, and how, he might be able to pull it off, he was quick to reply.

"Yes, yes of course I can. Leave it with me and I'll get it sorted out." He turned to blimp man. "And just to be clear, you are proposing that in return I will receive the dividend you mentioned as soon as your marketing gets into gear -- presumably some time in the New Year?"

"Exactly, Mr. Garter, one hundred thousand dollars by April at the latest."

"Very well, it's a deal." John Garter sat back in his chair, looked at Julia Miller, and returned her gentle smile with a satisfied beam.

"Some trifle anyone?" asked the young Indian man.

* * *

On the return journey to Julia Miller's apartment, they sat together in the back seat of a taxi speaking in hushed tones as they talked over the understandings that had been reached during their dinner with the inflatable man. Julia Miller's revelation of her contempt for conventional standards of morality, cemented now in their newly formed business relationship, had swept aside the anxiety that John Garter normally felt in her presence and replaced it with a feeling of intimacy and power. She was not the zealous guardian of virtue and truth he had taken her for, but instead, a calculating criminal, intent on selfish gain regardless of the human cost. And, she needed him as a partner to implement her plans! Their de-briefing conversation gave way to giggling, nuzzling, and then, as their lips edged together, a gentle, moist, and delightfully erotic, first time kiss: a kiss that to John Garter tasted every bit as soft, tender, and inviting, as anything he had imagined. Oblivious to the curious, rear view mirror stares of their cab driver, they spent the rest of their journey entwined in a tight embrace, their mouths pressed together, and their lips and tongues sliding in passionate exploration.

It was close to midnight, as the taxi deposited them at Julia Miller's building. They pushed through the revolving doors of the main entrance, returned the polite, but disinterested, greeting extended by the security desk attendant, and ran to catch a waiting elevator that immediately closed its doors and transported them to the seventh floor.

As she opened the door to her apartment, Julia Miller tugged at John Garter's hand and pulled him inside. Without speaking, or turning on the lights, she removed the topcoat that covered her black cocktail dress, tossed it onto a hallway chair and helped him unwrap from his belted gabardine raincoat and suit jacket. Despite the darkness of the hallway, her silhouette, etched against distant, softly lit windows, revealed with every movement her slim, long-legged elegance and perfectly proportioned body. She steered him backwards against the closed apartment door, pushed her body against him, and with an intensity that he found delightfully exciting, pressed her lips to his. She felt exquisitely firm and vital in his arms. Her hair and face exuded a subtle perfume that reminded him of something familiar--a fruit of some kind, he couldn't be sure. Her skin was soft and smooth and her body, now pressed into his, radiated a passionate energy. For several minutes they clung together tightly, only disengaging from their embrace to simplify the loosening and unfastening of garments that impeded their feeling and caressing explorations.

Soon they stood in an island of discarded clothing, their bodies pressed tightly together, and her soft, moist lips caressing his face and neck. At that moment, Garter felt as though he had no cares in the world; all those years spent in luckless solitude, surrounded by leeches and other ingrates, now seemed a distant reality. At last he had discovered someone with whom he could share thoughts and feelings: someone who deserved his loyalty and his passion.

Julia Miller's breasts slithered enticingly on his hair-covered chest as she rose on tiptoe, pulled his mouth to hers, and pressed tightly against him -- as eager as he, to speed onset of the intimacy they both sought. She bit at his lip and whispered in his ear. "I want you in my bed, now, Jonathan." She took his hand in hers. "That's right, it's this way, there's a good boy."

* * *

Except for one light in the hallway, the home of Mrs. Harry Jefferson senior, had been in darkness for more than three hours. Shortly before midnight she had completed her customary pre-retirement tour of electrical plugs and switches and, with her son still not home, had gone to bed resigned to the fact she would be awakened later by the sound of an uncooperative front door and a creaky hallway floor.

Prior to Harry Jefferson's expulsion from his marital love nest, his mother had always slept soundly at nights.

However, having been exposed for almost two weeks to her son's inconsistent daytime routines, his strange nocturnal patterns and, as she had reluctantly come to admit, his dubious attention to personal hygiene, she was discovering that sleep was now much more elusive. As annoying as it was to have her comfortable routines upset and to go to bed wondering how long she would have to wait before being disturbed, the truth of the matter was that her concerns stemmed mainly from worry over the state of her son's mental health. She had tried to broach with him the subject of his medication and enquire whether he was taking his prescription regularly but the discussion had led only to his assurance that all was fine. He had admitted to some angry feelings towards people who had turned his wife against him, but assured his mother that God would see to it that such malevolence would not go unpunished. In any event his wife would see the wisdom of forgiveness before long and he could then return home.

As it transpired, the sound that jarred her awake at three o'clock in the morning was not the front door, or creaking floorboards, but the sound of breaking glass. She called out nervously through the darkness, "Harry, is that you?"

"Yes mother. I lost my key and had to break-in. I'll make it safe though. Go to bed." With that, Harry Jefferson locked the door and pushed a coat stand to a position where it covered the missing pane of glass. Despite the hour he was not the least bit tired, but he was hungry. He headed towards the kitchen and searched through the refrigerator where he found a variety of suitable appetizers to load onto a plate. He carried the feast to his bedroom, shut the door, and began to stuff food into his mouth while simultaneously positioning his notebook on a small desk that occupied one corner. He sat down and scribbled furiously, not looking up from his work unless to better position his mouth around an item from his plate. He continued writing long after the food had all gone until, eventually, dawn rays began to flood the room and a feeling of drowsiness finally hit. He left his note book open on the desk, trundled to his bed, fell on it heavily, and immediately went to sleep. It was a deep, uninterrupted, sleep that remained undisturbed by the noise of traffic outside and the clatter of domestic chores inside. The sound of his door being opened did not cause the slightest stir, and neither did the footsteps of his mother who, propelled by a mixture of concern and curiosity, was at that very moment creeping across the room to check on his condition. She stopped, looked down at his unconscious form and enquired gently. "Are you all right dear?" Despite the absence of a reply she decided that he was, and made her way to the window where she closed the blind. As she turned to leave, her eyes alighted on the open note book. She peered down at the writing and began to read a passage of text. A puzzled expression accompanied her lip movements as she tried to make out the unpunctuated scrawl:

> *"...justice for all is God's will and the devil's torment shall notwithstanding the evidence of hypocrisy in the land be the proof of his living death and so it will be that all is pestilence and the wife will be atoned and those of the knowing and those of the unknowing will never come apart for financial gain and shall not be allowed to profit whether for the whore or the poor or the shore or the core or all four and more than that when the result is in it shall be ever the better and send the trend to mend...."*

She slapped shut the notebook, as if to expunge its contents from her mind, and abruptly left the room, dabbing at her eyes with a tissue as she did so.

Chapter Fifteen

While Harry Jefferson focused his attention on planning the demise of his two main enemies, one of them was preoccupied with the intractable problem of how to prevent his wife from ruining his life. Garter had been horrified to learn from Mr. Davies that there was to be no insurance settlement without the consent and involvement of his wife's lawyer. Even worse, he had just received from that same lawyer a divorce settlement proposal that would spell total financial ruin. On top of those problems he was once again indebted to the Fast Credit & Loan Approval Institute and, although it was less urgent and might even be avoidable, he was supposedly obligated to pay an extortionate debt to Tony Angle. The hundred thousand dollars he had been promised for his, now successful, resurrection of the Crylex project would not be realized for several months, leaving him with few options and an oppressive sense of déjà vu.

The idea that his life would be greatly simplified if his wife were no longer alive was not new. It was in fact an idea that had surfaced on a number of occasions in the past, but one that to date had not survived serious analysis--even though it had led to the precautionary step of a life policy. Now, however, it seemed the obvious course. Mary's death would leave him with all of their family assets, including the stolen jewellery settlement, and, provided the death was not ruled a suicide, the substantial proceeds from her life insurance policy. Moreover, as he now realized, his recent co-option to the Crylex project presented him with a heaven sent opportunity to acquire a sample and put it to immediate use. After that memorable dinner he had been quick to make contact with blimp man's scientist, and had left him in no doubt as to where his primary loyalty should lie. He had even received a full briefing on the product and now, confident of the man's assistance, he saw no reason for delay.

He picked up the telephone and dialled the laboratory. "It's Garter here. I need to see you."

*   *   *

At his desk in the police station, Inspector Ogopoulos knew in his bones that he was on the verge of a breakthrough. There was the dead Frenchman, the Garter burglary, and the car theft. He had long ago decided that all three incidents were inextricably tied together and that as soon as he could find either the burglar or the person responsible for the death of the Frenchman, then he would have found the lout responsible for the theft of his car. The problem was, he still had no clear suspect. For a while he thought it might have been the dead Frenchman himself; his hypothesis being that he had committed the burglary as an act of revenge after being dumped by Mrs. Garter, made off with the car, and then become the victim of a mugging or a double cross by an accomplice. But, that idea was quite unsatisfactory. If it was correct it was unlikely he could prove it without talking to the Frenchman. That of course he could not do since the Frenchman was dead. So, given that he felt sure he was about to prove something, his trusted logic circuits told him that he was on the wrong path and that the burglar and car thief could not have been the Frenchman.

The idea that the Garters might have carried out the burglary themselves, either separately or together, had also occurred to him. He had however dismissed the idea on the grounds that if, for whatever motive, either or both of them had carried out the burglary, they would not have stolen his car to make their escape. Instead, they would have faked the burglary, left by their own car and returned later. Besides, despite her philandering ways, Mrs. Garter was not that type of person.

Inspector Ogopoulos once again turned his attention to the possibility that Mary Garter's husband was the culprit. Clearly he had reason to be mad at the dead Frenchman. However, the question was, did he know that? Mary Garter was sure he was unaware of the relationship, but she may have been wrong. Her husband was an angry sort of man, and despite his homosexual tendencies would no doubt have been quite upset if he had found out. In that case, the car could have been stolen intentionally for use as a weapon. The burglary might have been some kind of diversionary tactic, or... The telephone interrupted his musings.

"Inspector Ogopoulos here." A male voice answered his greeting.

"I hear that there is a reward being offered for information about a burglary on Brookmead Crescent last month. Is that correct?" Inspector Ogopoulos switched on a tape recorder attached to his telephone.

"Yes, that is so, but the reward is linked to recovery of the stolen items. If your information leads to recovery then you might qualify. Otherwise, you will simply be doing your civic duty by assisting us with our enquiries. To whom am I speaking please?"

"My name is Burgess. I'm a taxi driver." He paused. "So, even if what I tell you is helpful, I don't necessarily get anything?"

"That is so Mr. Burgess. Why don't you just tell me what you know? We won't cheat you if you are entitled to some portion of the reward. You'll have to trust me on that." With pencil at the ready, the Inspector listened expectantly.

"Trust you! I don't know about that." He paused. "I suppose I don't have much choice though do I? All right, here goes. At about nine o'clock in the evening on the night of the burglary I dropped a drunken Frenchman close to the spot where the burglary happened. He said that he was going to number twenty eight. I left him a few doors down the street. The thing is, if I'm not mistaken, he is the same man who was in the paper dead. There… what do you think of that?"

"I think that is most interesting Mr. Burgess and I thank you for the information. Let me ask you, could you identify the man again-- let's say from a photograph?"

"Maybe. Would that help with the reward?"

"It might. I really can't say, but it would certainly help with my enquiries. Come and see me here tomorrow will you?" Having made the arrangement, Inspector Ogopoulos hung up the telephone and returned to his notes, confident that the evidence he needed to prove that the Frenchman was responsible for the theft of his car was now to hand.

*   *   *

The extraordinarily loud noise made by Mary Garter's telephone always served as a reminder that she had not yet learned how to turn down the ringer volume. Prompted once more by the insistent tone that filled her apartment, she pounced on the receiver, breathless from an across room dash.

"Hello, Mary Garter."

"Mrs. Garter, it's Kenneth Davies here, Regal Insurance. Look, there's been some action on the burglary. I've had a call from someone who says he may be able to find and return your jewellery provided the reward money is assured, and the police are kept out of it. He wants a straight anonymous deal, jewellery for reward and no questions asked."

"Oh, that's marvellous! How wonderful. Have you done it yet?"

"No, Mrs. Garter, not yet. It isn't that simple. I can't give him any guarantees about what the police will or won't do, so he may not want to go through with it. That's the tricky bit."

"Do the police have to know about it?"

"Well, yes. They're going to find out at some point. The only question is, when. I haven't told the Inspector yet as I know he's going to have a lot of questions and will want all kinds of conditions attached. I'm supposed to brief him right away if there are any developments from my end, but if I do, it probably means we'll lose the opportunity to deal."

"So what are you suggesting Mr. Davies?"

"Well, I'm prepared to tell the Inspector that I got an anonymous tip, and then do a little behind the scenes deal-making. He'll probably smell a rat, but I can't really help that. The thing is though, I will need you to take a

175

look at the property to confirm that everything is there before I pay out. I've made that much clear to the caller, and he's prepared to go along with something like that as long as I promise to keep the police out of it."

"It all sounds very sinister. Who is this man?"

"Oh, that I don't know. He says he is acting as an intermediary, which might well be the case. Whoever he is, he has to place his trust in me that if we get the goods back, that he'll get the reward money. I'm not doing it any other way. He knows that, and we've discussed a way to do it." He paused. "Sounds a bit cloak and dagger I know, but if you are in agreement, we can do it this morning."

"Yes, of course I'm in agreement. Tell me what I have to do."

"Well it's quite simple really. You'll meet me at the railway station. I'll open the combination lock on a predetermined locker, and we will then inspect the contents and make sure that it is your stolen property. If it is, and I'm assured it will be, I'll leave the reward money in the locker and we'll leave."

"Mr. Davies, have you told any of this to my husband?" There was an awkward silence.

"No, Mrs. Garter. I suppose I should given the circumstances, but I thought you would prefer to handle it alone for now."

"Yes, indeed! Thank you Mr. Davies. I appreciate that."

"I'll have to tell him of course, and Ogopoulos, but I'll do it after we've recovered everything. I'll say it was a tip-off, that I went to check it out expecting it to be a hoax, and there it was! We'll keep the rest of it to ourselves Mrs. Garter…agreed?"

"Of course. Let's get going then!"

"We'll have to wait a bit Mrs. Garter. He's going to call me back in about ten minutes from now, to confirm we have a deal, and nail down the details. So, you hold on there, and I'll call you back as soon as we're ready to go. I'll come by and pick you up if you like."

"Yes, thanks. I'll wait for your call then."

As she put down the telephone Mary Garter was elated. She had never lost hope that the jewellery would be recovered but had not dreamed that it would come this way rather than through the police. Perhaps there was a guardian angel looking out for her after all!

While she cleared away her breakfast dishes and waited for Mr. Davies' call, the man weaving his way through traffic, making his way towards her home, was most certainly no guardian angel. John Garter had conducted a successful transaction with the scientist on blimp man's payroll, and now intended to arrive, unannounced, at her door to ask for a private discussion about Ms. Juby's troublesome divorce settlement proposal. The lipstick container in his pocket housed a Crylex delivery mechanism, experimental, but guaranteed to be virtually risk-free to the user. He had been well briefed. To induce the desired effect, he need only to remove the cap, and surreptitiously dab the applicator head on any area of the target's bare skin. Death would follow one hour later: suddenly, painlessly, and without chemical trace.

He turned onto her street, passed by her car which was parked opposite her house, under one of several beech trees that lined the sidewalk, and drew to a stop a few doors beyond. It didn't matter if he was seen, he had told himself, but it might be preferable if his visit was unnoticed. He waited until there was no one in sight, opened the car door and walked towards the front entrance. A flagstone pathway led to the front porch. He stepped onto it and made his way to a set of steps leading up to the front door. Just as he was about to ring the bell, a silvery movement of light, in the frosted glass of the entranceway, indicated that someone on the other side was reaching for the door latch. An elderly woman, dressed in a heavy woollen coat and carrying a shopping bag over one arm, appeared into view, clearly on her way out of the house. "Yes," she demanded, "can I help you?"

"No, thank you. I'm visiting someone."

"If it's the woman on the top floor you want you've missed her. She just left with a man in a car." She sounded distinctly triumphant, as if he had just got what he deserved. She pointed at the door-bell. "That one, I mean, Mary Garter." Annoyed at his misfortune, he muttered indistinctly, turned on his heels, and stomped angrily back to his car. He had waited this long, he told himself. If it took a little longer then so be it.

* * *

The railway station locker responded immediately to the three digit code that Kenneth Davies twirled into its mechanical memory. He slipped off the lock and pulled at the catch. It was the bottom locker of a double-stacked tier, and he had to bend low to swing open the door.

"That looks like mine!" Mary, was peering over Kenneth Davies' shoulder, and had immediately recognized a familiar looking zipper bag: one that until that minute, she had not even missed. She felt instantly encouraged. She lifted a leather tab. "Yes, that's mine!" They must have taken it to put our things in I suppose."

"Well let's hope it's all still there." He reached for the handle, pulled out the bag, and un-zipped the top.

Mary craned forward to inspect. The jewelery sat in an open cardboard box and was surrounded by a variety of familiar looking ornaments, trinkets, silverware, crystal and other items.

"Oh yes!" she exclaimed. "All the other stuff too! I wasn't expecting that!" She began to sift through the jewellery, exclaiming excitedly when piece after missing piece came into view as she eagerly probed, prodded, turned and inspected. "It's all here! I'm sure it is. It all looks so familiar." She continued examining every piece, trying to identify missing components or any damage that might have occurred. After a few moments Mr. Davies interrupted her.

"Mrs. Garter," he said, in a serious voice, "without looking at the box, I want you to think of three particularly important items that were in your collection. Look away while you think of them, and describe them, out loud to me. I know you think everything is here, but this will help to ensure we aren't missing anything that is particularly desirable. Mary looked at him with a thoughtful expression.

"All right. I'd say the ruby and diamond brooch… but I know that's there I just saw it! Then, I'd say grandmother Martin's matching ring set, there's three altogether, all quite rare, and the gold chain and locket, and the dress ring with the large stones…" she broke off. "I've seen most of them I'm sure! Let's check." One after another the specified pieces were joyfully identified. "It's all here. I can't think of anything that is missing."

"All right then Mrs. Garter I'll complete the deal." Mr. Davies removed an envelope from his inside pocket, placed it in the locker, re-clasped the lock, and spun the dials. "Let me carry the bag to the car, just in case there's any nonsense, although I'm not expecting any."

He picked up the bag, and steered Mary towards the car park, feeling rather guilty as they walked knowing that Inspector Ogopoulos would not be pleased if he learned the truth about the transaction they had just completed. It had however saved his company at least forty thousand dollars and, after all was said and done, that was the whole point of the exercise. Mary, who harboured no such thoughts, remained elated at the recovery operation. "Can I take the jewellery home with me now?" she enquired of Mr. Davies, somehow expecting a negative response.

"That will be up to Ogopoulos, Mrs Garter, but I think you'll find he might want to hold onto it for a while in case it's needed as evidence. Mind you, I don't think he's got anything to go on, so he'll probably close the book on it pretty fast." He opened the passenger door of his car, watched her climb in, and walked around to the opposite side where he once again demonstrated his miraculous body folding technique, and edged himself into the driver's seat.

As Mr. Davies drove away from the station, Tony Angle lost no time making his way to the locker. He had positioned himself well out of view, in the car park, and had watched with great interest as the pair had arrived and carried out their work at the locker. Although acutely aware of his vulnerability, his various discussions with Mr. Davies had left him completely confident that no dirty tricks had been planned. Nevertheless, he could not quell the anxiety he felt as he approached the locker. He surveyed the scene carefully scanning for any sign that someone was laying in wait.

Satisfied there was no one waiting to clamp a hand on his shoulder, he turned his attention to the lock, quickly unfastened it, and swung open the door. A fat envelope lay on the floor of the locker. He scooped it into an inside coat pocket without looking inside. He removed the lock from the clasp, tucked that into an outside coat pocket, closed the door, and walked briskly through the lobby towards his car. No one had taken the slightest interest in his movements and by the time he reached his car he knew that no one intended to challenge, or restrain him. All the same, he left the car park quickly, not even stopping to open the envelope until he had traveled several blocks and pulled into a small shopping plaza. The envelope, pleasantly solid in his hand, sprung open easily and revealed a wad of one hundred dollar bills; all of them were used notes, just as they had agreed. He leafed through the bundle and satisfied himself that there were indeed two hundred, even though on his first count he had made it two less, and on his second count one more.

Tony Angle felt pleased with himself. The twenty thousand dollars reward money he had just obtained offset the money he had given to John Garter, so he was not out of pocket. Of course, he no longer had Mary's jewllery to sell, but he didn't mind. Garter owed him twenty thousand dollars, ten for his split of the sale price, and a ten thousand bonus for agreeing to make a quick sale and agreeing to wait for his share. Of course, now that there was to be no insurance pay out, his chances of seeing that money were not good. But, as he had told himself when he decided on this course, even if the insurance company had paid out, Mrs. Garter and her lawyer were going to make damn sure that none of it went into John Garter's pocket anyway, so neither partner in crime would have benefited.

By the time Tony Angle had counted his reward money, Kenneth Davies and Mary Garter were well on their way back to Mary's new home. On the return trip Mr. Davies seemed thoughtful. Eventually he broke the silence. "Look Mrs. Garter, I don't want you to have to lie about this, but I'm going to have to involve you a bit in my explanation to the good Inspector." He looked at her and smiled. "What I'm planning to say is that I checked out the tip, expecting it to be a hoax, found the bag-- obviously intact--called you and Mr. Garter, and asked you both to meet me, with Ogopoulos, at the police station. I'll actually make both of those calls, after I've dropped you off back home. I will then expect to see you both there, and we'll see how it plays out. You'll have to make as though you're seeing the stuff for the first time and do the ID thing all over again of course." He paused, "I'm sorry to ask this of you, but I can't think of any other way to do it without him knowing that I worked a deal and got you involved in it."

"Yes I understand. And don't worry, I think I can handle my part all right, I'm not entirely devoid of an ability to obfuscate." She smiled to herself. "By the way, please call me Mary, Mr. Davies." He seemed pleased.

"Mary. Yes of course! And please call me Kenneth." He pulled to a stop outside her house and waited while she got out of the car. "I'm going to stop here for a few minutes and make some calls," he told her. "I'm going to call Ogopoulos, then Mr. Garter, and then you. I'm going to suggest that we rendezvous at the police station at five. You have got your car haven't you? You can make your own way there I assume?" Mary confirmed that she could, thanked him for his help, and made off to her front door, leaving Kenneth Davies to prod at the dial of his cell 'phone.

Chapter Sixteen

"It's all here, there's no question about it." Mary looked directly at Inspector Ogopoulos. "I can't tell you how pleased this makes me. Thank you so much!"

"It isn't me you should be thanking, Mrs. Garter." He glared at Mr. Davies accusingly. "Your insurance agent seems to be the person deserving your gratitude." Mary smiled appreciatively, while the scowl on her husband's face suggested that what he actually deserved was to be hung up by his thumbs, with the incompetent Tony Angle similarly positioned alongside. How on earth could this have happened! It was a question he had asked himself repeatedly since first learning of the reason he had been summoned to join his wife and Kenneth Davies at the police station.

The idea that Tony Angle had retained and then returned the stolen goods did not even cross his mind. However, a recurring thought was that Angle had sold them to someone untrustworthy, who had somehow decided to not follow through. But for what motive he could not fathom. He placed his right hand in his jacket pocket and felt the lipstick container, solid and cool to his touch. He reproached himself for being too trusting. It seemed likely that Angle was out of his depth. But whatever the case, his whole refinancing plan was now shot to pieces. His fingers curled around the container. One goal at a time he told himself. There is no need to panic. The jewellery will soon be mine to dispose of on the open market quite legally.

"Well, whoever deserves the credit we are most grateful," he announced, in a surprisingly convincing voice. "I think we had both given it up for good, isn't that so Mary?" He paid no attention to her reply. It was time for intelligent action and he had to seize the moment. Mary held the box of jewellery on her lap, and her bare hand was not more than a few inches from his. This was the perfect opportunity. He held the slim tube in front of him, shielding it from view under the edge of OgoPogo's desk, and eased off the cap. He leaned towards her as if he intended to sift through the jewellery, wondering whether he might inconspicuously brush the applicator head on the back of her hand. He thought better of it, replaced the cap, and returned the container to his jacket pocket. He stood up. "Look, I have to go now. Unless there's something else either of you need from me I'll be off." Without waiting for approval, he turned to leave. "Can my wife take all this home with her now Inspector?"

"Yes Mr. Garter, she can. Technically speaking, you reported a theft, the stolen items have turned up, and the case is closed. However, that is not to say that my investigation is complete of course. There's still the matter of my car…and the Frenchman of course." He looked at Mary, and to her relief said nothing further on the subject of Daniel's death. John Garter turned to the door.

"Thank you again Inspector, and you Mr. Davies, we are most grateful. Good afternoon to you all." He glanced at his watch, and strode through the front entrance of the police station towards his car. It was five thirty exactly. The meeting with Ogopoulos was obviously drawing to a close and no doubt his wife would be returning home.

He would follow and meet her there. After pulling out of the police station car park, he drove around the corner and parked in a spot where he could see when she came out. Ten minutes passed. There...there she was! Mary and the towering figure of Kenneth Davies appeared in the parking area. They stood chatting together for a few minutes before shaking hands, and then making for their cars. Mary carried a bag under one arm and she held it awkwardly as she fumbled in her purse for her keys. He watched as she unlocked the door and climbed inside. Before she had positioned her seat belt, Mr. Davies, in his small, red Honda, zipped past her on his way out, waving as he did so. Mary reversed out of the parking space, drove to the entrance, and quickly slipped into a gap between two cars in the curb lane, both of which were slowing to stop for the traffic light ahead. He started his engine and moved off in pursuit.

The first stop she made was at a convenience store where she spent several minutes buying various items before emerging with them in two plastic carrier bags. Her next stop was at a bank. Five minutes later after her business was complete, she pulled out of the bank, and drove for three kilometers before turning off at the intersection that led to her road. Following cautiously, at a discreet distance, he watched her park, open and close the trunk of her car, and carry the plastic bags and the bag containing her jewellery across the road to her front entrance. She unlocked the door and closed it behind her. Garter stared at the door, wondering how best to proceed. As he pondered the question a small red Honda pulled up and parked next to Mary's car. The unmistakable figure of Kenneth Davies, carrying what looked distinctly like a bottle of wine, then walked briskly up the driveway, rang on the door bell, and after a few moments delay disappeared into the interior of Mary's house.

"Damn that man!" John Garter cursed out loud, giving vent to his frustration at once again being thwarted in his attempt to get at his wife. He started the car and drove off, a wave of frustration flooding over him.

Chapter Seventeen

Frustrated by his failure to make the planned contact with Mary, he returned home to eat and shower. He would be seeing Julia later that evening, and he knew that their time together would not be wasted on cooking or eating. In fact, if recent past encounters could be taken as a guide, their time would be spent in a near continuous stream of frenzied love making: intense, passionate intimacy, in the comfort of Julia's bed, interrupted only by occasional pauses to recover energy, whisper confidences, and share fantasies.

The chemistry that attracted him physically, bound him emotionally too. He thought of her constantly, eagerly anticipating meetings, and relishing whatever time they could spend together. He trusted her completely. He felt extraordinarily calm in her presence. There was no need to be wary, or to edit his conversation before he spoke. She allowed him to be himself and made him feel powerful. Never before had he experienced such a sense of wholeness and belonging: nor such contentment.

After his shower he dressed and made a sandwich. He bit into it enthusiastically and while still munching, sorted through the day's still unread mail. An envelope from Douglas, Douglas, Juby and Cross, leapt out from the others. He tossed it to one side, reluctant at that moment to review the latest absurd demand from Mary's lawyer. He poured a coffee, sat at the kitchen table, and finished eating while staring blankly through the kitchen window. Whatever the difficulties he might encounter, he was determined that his next attempt to administer Crylex to Mary would be successful.

He cleared up the kitchen, brushed his teeth, and then left the house. As always, his Volkswagen surged to life on demand; its faithfulness and reliability doing nothing dispel its owner's disdain for its fitness to serve him. However, as he now reminded himself, times would soon be different: a new car was long overdue and as soon as Mary's life insurance policy was paid out he could give serious thought to a replacement.

Before he reached the end of the road his cell 'phone rang.

"Jonathon, you're late. I hope you have a good explanation or I may have to chastise you again."

"Julia! Yes, I know…but I'm on my way now. I had to go to the police station they've found our stolen jewellery."

"Well, well, Mary will be pleased. Is she with you now?"

"No, I'm alone. Just coming though. I'll be there at about seven thirty."

"Very well Jonathon, I'm looking forward to your ministrations, so don't waste time will you." As always, her silky, purring, voice sent energy bolts of erotic anticipation coursing through his body. She ended the conversation without waiting for his reply.

The journey to Julia's apartment required navigation along some suburban side streets, a sprint along the Expressway and Lakeshore road, and some meandering through streets in the downtown core. Depending upon traffic, it was a twenty to thirty minute journey. He approached the Expressway doing mental arithmetic. Sixty thousand for the jewellery; two hundred thousand from Mary's life insurance policy; one hundred thousand for the Crylex operation; debt to Fast Credit twenty thousand; debt to Tony Angle… huggh, nothing! What the hell had happened there? Davies said he'd had a tip. Who would turn in stolen property like that when there was reward money to be had? No-one in their right mind! Maybe Davies was being coy about the reward. Yes, of course! Someone got the reward money. But, that made no sense either: twenty thousand for that lot. They'd be crazy!

While he continued the internal monologue, Harry Jefferson climbed the first flight of stairs on his way to the seventh floor of Julia Miller's building. He continued his climb, pausing at the top of the third flight before moving to the next.

Garter approached the Lakeshore turn-off and decided it would be faster to continue along the Expressway before making his exit turn.

Jefferson reached the seventh floor. He pushed open the landing door and walked purposefully along the corridor. He stopped at Unit 703, and knocked twice.

"John! Clever boy, you're here already." Julia swung open the door and immediately recoiled in shock as the rotund figure of Harry Jefferson stormed towards her, slamming the door behind him with one hand and swinging a punch to her head with the other. She staggered backwards, lost her footing, and fell to the ground, denied by the speed of his attack the opportunity to shout in protest, or cry for help. In a moment he was astride her, his hand pressed over her mouth reaching for the cloth in his pocket. She bit at his hand and tried to scream, but

189

the pressure on her mouth made it impossible. She felt herself choking, and retched. Gasping for breath, her head flayed from side to side until Jefferson forcibly restrained it and jammed the cloth over her mouth. Her struggling and writhing prevented air flow through her nose, and she was forced to stop fighting and focus all her energies on keeping her nasal passages open. She found a way to inhale air, and resisted the urge to struggle as he wound duct tape over the gag and round her head, forcing the cloth deep into her mouth. He yanked her to her feet, dragged her across the room, and pushed her down into an armchair. Still struggling for air, she was unable to resist. He grabbed her arms, pulled them behind her, and proceeded to wrap her wrists with more lengths of tape. He kneeled in front of her and stared into her face.

"You Satan," he hissed. "You child of the devil…you evil fiend! You may want to destroy me but you are not going to succeed. You are the one who is going die." Julia managed to fill her lungs, and her panic gave way to terror. She attempted to speak, but the words, stifled and unarticulated, came out like the whimpers of a dreaming dog.

"Mmmmng…mmngg…mmmmng."

Garter's Volkswagen pulled off the Expressway and turned onto Front Street.

"I intend to make the world a better place Mizz Mighty Miller." He clenched his teeth and thrust his head forward until his nose was no more than three inches from hers. "When you are gone, and your evil, devil-worshiping partner in sin has had his just desserts, God will smile and say, 'Well done, Harold, you have carried out my bidding.' He will heave a sigh of relief and mark my score card with expressions of gratitude."

The Volkswagen turned onto King Street.

"M m m m m n g … m m m m n g …. m m m m m n g!" Jefferson strode to the window and looked out, his back turned to his helpless victim. "Do you know what, Mizz Mighty Miller. I have followed your every move for the past four weeks. I know all about you and your filthy, adulterous lover, who cheats and manipulates our money with your help and your co-operation. Yes…I know, and God knows, and soon everyone will know." He turned and walked towards the back of the armchair in which her strapped figure twisted and contorted itself in a vain attempt to speak to him.

The Volkswagen turned into Church Street and into the underground car park below Julia's building.

"I know what you are trying to say, but it's no use. God will not forgive you Mizz Mighty Miller. Your pleading is a waste of time." He felt in his pocket and pulled out a length of nylon cord. He approached the front of her chair and waved the cord slowly from side to side brushing the ends against her face in a taunting, sadistic, display of his intent.

Garter pressed button number seven in the elevator.

Jefferson wrapped the cord around her neck and slowly pulled the ends until the resistance indicated it was in position. He rolled one end of the cord around his left hand and the other around his right. He bent over her shoulder, and hissed in her ear. "Good bye Mizz Mighty Miller." He tugged on the cord and forced his hands wide apart, giggling as he did so. Her feet stamped impotently on the floor. His grip tightened, and the tension on the rope increased until he could pull no more. The rope cut into her throat and her face turned to a deep shade of purple. He maintained the pressure, pulling as tightly as he could, his giggles increasing the more that he tugged. His arms ached, and the rope bit into his hands, but he made no attempt to loosen his grip.

Garter knocked on the door.

Jefferson loosened his grip, and allowed Julia Miller's lifeless body to slump forward. He stood, partially upright; hands outstretched, staring at the door like a puppet waiting to be animated by its master. Another knock.

"Julia, it's me."

The sound of Garter's evil voice triggered an immediate response. He picked up the length of nylon rope and crept towards the door. It was not the scenario he had planned, but the opportunity to finish his work had just been made that much easier. He quietly released the latch, opened the door an inch or two, and concealed himself behind it. John Garter gave it a gentle push, and stepped into the hallway. "Julia? It's me, are you there?"

He stopped immediately, and stared in amazement at the sight of her body sprawled on the floor ahead of him. Before he could run to her assistance, the door clicked shut and Jefferson leapt forward, hooking the rope around Garter's throat. He swung on the rope ends, using his weight and the element of surprise to bring his quarry to his knees. Garter managed to get three fingers under the nylon cord. He pulled against it and turned his head, trying desperately to see what kind of murderous ghoul he was grappling with. Jefferson stabbed a knee into Garter's back and pulled tightly on the rope, attempting to yank it free from the fingers that threatened to thwart his attack.

Garter struggled to his feet, and with Jefferson still clinging to his neck, swung his body in a wide arc crashing his attacker against the wall. Winded by the impact, Jefferson released his grip on the cord, allowing Garter to spin free, and for the first time, get a view of his attacker. "Jefferson! You stupid bastard! What the hell…" The sentence fizzled out as Jefferson swung a fist towards Garter's nose. It was easily blocked, and in the struggle that followed, Garter quickly gained the upper hand, grasping Jefferson in a painful headlock and driving him forward towards the spot where Julia's body lay crumpled and lifeless. They staggered sideways and Jefferson landed full weight on Garter's face. For a moment he could not breathe, and flailed about, helplessly unable to gain the leverage necessary to pry himself away. Jefferson stretched out his arm and reached for an onyx statuette that, if his idea had worked, would have split Garter's skull. The movement allowed Garter the opportunity to clamber onto one knee. From that position he lunged at Jefferson's feet, swept his legs from under him, and sent him crashing towards the floor. As he fell, Jefferson's head smashed against the corner of Julia's marble topped coffee table, opening a wide gash at his temple. He crashed to the ground, blood oozing from the jagged wound, and lay there perfectly still.

The room was eerily quiet: no crashing, no banging, no gasps, no cries--only the sound of his own panting breath, and the thump of his racing heart, indicated the presence of human life. He sat, for a moment, staring at Julia's gagged and bound body. He kneeled down beside her, tore away the cloth from her mouth, and ripped at the tape that bound her hands. Her eyes, open and bulging, stared grotesquely from her bruised and contorted face. He gazed on her body in disbelief, desperate to see some sign of life: a movement, a gasp perhaps, a twitching nerve, anything to disprove his fear that the delightful Julia--his lover, his tormentor, his soul mate, his liberator--was now dead. Finding none, he lifted her wrist and fumbled to locate her pulse, but without success. He breathed into her mouth, pressed on her chest, and repeated the cycle again and again, unsure how hard to blow, how hard to press, or how frequently to perform either operation. He continued the cycle for several minutes with a mounting urgency, and an increasing sense of despair. He commanded her to wake-up: he slipped his arm under her shoulders and raised her to a sitting position; he shook her by the shoulders as if attempting to rouse her from a deep sleep; he spoke, in a faltering, cracking voice, urging her to be strong; and finally, in silent resolution, he laid back her head and shoulders onto the carpet, stared at her lifeless, gorged face, and accepted the indisputable: she would never again draw breath.

He moved to where Jefferson lay, sprawled on his back, arms stretched outwards, legs apart, and his head on one side. With a furious burst of anger he launched a sweeping kick at his spread-eagled assailant, losing his balance in the process and almost toppling over. The blow landed with great force sinking into a boneless, midriff section, above the hip and below the ribs. It had no noticeable effect; he might as well have been kicking at a sack of flour. There was no movement, no sound; no reaction of any kind.

He bent over the lifeless form and felt for a wrist pulse. There was none. Feeling a sudden urge to vomit, he made for a bathroom across the hall, collapsed around the toilet bowl and heaved repeatedly into the pan. For several minutes he remained kneeling there, clinging to the bowl for support while he attempted to regain composure and clear his mind. The reality of his situation began to sink

194

in: Julia was dead, and Jefferson was dead. He staggered to his feet, reeled to the wash basin, and sloshed his face with cold water. He would have to call the police and explain what had happened. And what was that! He started to get the story straight. He would say that Jefferson had forced his way into Julia's apartment, and had then attacked and killed her. For his own part, he had arrived to discuss committee business with Julia and had got there just before Jefferson could make his escape...or, was it that Jefferson was lying in wait to kill him too? Yes, that was indeed possible: Jefferson had given every appearance of being completely deranged. They had struggled, and in his effort to fend off an attack--an attack that had nearly proved fatal--Jefferson had tripped, and fallen on the edge of the table. He ran over the story once again, checking for inconsistencies. As he did so, an amazing thought struck him: it was all true! He had no need to lie. No need to confabulate or to create rationales. He could handle everything with the certainty that he had done nothing wrong and need only tell the truth.

He walked back into the living room, and surveyed the scene, almost gagging once more at the sight of Julia's helpless, tormented face. He stepped around her body, walked towards Jefferson's lifeless form lying just a few feet away, and stared intently as if lost in deep thought. He walked towards a telephone and plumped into the adjacent armchair. He felt for his wallet, pulled out a business card, and dialed the number.

"Ogopoulos here."

"Inspector, it's me, John Garter. There's been a murder. I need your help."

"Where are you Mr. Garter?" Inspector Ogopoulos scribbled the address onto his notepad. "I'll be there in twenty minutes. A homicide crew will arrive before me. Don't touch anything." His unusually commanding tone was oddly reassuring.

"I won't. I'll be waiting in the corridor outside." He put down the telephone, and with a glazed expression walked to the kitchen, removed Julia's apartment key from a rack on the wall, stepped into the corridor, and allowed the door to slam behind him.

Chapter Eighteen

At *Tratorria Blanco*, Mary and Kenneth were seated at a corner table with a clear view of a flaming log fire. The celebratory drink of champagne at Mary's apartment had been a pleasant occasion, and had induced a comfortable, relaxed atmosphere between them: so much so that Mary did not hesitate to agree when Kenneth Davies had suggested they round out the occasion with dinner at his favourite restaurant.

By now, they had discovered they had much in common. Both were only-children born into a low income, single parent family, both had attended the University of Toronto, although they had overlapped for only one year, and both held political views they considered to be 'liberal-leftish'. Neither held strong religious convictions, but believed in a God of some kind. Both shared a passion for Italian food, red wine, world peace, and independent foreign movies. However, as they compared notes over coffee about the debilitating effects of unhappy marriages--a subject that in Mr. Davies case had led to a divorce two years previously--a difference of opinion began to emerge. Noticing Mary reach for the bill, Kenneth Davies grabbed at the folder.

"No, this is on me!"

"Oh no. Let me have it. I'm very grateful for what you have pulled off, and it's the least I can do." She held out a hand expectantly.

"No, Mary, I mean it…I want to treat you. You've been through a nerve-wracking time, and helped save my company a great deal of money. I'm indebted to you. Besides…" he smiled, "I invited you out on a date." She laughed, and not for the first time that night, Mary acknowledged to herself an increasing attraction.

"All right then, but on one condition: you let me return the treat on another occasion."

It was close to midnight, when Kenneth Davies dropped-off Mary at her apartment. He pulled to a stop outside her house and, not wishing to appear presumptuous, left the engine running while they said their farewells. Much to his relief, she responded willingly to his cautiously proffered kiss. The embrace that followed, enthusiastic but brief, had established a clear mutual understanding: more such intimacy lay ahead. She waved good-night and, while reporters and editors prepared to spread word of condominium murder, she, blissfully unaware of these events, returned to her apartment to find a telephone message from Inspector Ogopoulos: would she please call him when she returned that evening or, if that was after ten o'clock, on Saturday morning instead.

* * *

The Metro area newspapers all carried front page headlines about the death of a female bank executive, found strangled in a prestigious, downtown condominium building, alongside a retired supermarket executive, found dead with head wounds. A man was assisting police with their enquiries. The story also appeared on inside pages of two National newspapers. No names were released in any of the accounts.

"I've no idea who she was!" Mary was on the telephone to her friend Ellen, sharing the astonishing news that her husband had been detained for questioning following the discovery of two bodies in a downtown condominium. Still incredulous, she tempted to communicate the story that, thanks to her persistence and interviewing skills, she had finally pieced together that morning from information pried out of OgoPogo. Ellen, too, had difficulty in comprehending the news.

"So, is he in prison then?" Ellen sounded hopeful.

"No, he hasn't even been arrested. What I gather from Ogopoulos is that he is being held for questioning after he called in to tell them that he was in a condominium with two dead bodies."

"Well how did they die? And what was he doing there anyway?"

"I don't know! I asked him the same questions but he wouldn't say." Mary's bewilderment began to give way to amusement. Maybe they were having a ménage a trios or something and the chandelier collapsed!" They both laughed at the image. "You know, Ellen, I really don't give a damn. I don't feel anything for him at all. He can handle this without any help from me."

"I know, but it is interesting though." Ellen's view of the situation was coloured by different considerations. "I mean it's not every day your husband gets arrested is it!" Mary laughed.

"No, you're right. It is quite funny really.

"Are you allowed to visit him?"

"Ellen, why would I do that! Anyway, he hasn't been arrested. Ogopoulos said he'll probably be free to leave any time now. So, who knows what will happen. We'll see. By the way, I had dinner with Kenneth last night."

"Kenneth? Who's Kenneth?"

"You know, Kenneth Davies, our insurance investigator."

"No, I don't remember you talking about him before." She sounded offended. "What's he like? Is he married?"

"No, he's divorced. And…he's intelligent… sensitive…. a bit shy…very tall too."

"How tall?"

"I don't know! Six- six maybe." Mary wondered if she might be under-estimating by several inches. "Anyway, what I was going to say was that he thought Ogopoulos believed that John was covering-up something. Kenneth didn't know what he had in mind, but I certainly got the impression he thought the same thing." She paused, "I think he's being cautious about what he can say to me at this point, but I expect I'll find out later."

"Well, you know what I think about your husband, Mary, and I've never tried to hide the fact, I think he's a creepy guy…sorry to be so blunt…but, the truth is I've never trusted him!"

"I know that, Ellen. And listen, you don't have to apologize to me for saying so, I'm not into defending him you know."

"I know. All the same, I don't like to trash the man you married. Seems like poor taste somehow doesn't it? Anyway, to get back to your Kenneth, when are you seeing him again?"

"On Wednesday--unless of course he decides that my being married to someone in police custody makes me an undesirable! Look I'd better go now Ellen, I'll call you if I learn anything more."

"All right, keep me posted. And have a good time on Wednesday. What are you doing anyway?"

"We're going to see a play. It's an amateur production of a murder mystery…. something to do with arthritis… the funding benefit I mean, not the play." Ellen laughed.

"Have fun! And, don't forget to call me." Mary hung up the telephone and sat for a few minutes lost in thought. Tony Angle had suggested that John was being harassed by a loan shark. Ogopoulos didn't trust him. He was now being questioned about the death of a man and a woman. What on earth was going on?

*   *   *

Inspector Ogopoulos had not moved from his desk since speaking to Mary that morning. Not being part of the central homicide division his access to information was limited: legitimized only by virtue of his previous dealings with Garter, and the fact that Garter had called him in the first instance. That meant he was not at that moment privy to how Garter was explaining himself. He was, however, expecting to be updated through a call from a colleague in central homicide at any moment. In the meantime, as he reflected on the fact that John Garter had been found with two dead bodies in a condominium building, his belief that Garter was a thoroughly untrustworthy character intensified dramatically: so much so, that it precipitated a grand unifying theory regarding the dead Frenchman, the Garter burglary, and his stolen car; a theory so compelling that the more he thought about it the more he became convinced of its merit.

Inspector Ogopoulos, like John Garter before him, quickly figured out that Kenneth Davies had paid out reward money to retrieve Mary's jewellery. He was convinced of this on the basis that no-one in his right mind would call-in and give it up for nothing. He had then gone on to ask himself why anyone would take twenty thousand dollars for something worth more than sixty or seventy thousand dollars. He had then arrived at the only conclusion that made sense to him: the person to do that would be someone who would end up with twenty thousand dollars and the jewellery. It was a simple step of logic from there to conclude that only John Garter was in a position to pull off such a transaction since no-one else, Mary Garter excepted, could end up with the jewellery and a reward. It was an equally simple step of logic to establish that if John Garter was able to return the jewellery that he must have taken it himself in the first place or it wouldn't be in his possession.

The next connections had been more difficult to fathom, but they too had now become perfectly clear. According to the taxi driver, he had dropped the Frenchman at the Garter house at about nine thirty. Mary Garter was out that evening at her art class, so why was the Frenchman there? The reason he was there was quite simple: the cuckolded Garter had summoned him there on some pretext, possibly to talk or to discuss some kind of pay off to get rid of him. But, intent on revenge, Garter's plan was to kill the Frenchman when he arrived, stage a burglary, and then call the police saying that he had caught him in the act of stealing their jewels and that he had accidentally killed him in a self-defence struggle. Where it had all gone wrong, was that having been hit on the head by Garter, the Frenchman had regained consciousness and escaped in Garter's car making off towards the hospital to get treatment for the injury that Garter had inflicted. Garter had then stolen the Ogopoulos car to give chase. He had caught up with the Frenchman by the hospital, found him in a state of collapse, and driven the car into his head to finish him off. He then returned home in his own car leaving behind the dead Frenchman and the Ogopoulos Buick. A man out for a walk, possibly Scottish, came on the scene, decided that the quickest way to get help for the unfortunate accident victim was to drive the Ogopoulos car to the station and call for assistance. Not wishing to get further involved he left the car there and departed the scene. In the meantime, Garter returned home in his own car, concealed the stolen property and adjusted his story to fit with the new facts: quite simply that he had arrived home to find that there had been a burglary. Before calling the police he drove to the Aztec restaurant in an attempt to establish an alibi and returned to the house to make his discovery and to call the police.

As OgoPogo continued to connect-up the dots, the call he expected, broke his concentration.

"Ogie? It's me. Well, he's certainly an obnoxious sod, but his story holds up, so we're going to let him go."

"You are! I am surprised. I'm sure he's up to his neck in this." He paused. "What did he say then?"

"What he said was that he and Julia Miller were friends. He went to her place to meet her and found Jefferson in there. She'd been strangled by the time he arrived. Jefferson let him in and then attacked him too. They fought, and Jefferson died when he fell on the corner of the table."

"Why would Jefferson want to kill her though?"

"Good question. I asked him that, and he said he didn't know but he thought it might have something to do with a disagreement over investment strategy… apparently all three of them were executive members of the Aerial Golf Club. Garter thinks that had something to do with it… we're going to check all that out. He also thinks Jefferson was a bit of nutter too. Do you know anything about him?"

"Yes, he's French. How did he get in the apartment?"

"I don't know yet. We're checking the security tapes to see what they show. Garter says he arrived at about seven, Jefferson was inside and she was already dead. Anyway, Garter's story checks out as far as it goes, so we haven't got any real reason to hold him. He seems pretty upset too, and promises not to go anywhere. Did you talk to his wife by the way: he seems anxious to know what she's been told. Wants to cover up the affair I expect."

"Yes, she knows now, but she doesn't care. Tell him I haven't caught up with her yet. They're getting divorced you know. She was having an affair too – with that Frenchman I told you about: the one who suddenly turned up dead--killed by Garter if I'm not mistaken. I tell you, he's a nasty piece of work."

"All right, you tell me then. What have you got on him?"

Inspector Ogopoulos proceeded to outline his theory that Daniel had been lured to the Garter house, and that Garter had planned to kill him there. Garter's plan was to say that he had caught the Frenchman in an act of burglary and that he had died in the ensuing self-defense struggle. But the plan had gone wrong. Ogopoulos went on to elaborate his ideas about the escape, the chase, the killing, and the burglary. And then, in a flash of insight, OgoPogo had a new thought: that scenario in which Garter comes upon a crime in progress was an exact parallel to the Miller/Jefferson deaths; it was, as OgoPogo announced triumphantly, Garter's 'modus operandi'. "It all fits, Terrence, I'm sure that's what happened." His counterpart in homicide had listened attentively throughout OgoPogo's briefing, absorbing the details with a keen interest. When it was completed he remained silent for a few moments, before commenting.

"How did he start your car then?"

"What?" OgoPogo seemed to think it an unfair question. "Ah…well I'm not sure about that yet. It wasn't hot-wired so he might have used a key. Old worn ones often work on an old car you know."

"Yeah, right. I think you might have to do better than that Ogie. Anyway, It's all theory isn't it? What evidence have you got? There's nothing as far as I can see. I'll grant you it's an interesting hypothesis though. Look, I'm going to let him go now, we can always pick him up again later if needs be."

OgoPogo replaced the receiver and stared thoughtfully at the wall in front of him. If his theory about Garter was correct, and of that he now had no doubt, then it was just a matter of time before this desperado unleashed another murderous attack; where it would be directed and what would trigger it, were the key questions to be answered. Mmmm, keys. How did he start the car? As he leaned back in his chair, his musings quickly induced a comfortable state of *creative reflection*.

Chapter Nineteen

Although Tony Angle was pessimistic about recovering the twenty thousand dollars owed to him by John Garter, he was not one to give up easily. The reward money he had received covered the cost of his cash outlay to Garter to acquire the jewellery for himself, and so he was not out of pocket. However, Garter owed him for services rendered, and even though there would be no insurance settlement from which to pay that debt, that was Garter's problem to solve and not his. The question was: when and how should he make his approach? It was clear that Garter was in some major financial difficulty and so timing and strategy were important considerations.

It was in the middle of one such contemplation that Inspector Ogopoulos appeared at the door to his office.

"Mr. Angle?"

"Yes that's me. Inspector Ogopoulos isn't it?" He held out a hand.

"Yes, indeed it is. Have we met before?"

"Way back, just briefly once. But I've seen you around and knew who you were." The Inspector seemed pleased at his apparent celebrity status.

"Can I come in Mr. Angle? I have some questions I need to ask you regarding someone's claim to have been with you one evening at the Fox & Hounds pub."

"Wow, that could be a lot of people, I'm there quite a bit. Anyway, come in." He led the Inspector inside and watched as he plumped himself into the chair on which Mary Garter had settled two weeks previously.

"This was a Wednesday evening Mr. Angle, November 18th to be exact. According to a statement made to me by a Mr. John Garter, you were there with him from seven in the evening, until nine in the evening. Can you confirm that for me please?" Tony Angle had expected the visit at some time, and played his part well.

"Mr. Garter? Yes I did meet with him, a while back and it would have been about that time too. Here let me check." He reached for the diary on his desk that served as a business and personal appointment book, and flipped through the pages. "Yes, here it is, November 18th. I made a note to remind myself. It says, 'Garter, 7.00 p.m. Fox.' Here take a look for yourself." He pushed the diary towards OgoPogo's outstretched paws. The Inspector stared at the entry for a few moments and silently handed back the diary.

"Do you recall what time he arrived and when he left?"

"Yes, I do. He came at seven, like he said he would, and we chatted for a couple of hours. I'm not sure exactly what time he left, but it couldn't have been far off from nine, because I remember having to leave about that time myself to meet my brother."

"Is John Garter a friend of yours Mr. Angle?"

"No, I wouldn't say so. In fact I don't really like him that much." The Inspector nodded approvingly. "He asked to meet with me."

"May I ask what he wanted to meet you for?"

"He wanted to talk about his car. We were chatting one day when he came in for gas. He had a lot of questions about repairs and how long he should keep it. We didn't have time to get into it that much, and he asked if we could chat over a beer sometime. So, that's when we arranged to get together at the Fox."

"I see." The Inspector seemed very interested. "Does he know much about cars?"

"Depends on what you mean. He certainly knows about costs, and the relative merits of leasing versus purchasing." The Inspector interrupted.

"No, no, I don't mean that. I mean does he have knowledge about mechanics? Let's say, for example, how to drive off a locked car without breaking in?" The sudden realization that OgoPogo had somehow connected John Garter with the theft of the Ogopoulos Buick was quite alarming. Did that mean, he wondered, that the Inspector had determined it was all an inside job? He needed to tread carefully.

"Well, no. There's not many people who can Inspector- -at least, not without the keys."

"Yes, but it can be done can't it? You know, with a dummy key or something like that?"

"Maybe, depends on the car."

"So, do you think he might have that knowledge?"

"Nah! Not him. I doubt if he could put air in the tires! He's an accounting wonk. Knows everything about finance, but nothing about what makes cars go. Anyway, why would he need to? I don't think that's his line really. Do you?" OgoPogo ignored the question.

"Mr. Angle, did you know Harry Jefferson or Julia Miller?" The names sounded oddly familiar but Tony Angle could not place either one.

"I may have heard the names but I'm not sure I know either of them." He frowned. "Wait a minute! Aren't they the two that were killed in that condo? I read about it last week. I don't know them though. Why?"

"They were both acquaintances of Mr. Garter, so I wondered if you might know them too."

"No… I didn't know them. But, like I said he's not a friend of mine, I just know him from when he comes in here now and again." He paused. "So they were both his friends eh?"

"Mmmm. Well one of them was. The other one certainly wasn't." OgoPogo's mysterious air triggered a thought.

"Wasn't there someone who was there at the time… a man helping police with their enquiries? You're not telling me it was Garter are you?"

"No, Mr. Angle I'm not telling you that." But, the inspector's tone of voice made it quite clear that only protocol prevented him from confirming Tony Angle's supposition. He quickly reverted to his previous enquiry.

"So, if he was going to take a car that didn't belong to him he'd need a key?" Tony Angle did not reply; his mind busily churned over the astonishing information he had just gleaned.

"What was that?"

"A key. You're saying he'd need a key to take the car?"

"Oh! Yes, I'd say so. Either that or a chauffeur!" OgoPogo's eyes slowly widened in response to a burst of insight. A chauffeur! Of course, there may have been an accomplice. Someone who knew about cars; someone waiting to help Garter in case the plan went awry.

"That's a very interesting observation Mr. Angle." He appeared lost in thought. "Thank you. You've given me a whole new angle." He took his leave and ambled towards his car, leaving the source of his inspiration wondering whether the pun had been intentional, and what on earth John Garter had been up to. As he watched the inspector depart, he picked up the telephone and dialed Garter's home number.

"Is that you Mr. Garter?"

"Angle? Yes it's me. I'm glad you called, I've been meaning to call you."

"Look, we need to talk. Ogopoulos was just here and I think he's on to something."

"On to something? Like what? I should have thought the case was closed now that some imbecile returned all the jewellery. What do you know about that?"

"I don't want to discuss any of this on the telephone Mr. Garter. Let's get together somewhere. How about the Fox again? It's six now, I can be there at seven."

"All right. I'll meet you there then." Having confirmed the arrangement, John Garter hung up the telephone and returned to his planning exercise, irritated at the intrusion into his analysis of when, and where, to administer a Crylex dosage to his wife.

*   *   *

The visit from Inspector Ogopoulos to the Ambrosia Service station had left Tony Angle quite unnerved. He knew that despite the Inspector's fumbling, bumbling, style that Ogopoulos was no fool. If he did think Garter had some involvement in the break-in and the theft of his car, then that could easily lead to a finger pointing at himself. He needed to know what Garter had been up to, and what might have triggered any suspicions Ogopoulos held. There was also the matter of his twenty thousand dollars.

In combination, the two issues made for a full agenda. Now, however, as he sat across from Garter at the same table they had shared on November 18th, he was struggling to get either topic under discussion due to Garter's persistence in pursuing his own priority.

"So you've no idea at all why the jewellery was returned?"

"No, I haven't, unless the person who bought it thought it was too hot to market, and changed their mind. There was a reward being offered you know."

"Yes, twenty thousand for at least seventy thousand dollars worth of stuff! Who would go for that deal? And of course, the insurance representative said he didn't even have to make that payment. According to him, he found the stuff in a locker after getting a tip-off. That's even more incredible; I don't believe it for one moment. I doubt that Ogopoulos does either." He stared at Tony Angle with a hostile expression. "So, your purchaser, who paid a measly twenty thousand dollars for the jewellery, took twenty thousand in reward money in preference to keeping the stuff and cashing-in a big profit? It doesn't make sense! Who was this bozo anyway?"

"I can't tell you that. He's reliable though. I've known him a long time. I assume he just decided to backtrack on the sale and get his money back."

"Yes. But why would he do that? Didn't he know that might wreck an insurance claim?"

"Most people who get robbed want their stuff back. Maybe he assumed the owner would be pleased."

"It's incompetent! The whole thing is an amateurish bungle." He stared accusingly. "I have to say I'm very disappointed." He took a sip of his beer. " In fact, I don't feel the least bit obligated to pay that extra amount we talked about because you didn't deliver your end properly."

"The 'extra amount', as you call it Mr. Garter, was because you wanted all of the proceeds right away, including my share! I did everything I said I would. I told you we would only get twenty thousand for the sale, I got that for us, and I willingly gave it all to you instead of only half. You agreed to give me my share later with an extra ten thousand as a bonus. There was nothing about it being conditional on the insurance money coming through." Garter shifted uncomfortably in his seat, while Tony Angle pressed on. "Look I'm sorry you didn't get the insurance money, but that is not my worry. You owe me twenty thousand and I expect you to pay." Garter grunted into his beer mug.

"Well, don't expect it any time soon."

"Sorry Mr. Garter. That's not good enough. I want to know *when* you plan to pay me." Tony Angle gave him a sufficiently determined stare that a reply of some kind could not be avoided. Garter decided to negotiate.

"I don't agree with you when you say that the bonus money was not conditional on getting the insurance pay out. I told you at the time that I would pay you the extra ten thousand after I got reimbursed. So, it should be obvious to anyone that if I don't get reimbursed you don't get paid."

"Are you saying you don't intend to pay me anything?"

"No. I agree you haven't had your half of the twenty thousand yet. All I'm saying is that the other ten thousand is a non-issue since there's no fund to pay it from." Tony Angle said nothing for a moment. He was surprised to hear that Garter was even willing to concede that he owed ten thousand. He decided to press on with his claim nevertheless.

"Well I suggest you start looking for a fund, Mr. Garter, because as far as I am concerned your debt is twenty thousand, and that's what I expect."

"Well surely you can see the logic of what I'm saying? In response to Tony Angle's slow shake of the head and fixed stare, Garter continued to negotiate. "Look it's not right that you shouldn't share some of the pain from the failure of this plan. We were both in it together so why should I have to shoulder everything?" Tony Angle said nothing and allowed him to continue. "Look, how about if we agree to split the difference? We'll make the bonus five thousand, and then I'll owe you fifteen in total. What do you say to that?" For Tony Angle, the idea was actually quite captivating. Here was John Garter solemnly confirming that he owed him money and now promising to pay fifteen thousand dollars. That was certainly more than he had anticipated.

"When will you pay it?"

"Well, I've got several irons in the fire. You'll have to wait a bit, but it shouldn't be too long now. Actually, I'm expecting an inheritance shortly. Should be a couple of hundred thousand."

"I need a date Mr. Garter. Otherwise I'm going right back to where we started this discussion."

"All right. Let's say end of January at the latest. How's that?" Tony Angle feigned reluctance to accept.

"Well… I'll agree to that, but on one condition."
"What's that?"

"I want you to square with me completely about what's going on with you and Ogopoulos."
"How do you mean?

"He came to see me today, and he's definitely on to something. He also implied…" he paused, fumbling for the right approach "that you had some connection to those two murders in that downtown condo recently, and that…" Garter interrupted angrily.

"He has no right to be discussing my connection to those events! I'm to be a material witness at an inquest and I'm told I can't discuss the matter with anyone. And he most certainly shouldn't be talking about it to you, or to anyone else. This is quite out of line!" Tony Angle was quick to backtrack.

"No, no. Let me be clear. He didn't discuss anything… in fact he refused to discuss it. It's just that from some remark he made I put two and two together. And I got it right didn't I? You did have some involvement and I need to know what it is, in case any of this comes in my direction."

"There's nothing likely to affect you. A woman friend of mine was killed by a mutual acquaintance: someone with psychiatric problems. I arrived just after it had happened and he then attacked me. We struggled and he fell and hit his head and died. That's all there was to it." Tony Angle's mouth opened as if he was about to speak, but no words emerged, and it closed again. "That was all. I shouldn't be speaking about it and neither should Ogopoulos."

"No, no, I suppose not." Tony Angle paused assessing the news he had just heard. " Well, well, Mr. Garter, that must have been a bit traumatic all round."

"Yes, it was. She was very important to me."

"She was, eh?" Tony Angle's sympathetic tone triggered a surprising response. John Garter's eyes began to flood with tears. He reached in his pocket and pulled out a handkerchief, dabbed at his face, and blew his nose.

"Yes she was." He sniffled, dabbed, and blew, for a few moments longer, and then, much to Tony Angle's relief, seemed to regain his composure. "I loved her, you know…very much." Garter reached for his beer mug, and took a long swill. I'm going to miss her." Tony Angle remained silent waiting to see if there was more to come. A few moments later he decided there was not.

"That's very sad, Mr. Garter. To lose someone you love." He looked thoughtful, while John Garter reached into his pocket again. "Especially like that. What a shock you must have had." At that point, John Garter burst into a loud sob, stood up, and made a dash for the exit door, masking his nose, mouth, and grief, with his now moist handkerchief. Tony Angle looked up in astonishment, wondered whether to follow, and decided immediately that it would be polite to allow his partner some private time. He remained seated, and glanced around. The bar was full of people, but no-one seemed to have taken the slightest notice of what had just happened. He sipped at his beer, uncomfortably conscious of the vacant space on the opposite side of his table. He picked up some paper serviettes, mopped up drops of spilled ale around John Garter' now empty glass, and wondered whether his partner would be back. A waitress appeared at his elbow.

"Two more Tony?" she enquired.

"Yes please, Irene." He drained his glass and watched while she deftly cleared the table, wiped it clean, and departed with the two empty mugs. Left alone with his thoughts, Tony Angle turned his mind to his earlier discussion with Inspector Ogopoulos. Why was he so curious about whether John Garter had the technical knowledge to steal a car? Surely then he must suspect that he was connected to the burglary? Irene returned with the beer, arriving at the table at the exact same moment that John Garter returned to his seat.

"Let me know if you need anything else, won't you?" She turned, and left them staring at one another.

"You OK?" Tony Angle enquired cautiously.

"Yes. Sorry about that... I'm all right now." Garter appeared to be in full control of his emotions, and managed a sheepish smile. "I don't usually get sentimental. You'll have to forgive me."

"Of course! Think nothing of it." Tony Angle decided to shift their discussion to his concerns about Inspector Ogopoulos. "Look, I need to talk to you about Ogopoulos. He's got some notion in his head that you stole his car the night of the burglary."

"So what? I understand that he suspects everybody of stealing his car."

"Does he?"

"Yes, apparently. At least, that's what my wife told me. Anyway, I didn't steal it, so what does it matter?" As Tony Angle wondered whether to confess to the crime, John Garter had a flash of insight. "It wasn't you was it? It was, wasn't it! You never did tell me how you got away afterwards, and I forgot to ask." Tony Angle nodded and grinned.

"I didn't know it was his did I? Anyway, it doesn't make much difference whether it was his or someone else's. He would probably have made a connection between the car theft and the burglary at some point."

"Yes, I suppose so. But I see now why you were concerned. If he does think I stole it, it means he thinks it was me who was the burglar. Is that what you're saying?" Tony Angle nodded. "But so what?" continued John Garter. "I wasn't the burglar, I didn't steal the car, the jewellery is back, it's a finished episode. What is there to worry about?" He paused. "You know, I really can't help thinking that he's just clutching at straws and trying to make as many possible theories as he can. He's very odd you know. When I first met with him about the burglary he seemed to think I had some illicit relationship with a dead Frenchman!"

"A dead Frenchman?" Tony Angle managed to contain his alarm.

"Yes. He showed me a picture of some unshaven lout who'd been found dead, and wanted to know if I'd been with him recently! He couldn't seem to grasp that I'd never set eyes on him before and he couldn't explain to me why he thought otherwise. In the end I told him that he'd wasted enough of my time and that I was leaving, which I did." As John Garter sat back in his chair and reached for his beer, Tony Angle wondered whether to complete the missing pieces in John Garter's picture of events after the burglary. He decided against it. The less he knew about the dead Frenchman the better.

"I think I read about him in the paper."

"Yes, that's right," said John Garter, "there was a picture of him too." Tony Angle decided to change the topic once again.

"Mr Garter. Just to get back to what we were talking about before…the fifteen grand I mean. I'd appreciate formalizing that agreement if you don't mind." John Garter snorted.

"What did you have in mind? A legal contract?

"No, nothing like that. A simple IOU will do me."

"An IOU? Are you serious?

"Yes, I am. Here..." He rummaged in an inside pocket and produced a used envelope and a pen. "Write on the back of this. Just put 'Tony Angle, IOU Fifteen thousand dollars' and sign your name. Better date it too." He waited while John Garter reluctantly took the pen. "I don't mind waiting until the end of January for the payment, Mr. Garter, I think that's when you said you would have it, but I do need something in writing. Being an accountant I'm sure you'll appreciate the wisdom of that." John Garter grunted, and did as he had been asked, remembering vividly the last occasion when he had been asked to take dictation.

"You all right Mr. Garter?" Tony Angle noted the pained expression on John Garter's face.

"Yes, thank you. I was just thinking of someone." He looked at his watch. "It's time I was going. I think we've both said what we came to say, haven't we?" Tony Angle considered the question, and cautiously nodded his head. Garter stood up, and prepared to leave. "Well, take care of that IOU won't you. I wouldn't want you to lose it." Before Tony Angle could answer he added a final farewell. "It's your turn to get the tab, I believe, so I'll say good night."

CHAPTER TWENTY

In the days following Julia's death, John Garter was filled with a terrible sense of loss. The idea of being forever separated from her was almost unbearable. She had changed his life completely. In a few short weeks, she had become his lover, his friend, his therapist, his mentor, his captor, his alter-ego: she had consumed him. But, he had been devoured willingly: an eager participant in a mysterious, wondrous process still unfolding at the time of her death. And now it was over.

He thought of her constantly: her face, her smile, her hypnotic eyes; features etched in his memory and ever present in his mind. He replayed their conversations, haunted by the mesmerizing resonance of that gentle, commanding, purring voice, still alive in his head as if she were at his side. He marveled at the trust she had engendered in him: a trust that had allowed him to speak to her freely about his fears, his ambitions, his hatreds and his insecurities. He thought of her contempt for hypocrisy. He thought of her distaste for conventional standards of morality and her ability to embrace the unlawful without guilt, fear or remorse. He remembered the scent of her hair, the intensity of her passion when they made love, her clarity of thought, her confidence, and her unfailing wisdom in judging what had to be, and what had to be done.

The church pew where he now sat was about twenty rows back. To the front and on both sides of the centre aisle there were dozens of people: a mysterious mix of what he guessed to be Julia's relatives, colleagues, and business associates. At the front of the church a pastor dressed in white and black robes over a dark blue suit, stood before the assembled congregation, forcing a slight, reassuring, smile as he confidently explained God's purpose in allowing the brief but distinguished life of Julia Miller to be callously extinguished by an errant hand. The explanation made no sense, and gave him no comfort. He felt angry and powerless. Around him people stood up, preparing to sing the next hymn. He rose from the bench and stared ahead at the lonely oak coffin, partially visible behind the dutiful cleric. Organ music played and people sang, but without gusto or conviction. Then the congregation sat once more, heads bowed, listening to a final prayer: a prayer that failed to soothe, console, or offer hope. Tears forced their way into his eyes causing him to reach for a handkerchief. Now, the coffin was lifted. It came nearer, marched along the aisle on the shoulders of six people, all of them strangers to him: strangers who dared to proclaim themselves closer than he to the lovely Julia.

An usher appeared at his shoulder and gently directed him to lead his pew of mourners out to the entrance lobby. He stood up, and walked towards the exit, following the route taken by the pall bearers. In the distance and through the church doors he could see the coffin being negotiated towards a black hearse that patiently waited to receive its cargo. In a moment he was in the fresh, crisp air of the outside forecourt, watching as the hearse and official cars, lined-up to form a final procession to the cemetery where his lover was to be buried. A young man approached, and handed him a piece of paper containing directions to the cemetery. He stared at the drawing, failing to absorb its instructions, scale, or landmarks, and asked himself once more why he had come to this ridiculous ceremony. He had no expectation that he would derive spiritual comfort, but nevertheless, he had felt a compulsion to be there: a need to fulfill an obligation to her; an obligation to say, "Good-bye Julia, I love you."

In the minutes that had passed since he had first slipped into the back of the church, he had recognized no-one, and spoken to no-one. Now, as he stood staring after the procession of cars wending their way out to the road, wondering whether to travel on to the final grave-side ceremony, an elderly woman approached him and tugged at his arm.

"Are you Mr. John Garter?" He turned towards her, startled by the sudden interruption of his thoughts.

"Yes, I am." The woman said nothing, and stared into his face. Her bright eyes suggested alertness, and intelligence, while her wrinkled skin and bent posture, spoke to a lifetime of hard work and suffering. "And you are?" He looked at her enquiringly.

"I'm the mother of the man you killed. The man they say killed this poor young woman."

"You're Harry Jefferson's mother!"

"Yes, I am." She stared at him intently, observing the shocked expression on his face, and said nothing more.

"Mrs. Jefferson, I don't know what to say! Your son killed the woman I loved. He would have killed me too if I hadn't been able to stop him." He broke off, lost for words.

"Yes, that's what they say." She stared at him again.

" I'm sorry but that's how it was. It pains me to say so, but I hate your son for what he did, even though I know that he must have been sick." He returned her steady gaze. "Why did you come here anyway?"

"It was my son's cremation this morning. Nothing like this though. It was just me, my daughter-in-law, and a police Inspector. I thought you might be there, but you weren't." She paused noting his shocked expression. "I learned from the Inspector that there was a service for Ms. Miller today, so I came. Mr. Garter, I wanted to meet the man who killed my son. That's all." He looked away, embarrassed by her confrontation.

"Mrs. Jefferson, I don't think we should be having this conversation. It was an accident and I have nothing more to say on the matter. I'm sorry. Good day." He turned and walked quickly towards the spot where he had left his car, edging his way through the throng of people still crowding the front forecourt of the church. She trailed after him, valiantly urging her frail legs to catch up.

"Wait Mr. Garter, I need to talk to you!" But, it was too late. She reached the parking area in time to see him driving off through the main gates.

A woman standing nearby noticed Mrs Jefferson's agitation and asked if she could be of assistance. The offer was politely declined. "No, I don't think so thank you. It's just that I didn't want him to go away thinking that I blame him for something I know wasn't his fault. I'll find some other way to talk to him. Thank you all the same."

She made her way out to the main street, and waited for the bus that would take her to the train station. It was, she reminded herself, quite proper for her to have hidden her son's diary after his death. The police had searched his room, but they were too late to find the journal. Too late to see what was revealed in the lucidly written sections sandwiched between the ramblings: a clear account of how her son intended to kill Julia Miller and John Garter. But, those were confidential notes. No-one had the right to see them. It was his private diary. Those were his private thoughts. Even so, a disturbing puzzle remained and Mr. Garter might be able to explain it: why had her son wanted them dead?. There had to be some rationale!

∗   ∗   ∗

Alone in his car, driving slowly through the Saturday afternoon traffic, Garter felt anxious, and uncomfortable. Mrs. Jefferson's approach had unnerved him and her words now echoed in his head: "I wanted to meet the man who killed my son." He tried to recall the emotion behind the words, but she had given no clue as to what she felt: there had been no bitterness apparent in her voice, and no threat implied-- just a factual statement.

He wondered for a brief moment about his own mother. How would she have reacted if it had been he who had committed a murder, been killed in the aftermath, and cremated that morning? He shivered at the thought. She hadn't bothered to come to his wedding, or go to his father's funeral, so she was hardly likely to grieve the loss of a deranged, murderous son. He thought of Julia. What would she have made of Mrs. Jefferson's presence? Immediately, he heard her answer: "She only needs some closure Jonathon--just like you." Yes, closure! That was exactly what he needed. He had to find a way to escape from this awful episode–to put it all behind him and start afresh. Suddenly he felt much better: it was time for some serious planning. He would be home soon. Then, at the comfort of his desk, with a pencil in hand, a glass of Scotch, and clean fresh paper on which to write, he would invent the next stage of his life.

CHAPTER TWENTY ONE

Garter looked at his watch. It was seven thirty. He had been working late, trying to catch up on neglected correspondence, and he felt drained of all energy. The events of the past few days had left him feeling hollow and fragile. Julia's death had hurt him deeply, more so than he could ever have imagined. Even the fight with Jefferson had left its mark, but that was a physical bruising, one that he would soon be over. With Julia it was different. He could not begin to imagine a time when her death would no longer hold its present, agonizing, prominence in his consciousness.

He left the building, crossed the street, and walked towards a coffee lounge on the far corner of the block. The cold evening air made a pleasant contrast to the recycled fug that circulated throughout the office tower where he worked. An espresso would clear his mind and help him to refocus on the outstanding business to which he must attend -- that night, if possible.

Inside, there was no-one he recognized. He took his purchase to a corner table, sat down, and considered how to proceed. The best option would be to administer the Crylex dosage when some other people were around. He could then slip away and be far from the scene leaving those on hand to witness events and do any explaining that might be required. Unfortunately, it now seemed extremely unlikely that in the foreseeable future he and Mary would be hosting, or attending, any social functions together. He would have to call her and arrange a visit, possibly on the pretext of discussing their divorce settlement. Yes, that was the obvious thing to do.

There was a pay telephone at the entrance to the coffee lounge. He decided to call and see what she was doing. Leaving his unfinished coffee on the table, he walked to the lobby and fished in his pocket for the slip of paper on which he had recorded her new number. He tapped it into the keypad. Mary answered almost immediately, and waited patiently as he explained his purpose in calling.

"Well, I'm with Ellen at the moment. If you don't mind her being here while you say what you have to, then you could come now...provided you can get it all said in ten minutes. I don't want the whole evening spoiled with pointless bickering." He jumped at her offer of a brief visit and confirmed he would be there in less than one hour.

He returned to his table, and upon discovering that someone had cleared away his unfinished coffee, growled at the counter staff until he was provided with a replacement cup and a complimentary biscotti. He settled down to consume both items. Mary's response to his request for a meeting provided him with a heaven-sent opportunity. He considered what he would say when he arrived. If Ellen was going to be there too, then a conciliatory message wouldn't go amiss. Yes, he would say something along the lines that he was close to agreeing to all of her demands, apart from one or two minor issues. That way, Ellen would have no reason to report negatively on his visit when she explained later how Mary had inexplicably dropped dead. He removed the Crylex lipstick case from his pocket, glanced around to ensure that no-one was observing him, and with the cap pointing downwards, held it as if it was a piece of chalk: a grip that felt ideal for making a gentle dabbing motion. He made one or two practice prods in the direction of his coffee, noting as he did so that when the cap was removed, the stem of the container could be held safely and concealed from view with his hand, while the cap could be held in the other hand with a simple thumb and finger grip.

Satisfied that he was ready to implement his plan, he finished his coffee, sneered contemptuously in the direction of the counter staff, left the shop, and walked to retrieve his car from the parking space under his building. Thirty minutes later, he was once again standing on Mary's front porch, waiting for her to open the door. This time, when the door swung open, it was she who appeared.

"I meant it when I said only ten minutes, John." Mary's greeting was accompanied by a waving motion of her arm, gesturing him into the front hall. "Up those stairs to the top."

*   *   *

The dabbing procedure had been even simpler to implement than John Garter had imagined. Mary had asked Ellen if she would be kind enough to make coffee while she and John talked. Ellen, relieved at the opportunity to be inconspicuous but within earshot, had happily complied, leaving them sitting next to each other at the kitchen table. He had then unfolded a letter received from Mary's lawyer and spread it on the table in front of them, suggesting they use it as an agenda. At that point, Mary had edged closer to remind herself of its contents, and had obligingly placed her elbow and bare arm in a perfect position for him to strike. It had taken him less than thirty seconds to remove the lipstick container from his pocket, take off the cap, gently prod the tip onto her skin, just above the elbow, replace the cap and return the container to his pocket. Thirty seconds: that was all the time that had been required to set the stage for a complete new chapter in his life. Mary had shown no sign of having felt the prod on her arm. She had remained silent the whole time they sat together, and had listened attentively while he had explained - even during the delicate dabbing procedure - his very reasonable settlement proposals.

He had declined coffee when it was offered, on the grounds that he wanted to honour the ten-minute understanding, and because he had, in any event, already consumed more caffeine than was wise if he was going to sleep soundly. Then, with his adrenalin racing, he had taken his leave, returned to his car, and, eager to distance himself from the scene, made for the Fox and Hounds pub. Although he had no particular regard for pubs, or for Tony Angle, it seemed a suitable setting in which to calm his nerves and suppress any unwelcome twinges of conscience that might surface.

When he arrived, Tony Angle was propped against the bar watching a hockey game with a group of other men. He immediately noticed John Garter's arrival, waved his beer mug in greeting, and ambled across the room to meet him.

"Well, well, what are you doing here? This isn't your usual haunt is it?"

"No, but the last time we were here I did leave a little abruptly and I wanted to apologize." He noted Tony Angle's grin. "I've been a bit shaken up by lots of stuff going on, and I wasn't myself. Can I buy you a drink?" Tony Angle allowed that he could, and they settled down at a table, where, quite uncharacteristically, John Garter kept the conversation going with a flow of pleasantries and small talk. The change in Garter's disposition did not go unnoticed by Tony Angle, and neither did the regular glances he made at his watch. But, what piqued his curiosity the most was an occasion when, in mid sentence, Garter suddenly stopped speaking, mumbled something about the washroom, and scurried off at a brisk pace, leaving Tony Angle to wonder why his companion had left the visit so late, and whether he would make it on time.

The reason for this rapid departure was, in fact, that Garter had suddenly remembered the spent lipstick canister in his pocket and had hastened off to dispose of it as fast as possible, anywhere that he could. The washroom provided him with several options. He decided not to flush it down the toilet bowl in case it should float back up again. Burying it in the garbage can seemed the best plan. He grabbed a handful of paper towels, wiped the outside casing clean of his finger prints, wrapped it in the towels, and with a great sense of relief, pushed it deep inside the overflowing container, satisfied it would soon be lost in a far distant landfill. He looked at his watch and calculated that fifty minutes had passed since he had dabbed the Crylex pad on Mary's arm.

He washed his hands, and dried them carefully, wondering as he did so, whether the dosage had already taken effect, or if it would take the full one- hour to work. He was pensive as he returned to join Tony Angle.

"That was a close call wasn't it?" Tony Angle grinned across the table, trusting he would be spared any detailed account of whether John Garter's race against time had been successful.

"What?" He looked alarmed, and then realized the meaning of Tony Angle's enquiry. "Oh yes…that. Talking too much, I expect… suddenly had to go." He looked at his watch once more. "I'll have to be off soon, got to be up bright and early for work in the morning. I've got back to back meetings from eight o'clock onwards." He chattered on for a few more minutes, explaining in response to Tony Angle's questions that he did indeed enjoy his work, and that he found it a constant source of challenge and reward. He was proud to work in the pharmaceutical industry and to be associated with a company whose mission was to eliminate illness and save lives. He looked at his watch once more.

"OK, I'm off now." He placed a twenty-dollar bill on the table. "This should cover the tab, and our previous one I think." He stood up and shook hands with Tony Angle. "Thank you Tony, I enjoyed our talk. I'll see you again soon no doubt."

He left through the front entrance to the pub, and wandered out into the cold night air, wondering if he should take a taxi home. He decided that he should, and strolled along the sidewalk, eyes alert for a passing cab. As he approached the first corner he became aware of a slow moving vehicle to his right. He turned to glance at it and was surprised at the sight of a police cruiser. He watched it pass slowly by and draw to a halt at the curbside just ahead. The passenger door sprang open, closed for a moment, and then opened once again, revealing the lumbering form of Inspector Ogopoulos attempting to clamber to his feet while simultaneously trying to fasten his jacket and wave his hat.

"Mr. Garter, just a moment please!" The Inspector padded around to the back of the car, and approached him from the front. "Hello Mr. Garter…uggh it's cold isn't it! I'm glad I got you by yourself,, I didn't want to interrupt you in the pub; not with all those people about. Anyway, thanks for stopping." He pulled a piece of paper from his inside pocket, patted it lightly, and paused as if unsure how to proceed. "You won't be pleased to know this Mr. Garter, and I'm sorry to be the bearer of bad news, but I have to tell you that I have here a warrant for your arrest on a charge of embezzlement of funds from the Aerial Golf Club, and…" he took a deep breath, and continued slowly, "and, a detention order based on suspicion of murder." He replaced the paper in his breast pocket, and continued. "I'd like you to get into the police car with me now if you would, and I'll read you the full charge and explain your rights." He looked at Garter with a politely questioning air, much as he might had he just issued an invitation to someone to dance. When no response was forthcoming, he seemed a little perplexed. "Mr. Garter. Are you okay? Did you hear what I said?" John Garter managed to nod his head.

"What on earth is this all about Inspector?" The more he tried to remain calm, the more his head spun. "I haven't killed anyone… and I have no funds belonging to the Aerial Golf Club. I can explain everything! There must be a mistake."

"You'd be surprised, Mr. Garter, that's what everyone says. This way now please." He pointed to the back door of the cruiser, gave a light touch to Garter's elbow, and gently nudged him forward. "Just sit in there if you would please, and slide across. I have to sit next to you."

Chapter Twenty Two

"I'll leave you to think about it then, shall I, Mr. Garter?" Anthony Hampton, a short, overweight man, with a bald head, expensive teeth, and a remarkable inability to project either warmth or empathy, clipped shut his briefcase, stood up, and proffered a business card. "Good day, Mr. Garter. Call me at this number during office hours. If I'm in court Marcia Gould will assist you to make contact." He turned, walked briskly through the guarded door, and disappeared along the corridor, the sound of his clipping heels echoing in the stone hallway. As the door slammed shut behind him, Garter, inside his detention cell, and still in a state of shock, was left to reflect on the legal intelligence that had been imparted during the previous sixty minutes: including the encouraging news that blimp-man had offered to provide financial assistance to help with legal costs.

Mr. Hampton had spent a considerable portion of the interview reviewing fee structures and payment options. The estimated cost for defending John Garter against charges of embezzlement depended significantly on how he intended to plead. The least expensive option would be to plead *Guilty*. In that event, and for a fee of not more than six thousand dollars, court time would be structured to provide a plausible explanation and a sympathetic response. Given that all money had been repaid, such a plea might even draw a conditional discharge. Apart from being the least expensive option, a Guilty plea would obviate the necessity to explain the existence of an apparently authentic confession that the police had found in Julia Miller's apartment. On the other hand, given that a conviction for embezzlement would likely cost him his job, and expose him to public ridicule, he might consider it worthwhile to invest in the substantially more expensive *Not Guilty* plea. Just how much more expensive was difficult to assess, but a maximum cap could be established, probably in the order of thirty thousand dollars.

There were, however, other considerations. The good news was that it was entirely possible that the embezzlement charges would be dropped. The bad news was that this would probably mean that a decision had been taken to proceed with murder charges instead, and that the embezzlement evidence would be unveiled as part of the prosecution's case. It was not possible to estimate legal costs exactly, but a *Not Guilty* plea against two murder charges would be expensive, capped possibly at around a quarter of a million dollars, part of which might be recovered if his case was successfully defended. A *Guilty* plea would reduce costs to a bare minimum, but would of course have the disadvantage that he would probably spend the rest of his life in prison. Whatever the choices, the first priority was to seek his release on bail: a procedure that as far as legal costs were concerned, might be less than ten thousand dollars but which, as far as the bail guarantee was concerned, could be substantial and in excess of one hundred thousand dollars.

It was at that point in his discourse that Mr. Hampton had mentioned to John Garter a call he had received from one Marco Algenon, who, subject to some minor terms that would have to be agreed, had indicated his willingness to post all necessary bail guarantees, and to assist with legal fees. Although Mr. Hampton was not aware of the terms attaching to the offer, he had, in anticipation that it would be of interest, obtained permission for a meeting between them for later that same day. He had then left, directing John Garter to call him with his instructions when the meeting had taken place.

As the sound of Anthony Hampton's exit steps faded into distant walls, a sense of isolation and despair descended on him like a sickly fog. How could this be happening! It was, of course, all due to that damned confession note. If only he had thought to search for it and remove it from Julia's apartment when he had had the opportunity…then, the police would not have found it, and would not have drawn their absurd conclusion that he had murdered Julia and Harry to protect himself from threatened exposure. Why couldn't they see the craziness of it all?

He lay down on his bunk. Nearly fifteen hours had passed since his visit to Mary. He wondered how long it would take before someone came to advise him about her death. It had been quite evident from the moment he dabbed the applicator tip on her elbow that she was completely unaware of the contact. Ellen would have called the hospital and the police when she collapsed--assuming she was still there at the time. If not, it was possible that her body had not yet been discovered. The thought was disturbing. He wondered about the end: whether it had come swiftly and painlessly as he had been assured would be the case, or whether there had been an unpleasant reaction of the kind he had once observed when he saw a passenger at the train station clutching at his chest and groaning in agony before dying minutes later from a massive heart attack. He hoped that it had been swift and painless: after all, there was no need for nastiness. Nevertheless, the important thing was that it had happened. He was now sole owner of the Garter asset pool, including the jewellery, and before long, he would have an additional two hundred thousand dollars from Mary's life insurance policy to ease the pain of his bereavement.

With a growing sense of optimism he began to assess the situation. He hadn't murdered Julia, or Harry, so why should he be worried that he would be found guilty? Surely he could trust the justice system to protect the innocent! Had not Inspector Ogopoulos said that very same thing after he had arrested him the previous night? The thought had not been of any comfort when OgoPogo had made the observation, because at that time he was still under the impression that his attack on Mary had been discovered, and that it was her murder of which he was suspected. But, now that he knew otherwise, some comfort could indeed be drawn from the idea that an innocent man had nothing to fear. He had borrowed from the Golf Club of course, but that was all paid back long ago and was simply a convenience transaction that disadvantaged no-one. He would have to make it perfectly clear to his company President that there had been absolutely no impropriety in his conduct, and that would be a simple matter -- particularly after he was found not guilty. *Not guilty!* Of course he would plead not guilty. How could Hampton even contemplate the possibility that he would plead anything else? Didn't he believe the truth when he came across it! But, on the bright side, it seemed that blimp man intended to help him with legal costs, either as recompense for getting the Crylex project back on track or perhaps, in anticipation of other deals: as a kind of investment in the future.

He looked at his watch. Five minutes to noon. He would soon know what conditions were to be attached. It was in the middle of these reflections that he heard footsteps approaching his cell door, and then the voice of an officer advising him that he was to be allowed a five minute supervised visit. The door was unlocked and he was then accompanied to an adjacent interview room. The officer pointed towards the table and two chairs that occupied centre stage, directed him to sit, disappeared momentarily, and then re-appeared with the large and smiling blimp man close at his heels.

"Five minutes only" he informed them both. "I'll be here at the door."

Garter rose from his seat in greeting as blimp man stepped forward and extended a hand. "Dear boy! Good to see you--and looking surprisingly well in the circumstances, I must say. Well, well, well, what have we got ourselves into here." He sat down and before John Garter could answer, continued with his address. "Don't you worry about a thing old chap, we're going to get you out of here in no time at all. Just you wait and see." He leant back in his chair, put a hand in his inside jacket pocket and retrieved a document of some kind.

"So sad about Julia, she was a remarkable woman. I will miss her terribly." He stared at Garter. "Look, we don't have long, so just read this, and sign on the dotted line. I will explain things after if it's not clear." He pushed the paper across the table. Garter was surprised to see that it comprised only one small paragraph of typing:

My signature on this document signifies acceptance of the offer by Vista Foundation to pay all legal fees, costs, and guarantees related to my application for bail, and my defence against all current and pending charges associated with my present detention.

Below the wording was a signature block and date line. John Garter looked up in surprise. "No conditions then? That's excellent. Thank you – of course I will sign." Blimp man beamed. "Good. Sign it and date it then." He passed a fountain pen across to John Garter who unscrewed the cap, sprawled his signature across the line, and wrote in the date. He replaced the cap and then pushed the pen and paper across the table as if clearing away an empty dinner plate.

"It's just a formality to square everything with the foundation, John." Blimp man folded the document, and slipped it and the pen back into his jacket pocket. "There are no strings attached John--the foundation wants only to see that justice is done." He pulled out a handkerchief and blew his nose loudly. "But, as you will appreciate, we do of course have an interest in what happens to you." Garter smiled. So, his assumption had been correct. This was all about future considerations. He thought of the deal they had struck over dinner.

"I'm sure Julia wouldn't have wanted me floundering in this place, accused of her death. Don't you agree?" Blimp man stared at him before replying.

"Dear Julia. What a tragic loss. I couldn't bear to go to her funeral…so final. Besides I dislike pomp and ceremony." He stood up. "Well, I think that's my business here settled. I'll take my leave." Without further comment he turned on his heels, walked through the door, and on, out of sight. Garter looked towards the door, and politely enquired of his escort whether he might use the remaining few minutes of the visit to call his lawyer. The man nodded and pointed towards a telephone hanging on the wall across the room.

CHAPTER TWENTY THREE

It was the first time that Mary's friend, Ellen, had attended a cremation service, and she was finding it extremely upsetting. The proceedings had got off to a bad start when, as she had driven into the car park outside the chapel, she had observed a small easel with a white card on it that, with cold-hearted bluntness, proclaimed a simple message for all to see: 'Garter Funeral'. Ellen believed that whether they wanted it or not, everyone should be properly buried: in the ground, and with a headstone--if only for the comfort of others who should be able to visit the burial site, and express their grief privately whenever they wished. The thought of loved ones being incinerated in a furnace was too ghastly to entertain.

She had been a little late arriving for the service, although not so late as to miss any of the proceedings, and she now sat alone, a few rows from the back of the chapel. The service had been brisk and unimaginative, and as it now drew to a close, she was shocked to see the chaplain conclude the ceremony by triggering a mechanism that opened a small set of doors. To the accompaniment of eerie music, the coffin then began moving on rollers towards the blue velvet curtains that shrouded the opening. Slowly, the coffin edged forward into the waiting jaws, rolled steadily onwards, deeper and deeper, until it finally disappeared altogether, apparently swallowed-up into some raging furnace beyond. The sight sickened her. She turned to her right, noting the grim expression on the face of Kenneth Davies who, across the aisle, sat quietly, staring ahead.

The conveyer belt image caused Ellen to wonder whether someone was already changing the sign on the easel outside. Perhaps it no longer said 'Garter Funeral'. Perhaps it was now time for the Jackson funeral or the Singh funeral or the McKenzie funeral. She stood up and walked briskly towards the exit, anxious to breathe-in crisp, fresh air.

Ellen sat on a bench and looked out over a grassy bank towards the distant Toronto skyline, asking herself why it was that funerals were so unsettling. It was not simply a question of grief: sometimes that wasn't even a factor. It was more the stark reality and the inevitability of it all that was so disturbing. One minute there were people you knew: people who had a life, and a presence, and a history, and a place in the world. The next minute they were gone. It was quite disgusting really. How could you tell when it would be your turn? A woman's voice interrupted her thoughts.

"Move over Ellen, I need some air too." Ellen looked up and smiled.

"I'm sure you do Mary," she said, edging along the bench to make room for her friend. "As you well know, I wasn't your husband's greatest fan, but I still don't like to think of him dead, and burned to a crisp: it doesn't seem right somehow."

*   *   *

At that moment, only blimp man, and the scientist on his payroll, knew why Mary Garter was alive and well, while her husband, neither well, nor alive, was pointing feet first towards a blazing cylinder that waited patiently for an opportunity to reduce him to cinders. The answer, though, was quite simple. After being harassed by John Garter into agreeing to prepare him a Crylex product sample, the anxious scientist had wisely decided it would be prudent to seek further authorization from his other benefactor before actually releasing a dosage from the laboratory. He had then been instructed to give Garter a blank cartridge, and told that if he later complained that it didn't work, he was to be referred immediately to blimp man, who would deal with the matter from there on. With that directive clearly established, he had replaced the lipstick case with a harmless dummy before handing it over.

The matter might well have rested there because there had been no complaint about the effectiveness of the product. However, the news that Garter had been present at the death of both Julia Miller and Harry Jefferson, followed by the news that he had been arrested, could not be ignored. To blimp man, John Garter was a major liability.

It had been the scientist who suggested the fountain pen delivery system. Once the cap was unscrewed, anyone wishing to write would be obliged to hold the pen in the exact spot where they would be exposed to a fatal Crylex dosage. It had then been a simple matter for blimp man, in the guise of benefactor, to create the opportunity to strike and assess first hand the efficacy of his latest market investment.

Mary Garter had been the first to be informed. Inspector Ogopoulos had called at her door to break the sad news. That had been one week ago now. There would, he had told her, be an autopsy, but it appeared that

Garter had died from a heart attack. Later, Ogopoulos had returned to advise her of the autopsy result: death was indeed due to myocardial infarction. There was nothing to suggest additional contributory effect. The funeral could proceed any time she wished.

Despite her aversion to the process it was, oddly enough, Ellen who had suggested cremation having recalled that John Garter had once expressed the view that burial was a waste of valuable land. She also remembered having suppressed the urge to observe that some people deserved nothing less than cremation, and that for them it couldn't come soon enough. But now, as she sat on the bench with Mary, staring out on the Toronto skyline, she felt just a slight twinge of guilt at having wished him an early demise.

"Do you think you will miss him?" she enquired. Mary thought for a moment before replying.

"He didn't do it you know."

"Didn't do what?" asked Ellen.

"He didn't kill Harry Jefferson or Julia Miller."

"That's not what the police think, is it? Anyway, how do you know?"

"Harry Jefferson's mother told me. She said she had some proof that it was her son who was the killer. I believe her too."

"What kind of proof?" Ellen sounded skeptical.

"I don't know, she wouldn't say. But she did offer to show it to me, whatever it is. Here…" Mary reached in her purse and pulled out an envelope, "…she wrote down her telephone number. She said I could come by any time I wished."

"And you haven't done that yet? Wouldn't it clear his name?"

"Yes, I suppose it would," said Mary. "I haven't had time yet."

Chapter Twenty Four

Mary had arranged a post-funeral reception at the Garter house. Ellen, and Mrs. Bennett, had assisted in the preparations, and now, plates in hand, both of them were enjoying the fruits of their labour, while chatting with other mourners.

Ellen was engrossed in conversation with a man who had introduced himself as John's work colleague: a tall, good-looking, man in his forties whom she had just discovered was the vice-president of marketing. He was not wearing a wedding ring and Ellen's subtle attempts to steer the conversation in directions that would reveal his status were, thus far, proving unsuccessful, but she pressed on. "Were you able to fit in a summer vacation?"

Mary smiled to herself, but in the surrounding buzz of conversation was unable to catch the man's reply as she edged past on her way to the other side of the room.

In the far corner, Mr. Hampton, still saddened by the loss of his client – or more exactly, by the loss of his client's fees--shared with Kenneth Davies his assessment of Garter's situation. "I think they fully intended to proceed with the major charges," he confided. "The embezzlement thing would have just been evidence to reveal the motive." Kenneth Davies nodded his head and wondered whether to ask the question that he, and everyone familiar with the case, was dying to know. He decided there would never be a better opportunity.

"Would he have got off?" he asked in a low, confidential tone. His question drew an immediate response.

"Not a chance. But of course, you didn't hear that from me." At that point Mary arrived, and Kenneth Davies introduced her to Mr. Hampton.

"Mary, this is Mr. Hampton the lawyer that John was going to engage."

"Oh really! I'm pleased to meet you Mr. Hampton." Mary held out her hand. "I'm sorry you didn't have the opportunity to prove your worth." Mr. Hampton shook hands cautiously and stared at her before replying.

"Yes, I would have welcomed the opportunity to clear his name." Mary paused, and then laughed.

"Oh, I see! You're the defence lawyer. I thought you were the divorce one." Mr. Hampton frowned.

"No, that's not my line. However, I understand he's around somewhere." He nodded in the direction of a tall, angular man, who appeared to be demonstrating a golf swing to someone trapped in a corner. Mary turned to Kenneth Davies.

"Kenneth I want you to meet someone. Would you excuse us Mr. Hampton?" Mary led Kenneth Davies towards a table where Tony Angle, was inspecting a familiar looking set of silver spoons laid out on a table adjacent to two coffee urns. "Mr. Angle, I'd like you to meet Kenneth Davies. He's a friend of mine and our… or rather, I should say, *my* insurance agent." Although they had not met previously, Tony Angle knew precisely who he was, having spoken to Kenneth Davies on the telephone, and having watched him remove Mary's bag of jewellery from the station locker. He put down a silver spoon, and held out his hand.

"Nice to meet you." Tony Angle pointed to the coffee urns. "I was trying to figure out which is the genuine article and which the decaffeinated imposter." Mary steered him to the correct choice.

"Kenneth, Mr. Angle knew John socially, a bit. He was very helpful to me recently. Do you remember, I mentioned how he had suggested that John might have been having trouble with a loan shark?" Kenneth Davies nodded.

"Yes, of course. You have that service station on Grand Boulevard don't you?." Tony Angle confirmed the identification.

"I think you were right about the loan business, Mr. Angle" said Mary. "I'm not sure yet what debts he had and who has to be paid, but I expect I'll find out soon enough."

"Oh dear." Tony Angle's voice had a sympathetic edge. "I hope he hasn't left you in dire straits Mrs. Garter."

"Oh no! He had a most generous life insurance policy didn't he Kenneth. Five hundred thousand dollars in fact." Tony Angle's mouth opened in amazement.

"That's wonderful, Mrs. Garter, I'm very pleased for you. I mean it's unfortunate how it came about of course, but you know what I mean." He paused as if deep in thought, and then continued. "Look Mrs. Garter…" he fished in his pocket, "I wasn't going to mention this, but as you'll see from this IOU, he owed me some money too – fifteen thousand to be exact." He passed the note over to Mary who looked at it and handed it on to Kenneth Davies to read. "There's no rush Mrs. Garter. Whenever it's convenient. He told me that his money problems had to do with his stockbrokers. I was just trying to help him out. He was going to pay me back in January or February when he got the two hundred thousand he was expecting from an inheritance or something." Mary retrieved the note from Kenneth Davies and handed it back to Tony Angle.

"Mr. Angle, I have no idea why my husband would borrow money from you, or for that matter why you would give it to him. However, please rest assured, you will be paid in full."

"That's very good of you Mrs. Garter. Like I say, there's no rush."

Mary nodded, and left Kenneth Davies with Tony Angle while she made her way towards Inspector Ogopoulos on the far side of the room. Snatches of conversation reached her as she crossed towards him. "So what are the schools like in that area?" In the centre of the room, Ellen was still interviewing the marketing V.P. Mary continued her passage, catching more snippets:"… too bad really... good to expose him… always thought he was…" and then, an embarrassed silence as Mary's approach was noticed. And, from Mrs. Bennett, speaking to an Oriental man, "He could be quite a gentleman… most didn't understand him…" Mary continued her journey, arriving to find Inspector Ogopoulos pushing sausage rolls into his mouth with one hand, while cleverly concealing a cup and saucer in the other. He looked up as she approached and welcomed her with a pastry-adorned smile.

"Hello Mrs. Garter. Sad business for you. I thought I should come." Some crumbs fluttered harmlessly down to his chin.

"Yes, thank you Inspector, I do appreciate the gesture." He wiped his mouth and reached for a crab-filled pastry puff, before waving his arm around the room.

"Mostly relatives are they?"

"No, they are mostly just colleagues from work, and some acquaintances. He didn't have too many relatives."

"You know Mrs. Garter, and I hope this doesn't sound callous…but in some ways this is not such a bad outcome for him you know. Personally I can't imagine anything worse than spending the rest of one's life behind bars."

"So you're quite confident that's what would have happened Inspector?"

"Oh yes. Indeed…indeed. No question about that." The inspector looked triumphant as he nodded his head vigorously. "I'm sure this isn't the time Mrs. Garter, but I would be happy to outline the case for you later if you wish."

"Thank you Inspector, I'm not so sure that I do wish, but I'll bear that offer in mind."

"It's always money at the bottom of things isn't it?" The inspector's question was clearly rhetorical, but it led immediately to another thought. "I hope he left you, comfortably placed, Mrs. Garter?"

"Oh, I expect I'll be able to manage Inspector," she replied. "I think he may have had some life insurance."

*   *   *

After bidding farewell to the last of the mourners, Mary and Kenneth Davies cleared away all evidence of the post-funeral gathering, vacuumed floors, restored the house to its normal, orderly state, and then made off in Kenneth's car to Trattoria Blanco. Positioned at their favourite corner table, they both gazed vacantly at the log fire. Mary picked up her wine glass. "How are you feeling about all this Kenneth?"

"Feeling about all what?"

247

"You know! I'm talking about John's death... the funeral...his arrest....us!"

"Oh that! Well, right now I was just thinking how pleasant it is to be sitting here with you, in front of this lovely fire, waiting for what I am sure will be a wonderful meal, and trying not to think about John or his funeral." He frowned. "It does keeping popping into my mind though. How about you?" He covered her hand with his own. "How are you feeling?"

"Unsettled, is the best description I think. So much has happened in a short space of time, and it hasn't all sunk in yet." She sipped at her glass. "It's not the fact that he's dead. I wouldn't have wished that on him of course, but as he no longer meant anything to me I don't feel any pain or loss." She put down the glass. "You know what Kenneth, it's the stench surrounding it all that is so disturbing: everyone thinks I was married to a murderer!"

"Yes, I know--and that can't be a pleasant thought for you I'm sure."

"Do you think he was a murderer Kenneth?" He looked at her for a moment before replying.

"I don't know Mary. I know that his lawyer thought so. So did Ogopoulos of course." He thought of adding that everyone he had spoken to at the funeral reception also thought so, but decided against it. "And I have to tell you Mary, I got a cold tingle down my spine when Tony Angle said he had been talking about getting two hundred thousand dollars from an inheritance. I hate to tell you what sprang to my mind then."

"You don't have to" Mary replied. "It sprang to my mind too."

On the journey home Mary was quiet. Kenneth Davies decided not to break the silence recognizing that Mary was thinking, and sorting through the painful ideas and information they had processed during the previous two hours. Eventually she spoke.

"Will you stay with me tonight Kenneth?"

"Yes, of course I will, if that's what you want."

"It is. I want us to be together." She turned and looked at him directly. "Do you think I'm being awfully shabby to say that when I've just had my husband incinerated?"

"Of course not. In any case, it's what I want too." Mary smiled but did not reply.

When they arrived back at the house, Mary asked Kenneth to make them both a nightcap while she made a telephone call. Happy to oblige, he wandered off to a liquor cabinet in the living room, while Mary seated herself at the kitchen telephone. She opened her purse and pulled out the envelope with the telephone number of Mrs. Jefferson senior. If there was evidence to prove John innocent then perhaps she did owe it to his memory to clear his name. She picked up the telephone to dial Harry's mother, but paused when she heard the beeping noise that signaled a waiting message. She dialed into the message centre and listened. It was a male voice, with a central European accent. The message and the menacing tone in which it was delivered were all too familiar. She listened in silence as the message unfolded, through to a final warning: "So you'd better get it here quickly… or else."

Mary replaced the receiver, and stared at it for a few moments, recalling the last time she had heard that menacing voice, demanding that her husband live up to his obligations. She then picked up the envelope with

Mrs. Jefferson's number written on it, peered at it for a few moments, and then carefully tore it into tiny pieces. She walked across the room, and dropped the remnants into a trash can.

"I'm coming Kenneth," she called out, "I'm all done here!"

* * * * * * *